HIGH PRAISE FOR ELAINE VIETS AND
THE PINK FLAMINGO MURDERS
A FRANCESCA VIERLING MYSTERY

"Viets employs good local research, great dialogue, colorful repeat characters . . . and a deft hand at surprise endings."—Gannett News Service

"It's got plenty of laughs and likable characters."
—*Arizona Republic*

"IT'S FUN."—*St. Louis Journalism Review*

"Reading a book by Elaine Viets is like going to a concert by the London Symphony Orchestra—you know you are going to get more than your money's worth."—*Murder on Miami Beach Newsletter*

"Readers of amateur sleuth cozies will want to meet Ms. Viets in St. Louis with this wonderful novel."
—Harriet Klausner

"AN AMUSING STORY . . . has a universal ring of truth whether you're from the Midwest or South Florida. Viets . . . continues to look at the vibrancy of her hometown . . . to capture the real St. Louis."
—*Sun-Sentinel*, Fort Lauderdale

Dell Books by Elaine Viets

Backstab
Rubout
The Pink Flamingo Murders
Doc in the Box

Doc
in the
BOX

Elaine Viets

A Dell Book

Published by
Dell Publishing
Random House, Inc.
1540 Broadway
New York, New York 10036

Cover art by Marc Burckhardt

Dell® is a registered trademark of Random House, Inc., and the colophon is a trademark of Random House, Inc.

ISBN: 0-440-23620-7

Printed in the United States of America

Published simultaneously in Canada

July 2000

10 9 8 7 6 5 4 3 2 1

OPM

To Don, who researched this book the hard way

Acknowledgments

Special thanks to my agent, David Hendin, who's still the best.

To my editor, Mitch Hoffman.

To the staff of the St. Louis Public Library, and to Anne Watts, who has given me some deadly accurate ideas. Also, to the staff of the Broward County Library. Librarians are the next best thing to moms for knowing everything.

Many other people in St. Louis and around the country helped me with this book. I hope I've acknowledged them all. I certainly appreciate their help.

Barry Berry, retired St. Louis Police commander, veteran detective, and commander of the Police Academy. Diane Earhart, Jinny Gender, Kathy Gender, Lisa Gender, Kay Gordy, Karen Grace, Willetta L. Heising, author of "Detecting Women." Debbie Henson, Lt. Kathy Katerman, North Miami Beach Police. Marilyn Koehr, Cindy Lane, Betty Mattli, Paul Mattli, the ever-hip Alan Portman and Molly Portman. Dick Richmond, Janet Smith, John Spera, Sarah Watts, Julianna Yonan.

Finally, thanks to all those sources who must remain anonymous, including my favorite pathologist.

Doc
in the
BOX

1

Jack was buttoning up his shirt. I stared at his upper chest, a slab of tanned and toned muscle. As he tucked in his shirttail, I admired that rippling washboard stomach once more, and imagined those muscles moving the way I saw them last night. My mind wandered to other visions now concealed by his pants. Those strong legs and hot buns and . . .

"So, was I good?" he asked, combing his hair with his fingers. He didn't wait for me to answer. He knew he was. He was the sort of man who made women howl and claw his hide.

"Got any hair spray I can borrow?" he said.

"Nope, never use it," I said. That wasn't quite true, but if you let him, the guy borrowed more stuff than a sorority roommate. He'd already used my powder compact, my teasing comb, and my pink lipstick to make his heart-stopping lips more luscious. He used his own eyeliner, though. I don't lend that out. I wasn't taking a chance of getting pinkeye from the handsome Jack.

I shifted on my lopsided chair in the men's dressing room at the Heart's Desire, a strip club ten minutes across the river from downtown St. Louis. We like to go across the Mississippi River into Illinois for our sin. That way we can pretend we really don't have it in our city. But we keep it close to home.

Jack Hogenbaum, a.k.a. "Leo D. Nardo, Your Titanic Lover," was the star of Ladies' Nights at the club. He'd been packing them in since the movie. He looked like Leonardo DiCaprio. Well, sort of. At least his brown hair hung down over his forehead on the left side, he had soulful eyes, and when he danced, he could do stuff with a life preserver you never dreamed.

It was my job to follow him around for a day. My name is Francesca Vierling, and I'm a columnist for the *St. Louis City Gazette*. I'm six feet tall, dark hair, smart mouth. I'm generally in trouble with the newspaper management, but this last punishment from my sleazy managing editor had turned into an unexpected pleasure. Charlie, who was slime in a suit, had ordered me to do a story about "a day in the life of a stripper on the East Side. Human interest, you know."

Humans were a species Charlie knew very little about. He was sure he'd make me furious with this porky assignment. But he never said *which* stripper I should follow. So I did a day in the life of a male stripper, Leo D. Nardo. So far I'd managed to extend this assignment to two days, for a real in-depth look. Last night I watched the show with the women in the audience. Tonight, I was backstage with Leo.

The club had that down-at-heels look you find backstage everywhere. The men's dressing room had a big silver star on the door, but the door was covered with dirty handprints. The room smelled of Lysol and stale cigarette smoke, and the walls were painted an evil yellow. There were two stained sinks, a wall mirror losing its silvering, and a cigarette-burned countertop littered with more makeup than Dolly Parton's dressing table. A scuffed black swinging door led to the shower and stalls. I stayed in the dressing room, which was fetchingly decorated with prime beefcake. Officer Friendly, an arresting male dancer in a break-apart police uniform, was applying eyeliner in front of the glaringly lit mirror. He danced before Leo, getting the women warmed up for the star.

Leo was dressing for his eight o'clock show. He'd shown up at seven-ten, wearing a sleazy purple mesh muscle shirt cut so low it barely covered his nipples, and tight jeans with a big bulge in front. I figured he must have stuffed half his sock drawer in there. He was carrying a freshly dry-cleaned sailor suit. It was the break-apart costume for his act. Leo hung it carefully on a nail in the wall, right over his glitter-covered life preserver that had "Titanic" spelled out in dark blue sequins. Then he stripped off his shirt and pants while I interviewed him. He looked casual and comfortable taking off his clothes. I felt overdressed in my black Donna Karan suit. I was glad I was sitting down, even on that hard molded plastic chair. I wasn't used to carrying on conversations with men who wore only a well-filled G-string with "Titanic" on the front. It looked like the guy didn't lie, either, unless he was wearing the male equivalent of the WonderBra. My mind skittered away from awful puns about going down on the *Titanic*. I couldn't print them, anyway.

Any other man would have been embarrassed taking off his clothes and putting on makeup, but not

Leo. He just got naked naturally. That was part of his charm. He didn't strut, although he had plenty of reason to. I could feel a blush creeping up my neck. Damn. I wanted so badly to be hard-boiled, but I couldn't escape twelve years of Catholic schools. The nuns got me, no matter how hard I tried to be cool. And this was an occasion of sin, if I ever saw one. Impure thoughts buzzed pleasantly in my brain. I was going to hell. Oh, well. Might as well enjoy perdition. I got hold of myself, since I didn't have the nerve to get hold of Leo. I tuned into what he was saying.

". . . and while I don't want to say it's every guy's dream to take off his clothes in front of a lot of women, it's by no means a boring job." Good quote. I wrote it down on my clipboard. I never used a reporter's notebook, which looked like a skinny steno pad. I'm a big woman, and I like something I can hold. Argghh. That sounded wrong, too. I had to get those raging hormones under control.

Leo's next action didn't help. He rummaged in the clutter on the dressing table for a bottle of baby oil, and began oiling his golden brown chest and arms. They were smooth, hard, and hairless. I wondered if he shaved them. I could definitely see he worked out, but he didn't have a rubbery overmuscled weight-lifter's body, the kind with the veins sticking out on his neck and arms. I'd never known any woman who found those overdeveloped hard bodies attractive. Leo's muscles were well-defined, but not bulging. He slathered more oil on a perky pec and said, "I do this because the women like it."

Amen, brother, I thought. But I wrote that down, too.

"Did you pump up?" Officer Friendly asked him, as

he used a Q-Tip to flick away a stray bit of mascara. Officer Friendly had light eyelashes he was trying to darken. I wondered if he knew he could dye them, but before I could say anything, I heard sirens. That was Officer Friendly's cue to go onstage. He grabbed his nightstick and ran out the door.

Leo dropped to the floor like he was in basic training and began doing pushups. Ten. Twenty. Thirty. Forty. Fifty. The man wasn't winded. He didn't even break a sweat. "I pump up my chest and arms to give me a full feeling effect in my body," he said solemnly. I wasn't sure what he meant. His body looked the same to me. He jumped up and pulled the plastic off his sailor suit. He showed me the Velcro fastenings that let him smoothly fling it off.

"Why do you wear that?" I said. "In the movie, Leonardo didn't wear a sailor suit."

"His real movie costumes weren't very interesting," Leo said. "I mean, I could either wear his clunky poor guy's clothes, or a tux. Bor-ing. Besides, women like a man in uniform."

"They sure do," I said. "I saw the way they were grabbing for you last night." He'd been in grave danger of losing the *Titanic*, and it wouldn't have hit an iceberg.

"I try to enforce the rules," he said, batting his mascaraed eyelashes sincerely. "The women give me a tip on the hip and then I give them a kiss on the hand or something. I try to keep it as clean as possible, but sometimes you have to say, watch that. That's all part of the fun."

"So what did you do the night this place was raided?" I thought it was time to remind Leo he stripped for a living. The Heart's Desire had been raided last December. Four dancers were arrested for lewd and indecent conduct, and a lot of women customers were mighty embarrassed. All charges were dropped later.

"During the raid, I was able to escape out the back door," he said, looking me straight in the eye like a good liar. I saw the cash Leo had pulled in last night. I wondered how many cops he'd had to pay off.

"Does your mother know you do this?"

He looked hurt, and I felt like a rat for asking. But I was supposed to be a reporter, not an adoring fan. "She didn't for a long time, but I finally had to tell her after the raid. She seemed to take it pretty positively."

"So what are you going to be when you grow up, Leo? Are you going to college?"

"I'm not really college material," he said. Right. He looked like he was solid Kryptonite. "I flunked out of Forest Park."

That took some work. The local community college wasn't exactly Harvard.

"I don't want to do this forever," he said. "It's a business. I know I have a shelf life, and it's coming to an end soon. I'm thirty years old. I'm finding gray hairs and fighting a gut already. I'd like to find some nice woman who'd take care of me. We could settle down, maybe have a family if she wants. I'm not really interested in a business career."

"Are you kidding? You could do sales. You'd be a huge success." I wished my eyes didn't slide downward at the word huge. I wished he'd put on his sailor pants. He did.

"Wrong," he said. "I tried it. I was bad. I couldn't stand the rejection. Office work bores me. I can't sit at a desk all day."

I couldn't imagine Leo keeping his clothes on for eight hours at a stretch, either.

"But I wouldn't mind if she had a career. I wouldn't feel threatened by her success or anything," he said earnestly. "I'd enjoy taking care of her house while she went to work. I could cook dinner for her and clean and run errands. You know, pick up the dry cleaning and grocery shop for her." Amazing. Inside this stud muffin was a perfect 1950s wife, waiting to get out.

But instead of tying on his June Cleaver apron, he slipped on his flexible dancing shoes, then slipped them off several times. "Testing," the Titanic Lover said, with that iceberg-melting smile. "Sometimes the shoes are a little too tight and you can't get them off."

The first notes of the *Titanic* theme drifted through the door. Leo took one more look in the mirror and liked what he saw. "Time to go to work." Pumped and primped, Leo grabbed his glittering life preserver and ran out onstage. I followed, hanging back in the wings to watch. That's what I do as a newspaper columnist. I watch, while other people live their lives. The world was a show put on for my benefit, and most of the time, I was entertained. Now I was fascinated by how the women started screaming the minute he stepped onstage. It reminded me of those old videos of Beatles concerts. They were screaming so loud I could hardly hear the souped-up version of "My Heart Will Go On." If he looked good in the dressing room, he looked even better onstage. Stage was too grand a word for where Leo performed. It was a raised black plywood platform that in daylight showed every nick and scuff. But now it looked like a pedestal for a bronze god. The strobe lights on his white uniform were dazzling.

Sturdy chrome railings kept the fans at bay, and burly bare-chested guys wearing tight shorts and black bow ties kept the more athletic women from climbing over. But there was plenty of room for their hands to stretch out and wave those bills. Women are supposed to be poor tippers, but I saw fives, tens, and even twenty-dollar bills flapping in the breeze. But Leo knew how to play hard to get. He didn't go for the money right away. First he displayed the goods, that bronze body in the form-fitting sailor suit. Then, the music switched to one of those fast, thumpy songs with about seven words (I wanna, shake your booty, sex, body) that you hear in aerobics classes, and Leo ripped off his shirt with two hands. He made the gesture look powerful, like he was ripping a phone book in half. A nimble, dark-haired woman grabbed for the shirt. Leo artfully yanked it out of her hands—he'd told me he'd lost more than one custom-tailored costume that way—and flung it over his shoulder into the backstage safety zone. Then he gyrated, naked from the waist up. The women yowled like love-struck alley cats.

Their enthusiasm was touching. I'd seen female strippers at work, and the primary emotion for the women dancers and their male patrons was boredom. As the female strippers danced, you could almost feel their contempt for any man dumb enough to watch them. The men seemed equally contemptuous of any woman who would take off her clothes for them. The men nursed their watered drinks and stared blankly at the women, who went through the motions like badly made robots. This club had a split personality. Its Ladies' Nights with Leo and the other male dancers were high-energy events. The rest of the time, it had listless female strippers.

There was a kind of innocence to Leo and these women. He seemed so eager to please, and they . . . well, they were definitely pleased. If they were screaming over his looks, think what they'd do if they knew he wanted to cook and keep house for a working woman. I supposed that was his delicate way of saying he'd stay home and she'd be the breadwinner. Plenty of women my mother's age made that bargain in reverse with a man, and I knew lots of overworked women now who'd be happy to have their own deal with a hunky homemaker. I considered it myself. What would it be like to have the little man waiting for you at the door with your slippers and a dry martini, when you got home from the corporate wars? "How was your day, dear?" he'd say. "Dinner will be ready in five minutes."

Leo could put the sailor act in dry dock—being waited on by a handsome man was every woman's real fantasy. The Poplar Street Bridge would be jammed with women heading to the Heart's Desire to propose to Leo. I wondered if I could be happy with him. He was easy on the eyes. He'd never tax my brain, either. What would we talk about, once we exhausted the subject of makeup brands and hair spray? The only book Leo had opened since he flunked out of school was the Yellow Pages. I liked my men smart. Like Lyle. We could talk about anything—books, politics, music, even offbeat topics like how Michael Mann shot part of *Manhunter* at the St. Louis airport, and the gory details of Elvis's autopsy. Lyle could quote romantic poetry and Shakespeare by the yard, which wasn't a surprise, since he was an English professor. If we discussed *Hairspray*, it would be the movie, not the product.

We didn't just talk, either. Oh, no. I remembered our nights and long afternoons together. Lyle made Leo look like a prancing kid. But I pushed those scenes out of my mind. I couldn't think about that. There was no point in going on about it. We were through. We'd broken up at the end of last summer, and it was April now. We were finished. It was over.

I hadn't dated anyone since the breakup. What choices did I have at age thirty-seven? The good ones were either married or gay. Where would I meet men, anyway? At the *Gazette,* I could choose from a limited number of bitter divorced men who griped about their ex-wives and wanted me to watch their kids on custody weekends. The *Gazette* single men were a discouraging collection who lived with their mothers or in dingy bachelor apartments. One guy used his lampshade as an emergency sock drier. The man knew nothing about laundry. If you needed your socks dried in a hurry, you nuked them.

My other choices were Clayton lawyers who worked eighty-hour weeks, and corporate types whose idea of a casual evening was to loosen their tie. No thanks. I was through with men. Watching Leo was all the action I wanted.

Look at that guy whip those hips. The man had lost his pants and shoes, and was now moving those long, strong legs and taut buns. The women in the audience were either swooning, screaming, or stuffing money in his Titanic G-string.

They were a cross section of respectable women.

That group there, the thirty-somethings in the ma-
tronly flowered dresses and pantsuits, could be seen
at any PTA meeting. Those gray-haired women with
the sweet faces and soft, spreading figures looked like
they belonged to a women's sodality. Except I don't
think they ever yelled "Take it off. Take it all off!" in
the church basement.

There were four professional women in power
suits and wedge cuts, who'd probably come here
straight from the office. And that group of ten over
there, toasting a young woman seated at a table overflowing with balloons, champagne bottles, and un-
wrapped presents, was obviously a bachelorette
party. A slim, laughing redhead detached herself
from the group and ran down to the front row. Was
that a ten-dollar bill she was waving? Leo's G-string
was already bulging with so much money, I feared a
major cash flow problem. Sure enough, when an
older woman with hair the color of tarnished brass
slipped a fiver in at his shaking hip, some bills fluttered to the floor. Leo ignored them and kept dancing. A couple of thrifty types picked up the money
and recycled it as their tips. Talk about cheap behav-
ior. The redhead elbowed her way through the cheapskates, and stuffed a ten down Leo's Titanic front.
There was something familiar about her manicure.

Wait a minute. I knew that woman. I'd seen her
earlier today. She was a nurse. In the chemo ward at
Moorton Hospital.

"Valerie!" I yelled over the noise and the music.
"Valerie Cannata!"

"Francesca!" she yelled back. "How the heck are
you? And what are you doing here?"

We ducked into the lounge off the main entrance

to talk for a minute. "I'm doing a story for the *Gazette*," I said. "What's your excuse?"

"You get paid for covering this?" she said.

"Covering doesn't quite describe what's going on here. Yes, I get paid. It's a tough job, but someone has to do it."

She giggled. "We're here for Laura. She's an ER nurse who's getting married Saturday. This is her last night to howl."

"Why would an emergency room nurse who sees naked people all day want to see naked men at night?"

"She wants to see a healthy body, babe. One that's not shot, burned, or broken. Now I've got a question for you. It's plain nosy, so you can answer it or not. Are you related to that woman you came with to the chemo ward?"

"No," I said. "Georgia doesn't have any family here. She's a friend. More than a friend, actually. She's my mentor at the *Gazette*, the only decent editor I have. She was diagnosed with breast cancer. The doctor did a partial mastectomy, and now that she's recovered from the operation, she starts chemo and radiation. I don't want her to go alone for treatment. She's not herself right now. She's scared. I've never seen her like that before."

Valerie patted my arm. "You hang in there, sweetie," she said. "You'll get through it. She will, too. It's good that she doesn't have to go alone. You're doing the right thing."

Valerie had the gift of making people feel better, just by talking to them. She didn't ooze useless sympathy. I was glad she was working with Georgia. She also knew the right time to end things. "Hey, we're missing that heavenly body," she said. "Why don't you get back to work, and I'll get back to ogling Leo. Do you think if I ran my ATM card down the crack in his butt I could get some money?"

"Shame on you, repeating that old joke. Besides, I think the church ladies have already tried that." I told her about the recycled tips as we rejoined the crowd. By that time, the women were wild with lust, clapping their hands and shrieking "harder, harder, harder!" while Leo danced what we used to call the Dirty Dog with Laura, the bride-to-be. One of her friends videotaped them. At least I hoped the video taper was a friend. Otherwise, most of the bride's salary would be going for blackmail. Dollars were falling around Leo like green rain. Then, suddenly, the dancing was over. The music stopped and the strobe shut down. Leo made a graceful bow, scooped up the dropped dollars, and ran off stage.

I met him in the dressing room. Two big guys in shorts and black bow ties were barricading the dressing room door from enthusiastic fans, but the men had orders to let me in.

Sweat poured down Leo's back, and his damp hair clung to his neck. But he ignored it. He was taking bills out of his G-string—fives, tens, twenties.

"Hey, is that a fifty?" I said.

"You bet. Got that from the big blonde in the corner."

"The heavyset one in the green pantsuit?"

"That's her. The bigger they are, the better they tip. Love those big, beautiful women," he said, kissing President Grant full on the lips.

The sink was now overflowing with tip money. "I

haven't counted it all," he said, "but the take looks like about six hundred dollars."

"For one show?" I said, awestruck.

"Yep. I'll do another one at eleven. The ladies don't stay late. They're usually heading home by midnight."

"You make twelve hundred dollars a night?" I said.

"More when I do the rush-hour show," he said, stuffing the money into a blue nylon gym bag. "But, hey, I work for it."

Then he turned around. There were long, red scratches from his navel down into parts unknown, made by long, sharp fingernails cramming money into his G-string.

"My god, that looks painful," I said.

He shrugged and shoved the last of the money into the gym bag, then zipped it shut. He picked up his costume from the floor, smoothed the wrinkles, and carefully hung it back under the plastic bag.

I stayed in the dressing room with him until the eleven o'clock show. Officer Friendly came back with a bag from McDonald's, and ate Big Macs and fries. Neither one said much I could use in the story. Both were exhausted. Leo drank bottled water ("soda makes you fat"), ate a PowerBar, and showered. I didn't go with him for that. Then he and Officer Friendly went through the oiling and dressing routine again, with one extra step for Leo. He covered the bloody scratches on his hips and stomach with an aloe vera salve, and then hid them with makeup. "If you look close, you'll see some permanent scars," he said, but that was the last thing I wanted to do. I stuck around for the second show and picked up a couple of funny quotes from the women in the audience. One grandmother insisted that I *not* use her name. Her friend insisted that I *should*. "Time the grandkids learn there's still some life in Grandma," she said.

By midnight, Leo's show was over, and the Heart's Desire became an ordinary strip joint with tired women strippers and jaded male customers. The guys only acted enthusiastic at exactly twelve, when the club doors opened again to men. They rushed inside, eager to buy drinks for the women customers left over from Leo's show. It was plain that some of those guys were going to get lucky with women who'd been preheated by Leo's performance.

I left a message for Steve, the manager, asking about good times to have a *Gazette* photographer take pictures of Leo dressing and dancing. It was after one A.M. when I finally wandered out to my car. The last women customers were gone. Only a handful of men were watching the strippers, and the huge, dusty, crushed rock parking lot was almost empty. It was a warm spring night, and there had been an April shower. All around me, the powerful parking-lot floodlights highlighted brilliant pinks and greens. But these weren't tender spring colors. The Heart's Desire was down the road from a chemical plant, and the puddles were unnatural colors: slime green and Pepto-Bismol pink, eerie iridescent purples and sickly reds. We were less than half a mile from the Mississippi River, and the view of the St. Louis skyline, with the silver Arch backlit by the downtown office towers, was breathtaking. So were the chemical plant's noxious fumes. At this hour, it was belching yellow smoke. I hurried to my car, anxious to get out of the toxic air before I had two heads and tumors, like the catfish and frogs fishermen had pulled out of the nearby creeks.

In the darkest corner of the lot, where the employees had to park, I saw Leo D. Nardo talking to someone. She looked like a soft, slightly overweight woman with short gray hair. A nice, harmless person. There were a hundred like her in the audience. I didn't pay much attention to her.

That was my mistake. I was probably the last person to see Leo D. Nardo that night.

2

Something was wrong.

I could feel it when I walked into the newsroom that morning. There was dead silence when the staff saw me. Even the phones seemed to stop ringing. Then as I passed the reporters' desks, I could catch swirls of giggles, sneers, and snide comments. I heard ". . . wait till she opens the paper . . . she'll hit the . . . this will get her . . ." Staffers were smiling at me, but these were predatory smiles with too many teeth.

Something was wrong with my column, the one in today's paper. I knew it. I just didn't know what it was. Had I misspelled a name? Misquoted someone? Gotten some obvious fact wrong? Did someone call the paper and complain?

I'd slept late after staying at the Heart's Desire for the Leo D. Nardo story Monday night. Now it was ten A.M., long past the time I could make any corrections. I wanted to grab the first paper I saw and check, but I couldn't afford to look vulnerable. Not at the *Gazette*. So I held my head high, straightened my shoulders to dislodge the knives in my back, and ignored the sickly quivering in my stomach. I made myself walk slowly past the rest of the cityside reporters' desks, past Rotten Row, where the big editors sat, and go slowly to my desk, where I finally picked up a paper and opened it to the Family section.

I told myself I would handle the problem, if there was one, with quiet dignity. I would not yell, no matter what boneheaded stunt management pulled. I would calmly . . .

"WHERE THE HELL IS MY COLUMN!!!!!"

My column was supposed to be in the paper. It was Tuesday. It was always in on Tuesday. But in place of my locally written column was a wire-service piece on spring shoe styles. What the hell happened? I saw the proofs at two o'clock yesterday and everything was fine. I wouldn't have left work unless it was.

I marched over to the Family section editor, Wendy the Whiner. She nervously ran her fingers through her untidy, no-color hair. Her green flowered suit, which looked like it had been a slipcover in another life, complemented the slightly greenish tinge to her complexion. Wendy was expecting trouble. She was afraid.

"Now, don't get mad at me, Francesca," she whined. "It wasn't my decision. It was Charlie's." Wendy tried to look me in the eye, but at the last minute her gaze wavered and slid sideways.

"What kind of sneaky stuff is he pulling now?" I snarled.

"That's no way to speak of our managing editor. Charlie is measuring reader reaction to our columnists. He started with you. If we don't hear from any readers, then we'll know your column isn't as popular as you think it is."

"You know it's popular," I said. "Every readership

survey says so. Why didn't you tell me about this so-called test yesterday?"

"He made the decision to pull the column at the afternoon meeting."

"I was here at two o'clock."

"He called a special meeting for four," she said, her eyes shifting uneasily.

Four o'clock. When Georgia, the assistant managing editor for features, was at the hospital getting chemotherapy. And I was with her. If Georgia had been at the office, she would have stopped Charlie's latest scheme or at least warned me. Now I couldn't go running into Georgia's office about my column being pulled. She had real worries.

"I appreciate how you stick up for your staff," I said.

"You don't have to get sarcastic. It's only a test, Francesca."

I heard my phone ringing and ran to answer it. "Francesca, it's Janet. Janet Smith. Why isn't your column in today?"

"It's a test," I told my neighbor. Janet was furious.

"First, they make us vote for our favorite comics in the Comics Poll, so I have to fight to save 'For Better or Worse.' Then, they redesign the TV book, and the type is so small I can't read the listings. Now they're testing us by taking out your column. I've had enough. I'm getting the school calling tree going."

"What's a calling tree?" I interrupted.

"We each have a list of ten names to call, and those ten names have ten names, and so on. It adds up to three hundred parents, and they're already angry. Your paper will not print anything but bad news about our city schools, and we're tired of it. If your managing editor wants phone calls, he'll get them. And while we're on the phone, we'll tell him exactly what we think about the *Gazette*'s education reporting. We're sick of the rich kids in Parkway and Ladue getting all the good stories, while our city kids are branded as hoodlums."

As soon as she hung up, the phone rang again. It was Debbie, the manager at Uncle Bob's Pancake House, where I had breakfast almost every day.

"Hi, honey," she said. "Where were you today, and where is your column? We had a rush of customers this morning and when I finally got a chance to sit down with a paper and a cup of coffee, you weren't in. This is Tuesday, right?"

"Sorry, Debbie," I said. "I got up late and didn't make it in this morning. And my column didn't make it in, either. Charlie's pulled it as a test."

"Oh, he did, did he? Looks like I'll have to make a sign, informing everyone at Uncle Bob's what happened. What numbers should we call, honey?" she said.

I gave her Wendy's and Charlie's numbers, and hung up feeling much better. My readers always went to bat for me. Like a Tennessee Williams character, I relied on the kindness of strangers. I stayed at my desk, working on my column for Thursday and taking more phone calls from readers asking why I wasn't in the paper. I also called the Heart's Desire to talk to Leo D. Nardo, but he wasn't in yet. I'd call him tomorrow.

Occasionally, I'd look up and see a harried Wendy talking on the phone, apparently about my column. "It's just for a day," she'd say, sounding aggrieved. "She'll be back in the paper on Thursday. You don't have to get so upset. We gave her the day off." Way across the newsroom, I could also see Charlie's secretary, Evelyn, talking on one phone, while another line kept ringing. She looked exasperated. Good. By the time I was ready to leave at three-thirty to get Georgia, Wendy was not answering her phone anymore.

"Your phone is ringing, Wendy," I said, as I headed for the door.

"I can't deal with any more of your callers, Francesca," she said. "They're so angry."

"They're just testy," I said, sweetly.

I was supposed to meet Georgia in front of her apartment building at three forty-five. Apartment was an inadequate word for Georgia's fourteen-room penthouse overlooking Forest Park. It even had a terrace and a hot tub. That apartment was one of the things that kept her at the *Gazette*. She knew she couldn't live in high-rise splendor if she moved to the company headquarters in Boston. There wasn't much chance of her going to Boston, anyway, not since she'd told the publisher what she thought of his latest plans to cut the paper's staff and delay buying new equipment. Georgia was out of favor.

There was no one but a tiny old woman standing outside the massive stone building, huddled near the door to avoid the sharp spring winds. Then, with a shock, I realized that was Georgia. Georgia was fifty-five years old, and weighed maybe one-ten if you threw in the wet towel, but she was such a powerful presence I never saw her as any particular age, and never thought of her as small. Now she looked aged and shrunken. But when she saw my blue Jaguar, Ralph, round the corner, she straightened up and seemed like her old self again. She opened the door, took a deep snort, and said, "Damn, I love this car. Smells like money."

That was my old foul-mouthed friend. Georgia started at the paper when the highest compliment a woman could get was, "You think like a man." She cussed and drank like one to prove she could write like one. It worked. Georgia escaped the pink ghetto of the women's pages, and did some solid investigative reporting before she was promoted to editor. Her marriage fell apart years ago, and her ex-husband moved away. She had no children. The *Gazette* was her life, and now she was afraid she would lose it. That's why she had me pick her up at her apartment, so no one from the office would see us leaving together, and maybe follow out of curiosity. She didn't want anyone to know she was going to the hospital for treatment.

"Are you sure you want to keep hiding this from Charlie?" I said.

Her face set into a stubborn line. "I don't want that jackass weeping crocodile tears by my bedside," she said.

"Uh, I think you've mixed your metaphors."

"Animals," she corrected, ever the editor. Then she said, "I'm not going to die like Milt!"

"You aren't going to die, period," I snapped. I hated when she talked that way.

"How do you know?" she said.

"I won't let you," I said.

"I thought only editors mistook themselves for God. Listen, Francesca, you'd understand how I felt if you'd worked at the *Gazette* when Milt was dying of brain cancer."

"But I did. I was new, but I remember. Charlie had just started his rise."

"He climbed over Milt's dead body," she said. "Milt was a great editorial writer. If he hadn't been so sick, he'd have never let Charlie near him."

That wasn't quite true. Charlie could be charming when he wanted something, and he wanted the great man's blessing. He didn't have any integrity of his own, but he borrowed some from the dying Milt, and it would advance him.

"Charlie professed to be an admirer of Milt's," Georgia said. "He perched at his bedside like a vulture. He'd bring back weepy reports of poor Milt's suffering to the newsroom. He read stories to him when his eyesight failed. When Milt went into a final coma, Charlie left his side only once—to claim Milt's nearly new computer. Took it right off the dying man's desk."

"Charlie was only an assistant editor back then, wasn't he?" I said.

"That's right," she said. "He'd never have had a computer that good if he hadn't swiped it from a sick man. I keep my office door locked."

The dying Milt got the standard treatment for seriously sick staffers at the *Gazette*. The power grab went on while they were ailing: the plum assignments and the best beats were carved out of their workload. Sometimes, if their desks occupied prime newsroom real estate, those were taken, too. If the sick staffers survived, they often came back to find themselves shoved off in a corner, doing drudge work. Too tired to fight anymore, many of them took early retirement. If they died, their grieving family was shipped a stack of cardboard boxes containing their things—

or at least the things the other staffers didn't want. Readers never saw this side of the *Gazette*. The dead reporters got wonderfully weepy obituaries in the *Gazette*.

"I admit Charlie gutted Milt's office with the sensitivity of a starving sewer rat," I said. "Even took the guy's Waterman pen. And I've never forgotten what Hattie Harrigan tried to do to me when I broke my elbow. What a sweetheart she was. Called all my sources while I was laid up and said she was taking over my column. Fortunately, an outraged source called me, and I called you."

"And I nipped that ambitious little twerp's takeover in the bud. Columnist!" Georgia snorted. "My ass."

It was one reason why I helped cover up her illness now. She'd helped me when I'd needed it most. I was not going to lose her. Both my parents were dead. My grandparents, too. I'd already lost the one man I loved. But I wouldn't lose the one woman I cared about. If I had to drag her out of the grave with my bare hands, I was not going to let her die.

So far, Georgia had successfully kept her bout with cancer hidden from the *Gazette* staff. She always wore boxy gray suits, so it was hard to tell if she'd lost weight. She preferred expensive blouses in seriously ugly colors like mustard, and they made her look kind of unhealthy, anyway. She'd had her partial mastectomy and axillary lymph node dissection during her vacation, so nobody paid any attention to her absence. The chemo was making her queasy already, so she kept a supply of Hefty bags in her bottom desk drawer in case she barfed without warning, along with a huge bottle of Percocet for the pain.

"How did you do today?" I asked. "Did you need the Percocet?"

"Yeah," she said. "But I didn't realize what an advantage it was to sit through a *Gazette* meeting drugged. Should have done it years ago."

That sounded like my funny, don't-give-a-damn friend, the only person in the *Gazette* management I respected. But lately I'd been encountering a new Georgia, one who was sentimental and overgrateful and cried for no reason. The old Georgia never cried. I didn't recognize this weepy, grateful Georgia, and didn't like her as well as the old one.

"You don't have to do this," the new Georgia said, her voice wobbling under a heavy load of tears. "You have columns to write. How are you going to finish them?"

"I bought a laptop," I said.

"You did that for me?" she said.

"No, I did it for me," I said. "I needed one anyway." That stopped the tears, thank god.

Georgia was the smartest woman I knew. She made only one really dumb mistake. Her cancer was more advanced than it should have been because Georgia was terrified of mammograms. I'd been trying to get her to make an appointment for the last two years. She made excuses instead. "I'm too busy," she'd say. Or, "I hate those things. Talk about your tit in a wringer." Then she developed a lump she couldn't ignore. Too late, she learned the discomforts of a mammogram were nothing compared to what she was going through now. The cancer had spread to her lymph nodes.

"Dumbest damn thing I ever did, putting off that

mammogram," she said, "and that includes marrying my ex and joining the *Gazette*."

She gave me the bad news at Miss Lucy's Lunchroom. It was a safe place for us to talk. Nobody from the *Gazette* ever went there, even if it was just around the corner. Miss Lucy's specialized in tea and tiny sandwiches without crusts, served by sweet elderly women in ruffled pink uniforms. Georgia and I stood out there like a couple of streetwalkers at a finishing school, and it didn't help that Georgia sounded like one.

I arrived first, sat at a dainty pink table, and felt like the Incredible Hulk. The pink ruffled waitress brought a pot of cinnamon orange tea and a plate of cookies that tasted like ceiling insulation dipped in powdered sugar. I'd bet the paper doily they were on had more flavor. This must be bad news indeed if Georgia insisted on meeting me here, and I thought of a dozen different things that could go wrong, but I never guessed the truth.

When Georgia charged through the tearoom door in a fungus-colored suit, she looked so shaky, I wanted to pour her a stiff Scotch, her usual drink. Instead, she swallowed some tea, made a face, and said, "Might as well get used to this swill. I can't drink booze for eight months. I've got the Big C, Francesca."

"Cancer?" I was almost too frightened to say the word.

"Yes, I have cancer. I need surgery, chemo, and radiation."

"How do you feel?" I said, sounding like a talk-show shrink.

"Like shit," she said, and the two women in Laura Ashley at the next table looked up like startled deer.

I've always regretted I didn't check their table again before I asked my next question: "What kind of cancer?"

"Breast cancer," she said, in a voice loud enough to be heard over the roaring web presses, except it was perfectly, pinkly quiet in Miss Lucy's, so quiet I could hear one of the ladies at the next table pouring, and I knew both were eavesdropping. "Can you believe it? Tit cancer. Isn't that a joke? I finally get a lump on this flat chest of mine and they want to whack it off!"

I heard a teacup hit the floor and knew the ladies had been shocked to their Pappagallos. I called for the check, and drove Georgia home to her penthouse, stopping first for a bottle of Dewar's for medicinal purposes. Then I spent the rest of the evening listening to her talk, while the lights of St. Louis came on around us, and the city shone like a movie set against the black sky. Two million people were below us, but we were absolutely alone.

As the weeks wore on, Georgia's anger and defiance gave way occasionally to an emotion I'd never seen before: terror. She kept up a brave front at the *Gazette*. Even I couldn't tell she was fighting for her life. But sometimes, when she was with me, I saw the fear in her eyes. "I'm not afraid to die," she said once. "But I hate dying. The *Gazette* makes it so undignified. I can't stand to have Charlie slowly take away everything I've worked for."

I tried to tell her this was a curable cancer and she wouldn't die, but we'd both seen too much death at the *Gazette*. The paper had an inordinately high number of staffers with cancer. There were nine brain tumors and four breast cancers out of a newsroom with less than one hundred people. Eight of those cancers were fatal. The staff blamed it on the old, radiation-leaking computer terminals and tried to interest OSHA in a study of the situation, but OSHA brushed us off, saying the sampling was too small and newspaper people had an unhealthy lifestyle with lots of stress and alcohol. That was true for some, but not all. Milt, for instance, used to run four miles a day, played tennis twice a week, and rarely drank.

What we noticed was that the people who got cancer usually worked at their computers all day. Reporters who got out of the office frequently, and goof-offs like Charlie, our managing editor, who hardly touched a computer, remained free of symptoms. Georgia was a worker, and now she had it, too.

Physically, Georgia was well enough to drive to her chemo and radiation appointments, but her fear made her so absentminded, she was an accident risk. So I drove her. As a columnist, I had enough freedom that I could sneak out to drive her, as long as I turned in my column. I bought a laptop so I could write while Georgia was in treatment, and if I had to, I finished my column at home that night. Georgia may have been sick, but she still cared what happened at the paper, and soon turned her conversation back to work. "Oh, hell," she said. "You're right. I'm not dead yet. I'm certainly alive enough to notice that Charlie screwed with your column when I took an hour off Monday afternoon."

"He wanted to test reader reaction," I said.

"I think you passed the test," she said. "At

three-thirty today, we had five hundred eighty phone calls. Nice work, Francesca."

"Don't thank me," I said. "Thank the readers."

The Wendell C. Moorton General Hospital loomed in front of us on Lindell Boulevard, a jumble of fifty years of mediocre architectural styles. We found a parking spot in the garage, a near-miracle right there. It was almost always filled.

"Look at those bastards," Georgia said.

"Which ones?"

"The doctors. They've got the best parking spots, right near the entrance. It's one thing if they needed a close parking space because they had a medical emergency. But this is ridiculous. Two ground floors of parking reserved for perfectly healthy physicians, while seriously sick people have to park four and five levels up, then wait for the elevators. No wonder people hate doctors."

"The doctors get to park free, too," I said. "You know why God is God, don't you?"

She shook her head.

"Because he couldn't get into medical school."

At least I had her laughing by the time we got to the hospital lobby, a pompous eighties addition that was supposed to be impressive. Instead, it looked like the hospital was trying to drum up more business. The green marble floor seemed slick as a skating rink, and terrified the patients who used crutches and canes. The bubbling fountain tantalized wayward toddlers. About once a month one took a header into the water. The atrium ceiling allowed the hot St. Louis sun to beat down on anyone waiting on the spine-crippling benches.

Once out of the lobby, the hospital was a maze of

depressing tunnellike halls, bristling with heating ducts and pipes. There were so many new buildings and additions, the only way to find your way around was by following one of the red, blue, green, or yellow lines painted on the floor. Radiation oncology was on the blue line. Georgia and I made nervous chatter as we passed pathetic sights in wheelchairs and on gurneys. Both of us were too frightened to talk about what we were really seeing.

The radiation oncology center was in a separate wing of the hospital. We walked into a room that smelled stale and closed in. It was decorated in 1980s face-powder pink. The chairs were worn, the gray industrial carpet soiled, and the cheerful, anonymous pictures of pink flowers were crooked. The magazines were well-thumbed and six months old. The receptionist, a plump woman in a flowered smock uniform, could have been pretty, except for her dissatisfied expression. She was busy laughing with a radiation therapist, who was sitting on her desk. The receptionist ignored Georgia and me. We stood there for maybe five minutes while they talked and flirted, and Georgia, this new Georgia I didn't recognize, was curiously passive. She just stood there.

Finally, I couldn't take it anymore. "Excuse me," I said. "Can anyone here help us?"

The receptionist looked up, frowned, and said, "What do you want?" The flirtatious radiation therapist oozed away.

"We have an appointment for radiation therapy," I said.

"What's your insurance?" she asked.

"Medallion American Healthcare," Georgia said, sounding like she was sleepwalking.

"PPO or HMO?"

"HMO."

"Where's your referral sheet?" she said.

"My what?" Georgia said, finally coming to life.

"Your referral sheet. Your HMO requires it. If you don't have your referral sheet, you can't have treatment."

"But Dr. Partland said all I had to do was come over here. He didn't give me a sheet."

"Sorry, can't do it without the paperwork," the receptionist said, not sounding sorry at all.

"Dr. Partland's office is in the next building," I said. "We'll go get the paperwork and be right back."

"Too late," the receptionist said. "We're closing in ten minutes. We've been here since eight this morning, and we're not staying late. She can come in another day. Tomorrow, maybe."

"This is unconscionable," I said. "This woman has cancer. You're going to let her suffer because you don't want to stay five more minutes?"

"One day won't make any difference," the receptionist said in a snippy voice.

"Easy for you to say," I said. She shrugged in an irritating manner. I fixed her with a patented South Side glare and intoned: "I am a witch, and I curse you and your curse is that you will be treated the same way you treat these cancer patients."

"You're nuts," the receptionist said.

"Let's get out of here and get the paperwork," Georgia said.

"I can't believe you gave that woman the evil eye," Georgia said, as we walked to Dr. Partland's office. "Where'd you get that, from one of your weird South Side relatives?"

"The spirit just moved me."

"How did you do that stuff with your eyes? You looked like something in a horror movie."

"That's definitely from my weird South Side relatives," I said. "It's the South Side glare, the most powerful force known to woman. I think I scared that receptionist."

"You sure as hell scared me," she said.

Dr. Partland's office was next door in the Wellhaven Medical Arts Building, a yellow brick cube so filled with doctors' offices it was nicknamed Doc in the Box. Georgia picked up her paperwork at Dr. Partland's office, and a kindly receptionist called and rescheduled her radiation treatment for eleven-fifty the next day. I said I'd drive her to radiation oncology tomorrow and promised not to fight with the receptionist. I also promised not to fight with anyone at work, while I was making promises.

I was a model columnist the next day. I sat quietly at my desk and worked on the Leo D. Nardo story. I'd forgotten to ask him how he'd gotten into the business, a fairly crucial question. And I didn't ask where he went to high school. No St. Louis interview was complete without this revelation. The answers looked so harmless, but they revealed everything about you: your religion, your social position, and how much money your family had. My old high school, St. Philomena's, for instance, let everyone in St. Louis know I was South Side, blue-collar, and Catholic. I needed answers to those questions, and I knew Leo often had a lunch-hour performance. It was eleven now, so maybe I could catch him. I called the Heart's Desire.

"Leo's not here," Steve, the manager, said. "I can't

find him. I'm frantic. He didn't turn up yesterday. If he doesn't show again today, I'll have to put on a substitute again. I have Officer Friendly and his Arrested for Love routine, but the women don't like him as well as Leo D. Nardo. This isn't like him."

"Maybe he's taking off for a few days," I said, and realized what a horrible pun that was, considering Leo's line of work.

"Not without telling me," the manager said. "He's always so reliable."

Reliable was never a word I'd associate with Leo. He was a stripper, not a brain surgeon. He probably was with an enthusiastic admirer. He'd turn up soon.

I said I'd call again tomorrow. It was time to take Georgia to radiation oncology. This time, she had the right paperwork, and she was shown straight into a special interior waiting room. I waited outside in the "caregivers area," the depressing, down-at-heels, pink waiting room, and listened to the receptionist abusing other patients. She ignored a frail seventyish woman wearing a white turban that I knew was not a fashion statement. She'd temporarily lost her hair in the cancer wars. When Mrs. Turban asked for a cab, the receptionist snapped, "There's a pay phone down the hall. It's not my job to call cabs."

"But they always call one for me up in chemotherapy," Mrs. Turban said.

The receptionist shrugged. "Well, I'm too busy," she said. I doubted that. I'd seen the open paperback romance on her desk.

Next, a dignified old man with a four-legged cane hobbled up to her desk. He wore a white shirt and an old narrow-lapelled suit that was too big for him. "I'm here for my prescription from the doctor. He's supposed to give me some pain pills."

"We can't do that. Your primary care physician will have to do that," she said.

"But I called here and you said the doctor would write me a prescription."

"I said no such thing," the receptionist said. "It must have been the person who answers the phones while I'm at lunch. She told you wrong. You'll have to go to your primary care doctor."

"But I came here by bus," the old man said, about to burst into tears. I was grinding my teeth, listening to this conversation.

"You can stand there and whine, or you can get on the phone and do something about it," she said. "There's a pay phone down the hall."

"Can I have change for a dollar?" the man asked, resigned.

"No. I'm not a bank. You'll have to use the change machines in the cafeteria. Follow the yellow lines down the hall." She left him to shuffle and stump his way through the endless hospital corridors. I followed him out and gave him my pocket change. When I went back to the waiting room, the inner door opened and Georgia came out, looking pale and shaken. "Get me out of here," she said.

"Me, too," I said. I couldn't wait until we were out of radiation oncology. Even the air in the hospital hall seemed fresher. The atmosphere was certainly less poisonous.

"What a vision of hell. Are they as nasty inside as they are outside?"

"Worse," Georgia said. "I'm stuck in a *M*A*S*H* rerun. They joke around like I'm not there. I'm lying on a chilled table with my mutilated chest exposed to complete strangers and they're swapping jokes and talking about their hangovers. It's like I don't exist. It's horrible." For a minute, she seemed about to cry. But she didn't. I couldn't get used to this new Georgia, who was so often close to tears.

"I wouldn't be surprised if someone goes postal and takes a machine gun to that place," I said. "It's the meanest department in the hospital. They were really nice in X-ray, and the chemo nurses are angels. But this place seems to attract every sadist in the hospital."

"Well, if anyone loses it and starts shooting, a jury of their peers will give them a medal," she said. "Especially if I'm on it." That sounded more like the old Georgia.

3

"Do you know who I am?" the massive man demanded. He was irate that he had to stand in line with the rest of us at Uncle Bob's Pancake House. Breakfast goers were lined up out the door into the parking lot, but this guy was the only unhappy one. He was about the size of a rhino and just as mean. I figured anybody that big had the stamina to endure a ten-minute wait.

"Who is he?" I asked the brunette behind me in line. She shrugged. "Beats me."

Her twelve-year-old son was shocked by this ignorance. "Mom! Don't you recognize him? He's with the St. Louis Blues. That's the hockey team," he added in case we were too dumb to recognize that, too. "He's . . ."

Before we could learn his name, the rhino's voice grew louder and more insistent, drowning out all other conversation: "I SAID, DO YOU KNOW WHO I AM?"

The hostess was seating a party of four in the back room. Marlene, the waitress, appeared to deal with this emergency. "No, sir," she said politely, "but we can call some people at the state hospital who can help you find out."

The rhino angrily charged through the crowd, rudely shouldering his way out the door. "Sorry," Marlene said, but she wasn't really. The crowd cheered his departure. The Cardinals' Mark McGwire would have been recognized immediately, but even he would have had to wait in line at Uncle Bob's. Everyone did. The line was a handy place to gossip, network, or eavesdrop, depending on who you were. The mayor stood in line at Uncle Bob's. So did aldermen, congressmen, police, city attorneys, assorted crooks in and out of office, and lots of hardworking citizens.

For me, Uncle Bob's was a combination office and family substitute, and you could find me there most mornings. If there was no line out front, Tom the cook had my one egg scrambled before my car was even parked. Marlene the waitress popped in two pieces of wheat toast and poured my decaf coffee by the time I took off my coat. That had been my breakfast routine for the last eight years. Readers who couldn't get through the *Gazette* switchboard knew they could reach me at Uncle Bob's most mornings, and the waitresses took more accurate messages for me than Scarlette, our department secretary.

It was another ten minutes before Cheryl the hostess could seat me, plenty of time to find out what caused the crowd this morning. St. Philomena's Catholic Church had a Recognition Day for students and parents, then gave the kids the rest of the day off. All those proud parents and their offspring had worked up an appetite picking up their achievement certificates.

"No booth for you today, Francesca," Cheryl said. "It's too crowded. I'm gonna have to stick you at the little table in the corner, but it's in Marlene's station."

Marlene was my favorite server, a generously proportioned woman with an innocent Irish face and a wicked comeback for everything. Today she barely had time to pour my coffee and plop down my plate. I buried my face in a murder mystery. I'm an addict. I read five a week.

A few minutes later, Cheryl the hostess came over. "There's a call for you," she said. "You can take it at the front desk."

It was Georgia.

"What's wrong?" I said.

"Nothing," she said. "I just don't want to call you at the *Gazette*. You know the phones are bugged there. Listen, can you pick me up an hour earlier for my radiation appointment?"

"No problem," I said.

"Are you sure? How are you going to get your stripper story finished?"

"I worked on it at home on my laptop. It's nearly done. I just have to ask Leo a couple of questions."

"Good. I need to buy a wig. I'll be losing my hair in another week or two. I want to have my wig styled and ready."

"Sure, I'll be glad to go with you," I lied. I'd hate it. But I couldn't tell her that. The woman's hair was going to fall out, and I was whining because it made me feel uncomfortable. She needed me to be with her, and I would. Friends don't let friends go bald alone.

"Is an hour going to be enough time?" I said. "I can leave earlier."

"I have dyed blond hair in a wedge cut, like every other woman my age. How difficult can it be?"

I thought it was going to be very difficult. I hung up, dreading the wig appointment. It wasn't even ten o'clock, and the day was already in a nosedive.

By the time I sat down again to cold coffee, Marlene's tables had cleared out enough that she could join me on her break. She poured me a fresh cup. Then she sympathized about Georgia's hair. To lighten things up, I told her the story about the missing stripper, Leo D. Nardo. But Marlene didn't laugh. "Monday night was the last time anyone saw him," she said. "This is Thursday. If he doesn't show up for work today, I'd say it's time to get seriously worried."

"Oh, come on, Marlene. This is a stripper. An absolute airhead."

"Francesca," she said, "if a man said that about a woman stripper, you'd be indignant. You'd say he was discounting her because she was a woman in a marginal profession. Men deserve equal treatment."

"But it's different."

"Why? Male and female strippers are both in businesses that attract a lot of weirdos."

"But he's . . ."

"He's a sex object. He just happens to be a male sex object. But he deserves equal treatment. How do you know he even went anywhere with a woman? Does he have a girlfriend? Did anyone see him with a special admirer that night? Did he have any money with him so he could take a sudden trip or get a hotel room for several days?"

"Just his tips," I said.

"How much is that—a couple hundred?"

"More than twelve hundred dollars in cash," I said.

"In a blue nylon gym bag." Even as I said it, I knew it sounded bizarre.

Marlene stared at me like I was thicker than Uncle Bob's knotty pine paneling. "A guy built like a Greek god who's been dancing nearly naked for a room full of screaming women walks out at one A.M. with twelve hundred dollars in untraceable cash, and hasn't been seen since—and you don't think anything is wrong? What's the matter with you, Francesca?"

She was right. What was wrong with me today? Might as well go to the *Gazette,* where I was expected to be wrong. I wasn't disappointed. I'd hardly reached my desk when my editor, Wendy the Whiner, came over wearing a wrinkled suit that looked like it had been swiped from a Goodwill donation box. "Charlie's been looking for you all morning. I didn't know where to find you," she said, accusingly.

"Where you'll find me every morning, at Uncle Bob's looking for stories," I said.

"He's not happy with you," she said, with satisfaction.

Charlie's door was open, and he was sitting at his vast, empty black desk in his huge sterile office. I'd always suspected his chair was built up to make the sawed-off little hairbag seem taller. He was smiling, a bad sign. His blue suit was styled to hide his paunch. His red tie matched his nose.

"Sit down, Francesca," he said. "You're late. Most people start work at the *Gazette* at nine A.M."

"I do, too, Charlie," I said, still standing, because I knew it irritated him. He hated any reminder that I was considerably taller than he was. "I was at Uncle Bob's."

"You count eating breakfast as work?"

He counted expense account lunches as work, but I didn't remind him of that. "That's where I meet readers, Charlie, and they tell me stories for my column."

"Well, see if you can eat your breakfast on your own time in the future," he said. I figured I could ignore that as bluster. He was too eager to deliver his bad news. The man was practically wiggling in anticipation like a puppy. Either that, or he had to use the john.

"In order to have a closer link with our readership," he began, with a solemnity usually reserved for Vatican Square, "we at the *Gazette* want to publish something with the common touch. Of course, we thought of you."

I knew this was insulting. I just wasn't sure how.

"We are doing a compendium of St. Louis recipes. We'd like you to write the foreword and contribute a recipe."

"I don't cook, Charlie," I said.

"What do you mean, you don't cook? You're a woman, aren't you?"

"Cooking isn't a sex-linked gene. That is an incredibly sexist statement."

"I figured you'd try to hide behind that EEOC stuff," he said. "So I'm offering you this choice: if you find a recipe too offensively female, you can do a Dialog St. Louis page."

Oh, my god, not that. Anything but that.

Charlie must have seen the look of horror on my face. It was why I don't play poker. "It's your decision, Francesca. If I don't have your recipe by tomorrow, I'll expect you to begin working on the next

Dialog St. Louis. That subject is: The Information Highway."

Trust the *Gazette* to go down that well-worn road where no reader wanted to follow. Charlie had been sold on something called "public journalism" at a newspaper conference he attended in South Carolina. Nobody was quite sure what public journalism was, but we could recognize it by its catch phrases: "solution-oriented stories," "focusing on community resources," "deliberative conversations," "citizen commitment."

We knew what that meant. Expensive and time-consuming investigative reporting was out. Blather by city planners, sociologists, and other experts was in. The *Gazette* would no longer attack corruption in City Hall, the state legislature, and the school system. Advertisers found that so upsetting. Instead, the paper would discuss what a fine future the city would have if we all pulled together. Public journalism turned a newspaper into a Miss Manners' dinner party. Unsettling topics such as deadbeat dads, killer kids, and alcoholic moms would not be polite. So they were never mentioned in any Dialog St. Louis.

Its appeal to management was immediate: public journalism was cheap and noncontroversial. It was also shallow and stupid, and *Gazette* readers, at least those old enough to remember its glory days when it was one of the first papers to fight against the Vietnam War, resented this drivel. The last Dialog St. Louis was "The Importance of Teaching Phonics." Another featured this controversial subject: "Should St. Louis Parks Have Separate Paths for Bikers and Bladers?"

The *Weekly Reader* was more controversial.

Smarter, too. And it had more circulation. Charlie failed to realize public journalism was practiced by Podunk papers. I'd do anything to keep my name from appearing on that page of pablum. Even find a recipe. But I wasn't lying to Charlie. I didn't cook. Some would say I didn't even eat. Breakfast was usually a scrambled egg and toast at Uncle Bob's. Lunch was something pale and gray out of a *Gazette* sandwich machine. I ate well if I went out for dinner, but I did that less and less since I'd split with Lyle. Instead, I'd stop for pork fried rice or order up a pepperoni pizza. Maybe I could publish "Francesca's Top Five Food Delivery Phone Numbers." Sometimes, I just opened a can of tuna and ate it over the sink, or dredged pretzels through peanut butter. Wouldn't that make a *Martha Stewart Living* layout?

If my grandmother were alive, I wouldn't have this problem. She was a superb cook. Of course, she never used recipes. She never even measured. She'd take a handful of flour or sugar, a lump of butter, a pinch of salt, or a dash of vanilla and whip up the best pies, cakes, and biscuits. I tried to watch and duplicate what she did, but I never could. I guess my hands weren't the right size. Once I asked her for her recipe for biscuits. Her scratch biscuits were like fresh-baked clouds, light, fluffy, and warm. She handed me a box of Bisquick and said, "Don't waste your time. Here's your old family recipe." I followed the directions on the box and made something that tasted like crunchy hockey pucks.

Where was I going to find a St. Louis recipe? I grew up in the old German section, but strudel or sauerkraut were beyond me. I certainly couldn't whip

up something French as a tribute to our earliest set-
tlers, or make collards and cornbread to honor our
black population. A stove was foreign territory. I had
till tomorrow to think of something, or I was condemned to serve on that mindless Dialog St. Louis
page.

Well, I'd think of some way out. I'd been at the
paper less than half an hour and managed to get myself in trouble. It was ten-forty, time to pick up Georgia. I told Scarlette the department secretary that I
was at the library doing research. That was the *Gazette* code for ducking out of the office. Once I actually ran into another reporter at the downtown
library and we were both really doing research. It was
very embarrassing.

I blinked in the strong sunlight when I stepped
outside the *Gazette* building. It was one of those
heartbreakingly beautiful spring days. The trees were
that tender yellow green you see only in spring. The
white dogwoods were lush, romantic drifts of pearly
petals. The pink dogwoods were like cotton candy.
Even the dandelions looked perky on the fresh green
lawns. I wondered why they were branded as weeds. I
liked dandelions. There was still enough cold air under the warm spring day to remind you that a sudden
cold snap could take everything away. I shivered. I
didn't need any reminders. Not when I was taking
Georgia to buy a wig.

When I picked her up in front of her building, she
seemed surprisingly chipper. On the drive there, she
talked about buying her wig. She was definite about
what she wanted: "My hairdresser says I should have
some fun, and get a couple of wigs in different styles.

A long one, maybe, or something red and curly instead of my usual straight blond hair. I know she was
being nice and trying to cheer me up, but I don't want
anyone to notice any difference. If I show up with red
hair, Charlie will figure I've flipped, and start scheming to put me out to pasture.

"So I want two wigs, both the same color and style
as I have now. That way I can have one washed and
set while I'm wearing the other."

She talked matter-of-factly. There were no tears or
self-pity. Hair loss was a problem, but it was one she
could solve, and right now so many of her problems
had no answers. Tarkington's Fine Wigs and Hair
Fashions, a few blocks from the hospital, was exactly
the right place to go. It was dignified and low-key.
The quiet, helpful, older woman with the light blue
eyes was used to dealing with chemo patients. Her
voice was soft and soothing. "Are you in therapy,
dear?" she asked, then sat Georgia down before a flat-
tering mirror and showed her wigs that were the
same shade as her own hair. I wandered around the
store, looking at wild red wigs and a fascinating black
Morticia Addams number. I longed to try on a jolly
Dolly Parton wig and see how I'd look as a trashy
blonde, but it seemed too frivolous under the circum-
stances.

After about twenty minutes, Georgia found a short
blond wig that could easily be trimmed into her regular style. The saleswoman made it fit nicely, then
brought another one just like it. She also sold Georgia
several turbans and a blue paisley scarf with blond
bangs, "because nobody wants to wear a wig
twenty-four hours a day, dear, and you can just throw
these on if the UPS delivery person is at the door.

Turbans are so glamorous, don't you think? They always make me think of marabou and movie stars."

I loaded the wigs, stands, boxes, and packages into Ralph's trunk. We still had plenty of time to get to the hospital for her radiation appointment.

"That was painless," Georgia said, combing her hair back in place with her fingers. I couldn't believe it would be gone soon. It seemed so solidly rooted to her head. She must have seen me staring at it.

"It just comes out, you know, all at once," she said. "That's what the chemo nurses told me. I'll probably find it all over the floor of the shower one morning. All your hair falls out. Everything. Everywhere. Eyelashes, eyebrows, pubic hair, armpits, legs. It all goes. My eyelashes are so pale they're hardly there anyway, and I think I can hide my missing eyebrows with big Sally Jessy glasses. I've been putting off getting my prescription changed for too long. This will give me an excuse to get new frames."

"Your arm and leg hair goes, too?" I said.

"All of it," she said.

"Wow! Then you won't have to shave your legs," I said.

"That's what I like about you," she said. "Always looking on the bright side."

I started laughing. She did, too. I could hardly drive the car around the parking garage, we were both laughing so hard. Snort. Giggle. Guffaw. It wasn't that funny, but I had tears in my eyes. When I almost sideswiped a minivan pulling out of a parking spot on level six, I finally straightened up and behaved myself. I also grabbed the minivan's spot.

"This day isn't going to be so bad after all," I

thought, as we headed for the hospital elevator. I was wrong again.

Georgia had chemotherapy once every three weeks. She had radiation every day for six weeks. This was only the second radiation treatment, and I felt sick walking into the hospital. It was the smell. It hit me when the automatic doors opened. I felt my stomach lurch. It must have bothered Georgia, too. I could feel her stiffen beside me, but she didn't say anything. What was that odor? Some compound of chilled air, cherry-scented disinfectant, something chemical, and something else—hospital lotion? A bleach-based cleaner? Whatever it was, the separate smells weren't bad, but mixed together, they turned my stomach.

We followed the blue line and opened the door to the radiation oncology waiting room. This time, the nasty receptionist wouldn't let Georgia walk back into the patients' waiting room. She had to wait with me. No reason was given, just a rude "you can't go back there now." It was almost noon, and the department must close around twelve or twelve-thirty for a lunch hour. The dreary pink "caregivers" room was empty except for the two of us and the exhausted magazines. We sat with our backs to the receptionist, so we wouldn't have to look at her, but we could still hear her talking on the phone to a friend about her date last night. I heard her say, ". . . and then I said, 'Listen, I just met you. What makes you think I'm so hard up, I'd . . .'"

"Can you do me a favor?" Georgia asked, and I abandoned my easy listening.

"Sure," I said.

"Would you go to the cafeteria and get me a Coke? I have this funny chemical taste in my mouth and soda helps get rid of it."

"Sure. I have to make a call and see if Leo's turned up yet, anyway. I'll be back in five."

I was back in fifteen, actually. The cafeteria was busy. The Heart's Desire phone was busy. Everything took longer than I expected. A skinny bald guy in a hurry brushed by me and I knocked part of Georgia's Coke down the back of a tall blond woman. I apologized, but her even bigger blond husband looked like he wanted the death penalty for spilling a spoonful of Coke on a silk blouse. At least I missed the woman in the wheelchair. The boney guy pushing her gave me a dirty look.

I balanced the rest of the Coke on a metal shelf at a pay phone, dug out my phone card again, and called the Heart's Desire, hoping I could get my two questions answered: Where did Leo go to school? And what made him start stripping? Damn, I was getting careless. I'd spent all that time with the guy and didn't bother to ask. I wanted to believe it was because I was worried about Georgia. But there was no point in being noble. I knew the sight of a seminude stripper had shorted out my brain cells.

I finally got through to the Heart's Desire and talked with Steve the manager. No one had seen hide nor hair of Leo D. Nardo. He hadn't called in yet, Steve said. Officer Friendly was scheduled as the main act for that evening, unless they heard from Leo, of course. Marlene had raised my consciousness, and I was really starting to worry. This was a long time for Leo to be missing: two days at the rate of twelve hundred dollars minimum. This vacation was costing him at least twenty-four hundred in lost income. I wanted him back for purely selfish reasons. If he didn't show up soon, I'd have to do a day in another stripper's life.

It was twelve-fifteen when I made it back to radiation oncology. I opened the door, balancing the Coke carefully. The place was dead quiet. No patients were in the waiting room. Georgia was not in her chair. They must have called her inside, finally. I went to ask the receptionist how long it would be. She was sitting at her desk, with an open romance novel in front of her. She didn't look up.

She never would again. She'd been shot in the back of the head.

"Oh, my god," I said, the horrifying sight finally registering. "Oh, my god. Georgia! Georgia! Where are you, Georgia?"

I ran inside to the patients' waiting area, but she wasn't there. I ran down the inner hall, calling her name, and threw open the door to the radiation therapy room. The flirtatious radiation therapist from yesterday was lying on the floor, shot in the chest. A doctor was lying crumpled behind him, shot in the head. It looked like the doctor had his hands on the therapist's shoulders. Had he been using the therapist as a human shield? If so, it didn't work.

There was a funny fresh smell, a rusty smell. The floor and walls were splashed and spattered with blood. For one weird moment, I thought of a charity paintball game I'd covered, where grown guys ran around and shot each other with red paint. Then I saw the pooled blood on the floor and remembered that wasn't paint.

"Georgia!" I screamed. No one heard me. We were

cut off from the rest of the hospital, and the office was supposed to be closed for lunch. No one would come through the doors anytime soon, except maybe the killer. I ran blindly through the warren of rooms and halls, and somehow came back out into the waiting room, where I heard a mewling whimper, and found Georgia curled into a ball under the magazine table. She looked so tiny and helpless. "He didn't kill me," she kept saying. "He killed everyone else but he didn't kill me."

I pulled her out. She sobbed on my shoulder and I rocked her in my arms like a baby. I was bewildered. The fiercest woman I knew had become this soggy, sobbing creature. I don't know how long I sat on the floor with her, but it was probably only a minute or so. I felt oddly calm, like I was moving in slow motion. I had to get help. How do you do that in a hospital? Call 911 and tell the police to follow the blue line to radiation oncology? Run screaming down the hall? Wait. The hospital had a switchboard operator. She would know what to do. I used the receptionist's phone and told the operator three people in radiation oncology had been shot and I thought they were all dead. My voice only shook a little. Next, I called the *Gazette* city desk and gave them a brief account of what I knew, which wasn't much. By that time I heard the hospital operator say, "Code Yellow, Radiation Oncology. Code Yellow, Radiation Oncology," and the first of the hospital security came running through the door.

Soon the place was crawling with police in uniforms, homicide detectives, police brass, evidence techs, police photographers with regular and video cameras. The EMTs couldn't do anything but fuss over Georgia. The other three were beyond help. The police blocked off the hall and the emergency exits, but the TV reporters, the *Gazette* staffers, the weeklies, the AP stringer, even the radio stations, were all there, waiting in the main corridor for the body bags to be hauled out and yelling questions that nobody could answer every time they saw someone. But that was their job.

This was going to be a high-profile case, and I was right in the middle of it. Mark Mayhew was one of the homicide detectives. We'd known each other a long time, but he was all business today. He took me to an empty office down the hall, and kept asking me questions. I repeated my story until I was sick of it. I hadn't seen anyone. I hadn't heard anyone. I hadn't heard anything, period. By the time I'd come back with Georgia's Coke, the shooting was all over.

Mayhew had plenty of evidence to corroborate my story. I was still clutching the cafeteria receipt with the time (12:03 P.M.) printed on it, although I'd dropped the Coke by the receptionist's desk. My bloody footprints were all over the back rooms and hall, trampling the crime scene, so he could see I'd run around there like a chicken with its head cut off.

From the questions he asked, I knew one thing puzzled Mayhew: Why didn't anyone hear the shots?

I wasn't surprised. The radiation oncology department was isolated in a separate wing, off a dead-end hallway. There were no phones, restrooms, or other reasons to wander down there. There weren't even any benches to sit on. The heavy wooden door was always closed. It was easy to pass by this grim department, when the main corridors were bright and noisy with people talking, babies crying, and food carts rattling by.

A uniformed officer poked his head in the office and asked Mayhew to come with him.

"I'll be right back," he said. "Why don't you write down what you just told me? And don't leave."

I finished writing my statement, and he wasn't back yet. I shivered in the uncomfortable chair for a while, and when I got tired of that, I got up and looked down the hallway. It was still blocked off, and I figured the bodies hadn't been moved yet. I heard the police photographers talking in the hall. They'd seen the same thing I did: the doctor had used the radiation therapist for a human shield. He'd died a coward, and everyone knew it. I wondered: If the doc had dropped the therapist and run for it, would he have made it out the door and lived?

I'd covered other random shootings over the years: convenience store holdups, a gunman who went crazy in a cafeteria, another who shot up a supermarket late one night. I did some of the victim profiles. They were the kind of good people that bad things happen to. I still remembered one of the convenience store victims with particular sadness. He was a thirty-six-year-old African American teacher who stopped to buy his wife a rose. That romantic gesture cost him his life. The cafeteria victims included a seventy-year-old nun having lunch with three friends from high school. Yes, high school. St. Louis friendships lasted a long time. In this case, until death. All four women died together. One of the victims in the supermarket holdup was a mother of two who ran out of Pampers at the wrong time. Her husband had stayed home with the kids. The checker who died with her was working her way through college. She was twenty-one.

These people had no connection with the crimes or the shooters. Nobody had anything bad to say about them, and you'd be surprised how eager people are to speak ill of the dead, as long as it's not for attribution.

That's what was different about these hospital murders. These victims had been cruel, or at the very least, thoughtless to their patients. It was almost like someone killed them deliberately. If so, the cops were going to have a heck of a time tracking all their enemies. Might as well open the phone book and point.

When Mayhew finally came back, we went over my statement again, and I signed it.

"Now can I see Georgia?" I asked.

"You can see her after she gives us a statement downtown."

"Downtown? You're dragging a woman with cancer to police headquarters?"

"The doctors checked her out. She's fine, Francesca," Mayhew said. "She's sitting up cracking jokes."

"It's an act," I said. I'd seen her collapsed and crying. "She's sick and upset. She needs me to be with her."

"She needs a shot of Scotch," Mayhew said. "Quit worrying. I'm not going to beat her with a rubber hose. We just need her statement, and she'll be more relaxed giving it downtown."

"At least let me talk to her, so I know she's okay."

"After we talk to her, you can see her. You can even take her home."

"She'd better be okay," I said, but my threat sounded pointless. The police let me out a back exit, away from the press. I didn't want to scoop my paper by showing up on TV. I couldn't believe the sun was shining. I felt like I'd been cooped up in there for a month.

I drove to police headquarters on Clark and Tucker, but Mayhew wouldn't let me upstairs. I paced around in the lobby. It had that gray-brown marble that's supposed to be impressive but has been used in too many public restrooms. I saw other worried people who looked like they'd grabbed the first thing in their closet and run out the door. They were waiting, like me. No one said much.

Georgia finally came out of the elevator. She looked wrinkled and worn as a charity suit, but she said she was fine, dammit, and would I quit fussing and take her home. Didn't I have a story to write for the next edition?

"If I'm writing the story, at least tell me what happened," I said, opening the car door. "I didn't see anything."

She took a deep breath, as if the subject was still painful to talk about, and said, "I didn't see anything, either. After you left for the cafeteria, the receptionist hung up the phone and probably returned to her book. She was quiet, anyway, and there wasn't anyone else around for her to torment. I was reading an old *Time* magazine from December. You'd think for what I'm paying here, they could afford newer magazines.

"I heard a loud pop about five minutes later, and didn't look up. I thought it was kids setting off firecrackers. Then I heard more pops coming from a back room and a voice begging, 'Don't kill me! Please don't kill me!' Then there were more pops and silence. By this time, I'd figured out somebody had a gun and I was probably next. I threw myself down on the floor and crawled under the table, expecting him to come back out and kill me, too."

"You keep calling the killer he," I said. "Do you think the shooter was male? Can you give a description?"

"You sound like a cop," she said, and in her present mood, that was no compliment. "No, I never saw him. I never even saw his shoes when I hid under the table and he ran out the door. I keep saying him, but it could be a her. But it would have to be a big woman. Maybe it was the footsteps that made me think it was a man. They seemed heavy. The person definitely wasn't wearing heels. But lots of women don't wear heels, especially at a hospital.

"I'm so useless as a witness. I couldn't even remember how many shots were fired. And I'm supposed to be a trained observer."

Her voice was getting weak and wavery. She sank back in the car seat, and her thin bluish eyelids fluttered shut. Her next sentence was almost a wail. "I don't know. I just don't know. I was sitting right by the receptionist. He could have popped me in the back of the head and I'd have never known what hit me. I don't understand why he didn't shoot me like he shot her. No one else could figure out why, either."

Her hopelessness alarmed me. "You're not a suspect, are you?"

"No, I'm a witness, but no thanks to me. I didn't help things much at the hospital. The paramedics were crawling all over me in the waiting room, annoying the hell out of me, and this uniformed cop

who looked about twelve years old was standing next
to the dead receptionist. He said, 'Who would want to
kill this poor woman?'

"And I said, 'Everyone who ever met her.' "

I knew Georgia would be okay.

4

The dreams started again that night. I knew they would. They always came when something bad happened.

I did everything I could to ward them off. I didn't go to bed. I knew that was a bad idea. Instead, I sat up in my grandfather's recliner and wrapped myself in my grandmother's yellow-and-brown afghan. Then I stacked my books around me. I told myself I wanted to read my favorites, but I piled them up like a barricade. Comforting old hardbacks by Agatha Christie and Dorothy L. Sayers, early Sue Grafton, and in my lap, a fat brown volume of Dorothy Parker opened to "You Were Perfectly Fine." I gathered these strong women to protect me: Agatha, Dorothy L., Sue G., and Dorothy P. But they couldn't help me. Nothing could.

No matter how much I stared at the pages, the words wouldn't register. Instead, I kept opening the door to the radiation oncology department. I'd walk up to the receptionist's desk and see her bloody head. Then I'd race into the back rooms, looking for Georgia, and find the therapist and the doctor. And the blood. So much blood spattered and dripped and splashed. It was horrible. But at least I was awake, and as long as I was awake, I was safe.

Then I opened the door again, except this time, I wasn't in radiation oncology. I was in my parents' house. I was coming home from school, and I was nine years old, and I knew in some despairing part of me that the dream had started and I couldn't get away. I knew there was something wrong in the house, just like I knew there was something wrong in radiation oncology. It was very still, except for this odd dripping noise. My mother wasn't in the kitchen fixing dinner and my father's car was in the driveway. He never came home from work this early. I went up the stairs, which were tilted at the funhouse angle you find only in dreams, and I opened the door to my parents' bedroom. I wondered why my mother had a new red bedspread, and why she and Dad were taking a nap in the afternoon on a weekday. I heard the dripping noise, and then I saw the blood. It was dripping off the ceiling light. And I was running screaming from the room and out into the street.

But I didn't wake up. Instead I ran and ran until I was in the cemetery at their funeral, and now I knew what had happened. My mother had killed my father and herself. Everyone was shocked, except me, because they were supposed to be such a perfect suburban couple. But I knew they drank a lot, and she hit me when she was mad at my father, and she was mad all the time. He fooled around. Sometimes he'd take me along when he saw his lady friends, and I'd have to play outside. I think he liked betrayals even better than he liked sex. Betraying my mother wasn't enough. He had to have the affair with a neighbor or a woman at church or the wife of a man he worked with. The cruelest thing he ever did was have an affair with my mother's best friend, Marcie. That made my mother crazy and she shot him and killed herself.

Now I was running through the cemetery's gray granite tombstones, and everything was gray, grass and sky and graveside flowers, and I was trapped inside that famous photo of me at their funeral, the one in *Life* magazine. It showed me standing at their grave, in my little blue coat, except in the dream it was gray, too. I was supposed to be the picture of grief, but I was glad they were dead. I never told anyone that, but now I got to live with my grandparents, who never hit me.

In the dream, I was looking down into my parents' grave. But I didn't see the two steel caskets. I saw nothing. Just black. The blackest black. The black was closing in on me, coming for me. It was going to swallow me up. That's when I began screaming.

Then I woke up.

What time was it? The time glowed green on the digital clock: four-oh-three. Ugh. How long had I been asleep? I didn't know, but I felt awful. I brushed my hair out of my face and sat up. The recliner squeaked and suddenly lurched shut, almost toppling me out of the chair. My head felt like it was stuffed with old cobwebs and I'd left a little puddle of drool where the afghan was bunched around my face. Lovely. No wonder I lived alone.

My stomach rumbled and gurgled. I was hungry. It was almost breakfast time, except I wanted dinner. I hadn't eaten anything since lunch, and god knows what was in a *Gazette* sandwich. It had tasted like cold, wet newsprint. My system craved the comfort of

the four basic food groups: grease, calories, cholesterol, and chocolate. I knew where I could get all four
at this hour. There was a twenty-four-hour White
Castle a few blocks away. I dressed and drove there.
The chilly air chased the last ghosts away, and Ralph,
my blue Jaguar, felt smooth and powerful as he
prowled the empty streets.

The sky had the eerie blackness that was almost
ready to fade into dawn. The people in the stark
White Castle interior looked like characters in a Fel-
lini movie. There was an old woman wearing a tight
black dress and bottle-blond hair in a glamorous Ve-
ronica Lake style. Bright orange lipstick was creeping
up the cracks in her lips. Two pale young men, who
looked like they'd borrowed the same bottle for their
own dandelion-dyed locks, were taking a break from
selling their skinny bodies. A workman in khakis was
getting his thermos filled with coffee, and a dark-
skinned woman in a white uniform was dipping fries
in ketchup. I ordered four of the oniony sliders, fries,
and a chocolate shake. This food was more soothing
than the finest lobster and pâté. Pâté. Wait a minute.
Didn't I see a recipe for an offbeat pâté somewhere?
Sure. A wire service story about White Castle pâté.
Now that was a recipe.

"Make that to go," I yelled. Two minutes later, I
grabbed the grease-spotted bag and headed back to
my flat.

The salt-spangled fries and sliders glistening with
hot grease slid down easily while I did my Internet
search. I found several recipes using the little
burgers, including a White Castle turkey stuffing.
(Belly Bomber Thanksgiving dressing. The folks at
Tums would be thankful indeed.) I was tempted by

the Broccoli "Castlerole" recipe, which used ten White Castles, four packages of chopped frozen broccoli, a box of Velveeta, and Ritz crackers.

But the White Castle pâté had classic simplicity. I'd need a blender, but I thought I had one somewhere that belonged to my grandmother. I rummaged around in the kitchen cabinets, shoving aside dusty Dutch ovens, a meat grinder, and an ancient turkey roaster, until I found a blender from a long-ago margarita party. That had been a real success. Grandma had misread the directions on the mix, doubled the booze, and sent half the party home in cabs. The rest went home on all fours.

I lived in my grandparents' South Side flat, and I hadn't changed anything since they died. I still had the same slipcovers on the sofa and all my grandfather's bowling trophies in the living room. Over the old Magnavox console TV hung a picture of Jesus whose eyes followed you around the room. Plastic roses were twined in the picture frame. The kitchen had a massive gas refrigerator, a Sunbeam toaster shiny as a chrome bumper, and a monster Magic Chef stove with a warming oven. Just looking at that thing gave me delusions I could cook. On the bathroom wall were Grandma's plaster fish with the three gold bubbles and a top-hat toilet paper cozy she'd knitted herself. A decorator friend called the place a perfect museum of kitsch. I couldn't see buying all new stuff at Crate & Barrel. Besides, I admired my grandparents' good, honest lives. I guess it was a way of keeping them with me.

I checked the clock. Six-eleven. Mrs. Indelicato's confectionary was just opening downstairs. That used to be my grandparents', too. A confectionary was the St. Louis precursor to the convenience store. Most are gone now, but not my grandparents'. Some of the same families they waited on still stop in the store for six-packs, Pampers, and a pound of boiled ham. Mrs. I took it over and ran it the way they did, which meant she didn't make any money, either. She lived in three rooms in back of the store, and had appointed herself my guardian. Mrs. I was furious when I broke up with Lyle, and hardly spoke to me for months. She was finally beginning to thaw, but she still gave me the cold shoulder sometimes. I gave her a cheery morning greeting. She waved back, and I relaxed. She was busy unpacking Campbell's soup, and even at that hour her shirtwaist was perfectly starched and every iron gray hair was in place. I bought bacon, yogurt, sour cream, and a bunch of rather elderly parsley.

"You're cooking, I see," she said, approvingly. She hoped I would settle down and embrace the womanly virtues, or at least a good man.

"Yes, I'm making pâté," I said. I didn't add that the other ingredients were fifteen White Castles.

Half an hour later, I was back home, slowly grinding up White Castles in the whirring blender. The recipe called for the whole burger, including bun, pickle, and onion. I fed in three at a time, adding a little water to help them blend. The resulting mush was pretty gross-looking. Next, I buttered a loaf baking pan, and put the bacon strips on the bottom. I figured the cholesterol level was now up there with Brazil's national debt. I poured the glop into the pan, and baked it at three twenty-five for forty-five minutes. When I opened the oven, I swear it burped. This pâté definitely didn't look like it came out of a can. Not unless it had "dog food" on the label. It looked better after it cooled and I covered it with sour cream and yogurt, and sprinkled parsley on top. Then I shoved it down the garbage disposal. No way was I going to eat that.

But Charlie had his tested recipe, and I wouldn't have to do a Dialog St. Louis. And somewhere during this foolishness, the blood-soaked visions of yesterday vanished. I was tired, but no longer afraid. I went to bed—my real bed, not a chair—and fell into a dreamless sleep until ten A.M., when a truck in the alley woke me up. Damn. Late again. I called the *Gazette* and left a message that I was working on a project for Charlie. Then I went to Uncle Bob's, where I tested their recipe for scrambled eggs and toast. Perfect. I'd have to write it down sometime.

I picked up a newspaper from the box outside. The Moorton Massacre, as the *Gazette* called the hospital shootings, took up almost the whole front section. The police had been concerned for Georgia's safety. They said they would not release her name to the other media, and urged us to keep her name out of our stories. She'd said the hell with that, news was news. But I had called Charlie from the scene on Mayhew's cell phone, and for once he made a decent executive decision, although for the wrong reason. "Shit yes, keep her name out of it and where she works, too," he said. "Especially where she works. I don't want some nut with a gun coming up to the newsroom. My office is too close to hers."

Now I saw my story on the front page, and winced. I'd written the eyewitness account last night, although I didn't see a darn thing, and our police reporter wrote an equally informative news story, and we'd run a four-column photo of a body bag being wheeled out that looked like all body-bag photos. For all I knew, we had a stock photo we ran with all shooting stories.

The victim profiles had emotional quotes from hospital spokespeople about what healers and helpers the deceased were. I noticed no colleagues or patients seconded that emotion. No one mentioned the receptionist's nearly criminal cruelty, or said the doctor and the radiation therapist behaved like unfeeling jackasses with their patients. No one said the esteemed doc probably used the therapist as a human shield, either.

The few facts I did see indicated the three victims did not have deep roots in St. Louis. The receptionist was forty-seven, single, and lived alone in an apartment in Brentwood. Her parents and one sister lived in Lansing, Michigan. The doctor, a radiation oncologist, had moved here from Boston a year ago, leaving his ex-wife and child back in Massachusetts. The therapist was also divorced. He'd recently graduated with an associate degree and radiation therapy certification from North Oregon Community College. No clubs, hobbies, organizations, or churches were mentioned. Take away their cruelties and carelessness, and these people almost didn't exist.

I guess I should have volunteered to write the victim profiles, and given the *Gazette* a more truthful story. But the paper would have never printed it. Readers would have been fascinated and outraged and our phones would have rung off the hook, but editors found polite fairy tales easier to deal with. So I'd batted out my first person non-account and gone home. I'd driven Georgia home after the police took her statement yesterday, and she'd sent me straight to the *Gazette* after I got her upstairs. She promised she'd take a sedative that would knock her out for the night. I wondered if she'd even come in to work today. I was worried. How would she hold up during her treatment ordeal, now that her secret was out at the *Gazette*? I was afraid she'd be too sick and upset to work. I could see the ambitious staffers circling like vultures.

I underestimated Georgia. When I got to the *Gazette* that Friday morning, she was sitting at her desk, briskly going through a stack of papers, her usual fearless self. I heard from several reliable sources, who just happened to be hanging around outside Charlie's office, that she had marched in there and announced that yes she had cancer but the doctors had removed it. She was in treatment now, but she was recovering and she'd sue his socks off if he tried any shenanigans. She looked better than I'd seen her in months.

I poked my head in the door and asked how she was. "Fucking fine and dandy," she'd answered in her finest foul-mouthed style. "What the hell are you grinning about? Don't you have work to do?"

I did. Besides, I'd just appointed myself head of a new project. I was going to solve the Moorton Massacre. Might as well use the time I was there with Georgia. If I succeeded, Charlie would quit sending me on foolish and demeaning assignments. I could interview people who kept their clothes on for a living. Not that I minded Leo D. Nardo. The lad was decorative. But Charlie had originally wanted me to interview a female stripper. That story would have been illustrated with a page of porky photos, guaranteed to turn off women readers. Next he wanted me to write for that snore, Dialog St. Louis. I'd successfully evaded that, too. But how long could I keep dodging Charlie's turkeys? If my name was on too many bad stories, I'd start losing readers. I was tired of fighting, but I couldn't stop, or I'd be one more burned-out *Gazette* writer. A major success would let me win the Charlie wars.

Poor lost Leo. I could write about the strange case of the male stripper who took off—maybe for good— and it would be an interesting story. But if I could solve the Moorton Massacre, I was looking at major prizes. Fame and freedom would be mine. Then I thought, what a sweetheart I was, using three dead people to advance my career. Maybe I was more of a *Gazette* employee than I wanted to admit, even to myself. On the other hand, I had to be at the hospital, anyway. Why not ask some questions?

I ran into Charlie lurking in the back hall by my department. "Well, Francesca," he oozed, "where's your recipe? Or are you ready to start on the Dialog St. Louis page?"

"I have a recipe, a good one," I said. His face fell. "You'll love it, Charlie. It's a pâté. Uses fifteen ingredients from a major advertiser. Has a classy name, too: Pâté du Chateau Blanc."

"Have it on my desk by noon," he said, gruffly. Charlie was a sore loser. He immediately turned on me. "Where's your day in the life of a stripper story? I assigned that weeks ago. I want it by noon Monday."

"That's when my regular column is due," I said. "But I'd love the overtime." Overtime was against Charlie's religion.

"Noon Tuesday then," he said.

At eleven-thirty, I left to take Georgia for her radiation treatment. Moorton's radiation oncology center was temporarily closed, so we went to nearby Barnes-Jewish Hospital. The staff was fast, efficient, and professional. But it was two-thirty by the time I got Georgia back to the office. Then I worked on my column, so I'd have Monday free to do the legwork on Leo.

Friday night found me heading across the river to the Heart's Desire strip joint. Leo had been gone four days now. I talked with Steve, the club manager. He was a paunchy guy whose hair was dyed that brassy blond you see on pro wrestlers. Tight pants and a shiny black shirt, gold chains, and black chest hair completed the ensemble. Steve had a sleazy, night-crawler look. But I'll give him this: he seemed sincerely worried about Leo.

"Something's wrong," Steve said. "Leo would never just up and leave. He was a professional. He never missed a performance, even when he had the flu. I filed a missing person's report. The police sent someone out to talk to me, but the guy seemed to be going through the motions. I don't think the police are taking it seriously."

But his customers were. Business was down without the Titanic Lover. We were sitting in the bar, a half hour before show time, surrounded by empty seats. No wonder Steve was desperate to find Leo D. Nardo.

"Did Leo have any girlfriends?" I asked.

"Not really. Leo was a healthy red-blooded young man, nothing funny about him. But he never dated one woman long. And a lot of them were customers."

"You didn't mind?"

"Mind? I loved it. Word was getting out that a girl might have a chance with Leo, especially if she was generous." He winked at me. Yuck. "If they even thought they could take a stud like Leo home, they tipped like crazy and bought premium drinks."

"Was Leo seen with anyone the night he disappeared?"

"Nah. Just some old lady. Officer Friendly saw them talking. Listen, anything you can do to locate Leo, I'd sure appreciate it. My business is dropping like a rock out a high-rise window."

He gave me Leo's address and phone, and two photos: a fetching headshot and one of Leo in mid-strip. Then Steve let me backstage to talk to Officer Friendly. The poor officer looked hangdog. He was the perfect second banana, and pushing him into top billing seemed too much pressure. He was spreading oil on his body with a hopeless "we who are about to die" air. But he tried to be helpful about the woman he'd seen with Leo.

"I didn't get a good look at her," he said. "She was seventy-something, I'd guess. About five-five or six, a little on the chunky side, shortish gray hair, pantsuit, flat old-lady shoes."

Sounded like the woman I saw. Sounded like half the older women in St. Louis.

"Do you think she was asking him for a date?"

Officer Friendly snorted. "No way. She was *old*. Anyway, most old ladies don't have money. They live on Social Security. The ones with the bucks are in their forties and fifties. They're not bad-looking, they tip big, and they're horny as hell, pardon my French. Some of the divorced ladies, or even the married ones with husbands who ignore 'em, they can get pretty grabby with a guy. They'd give Leo little presents or help pay the rent, and he'd go out with them. He also dated real young, pretty ones sometimes, but they had no money. But this lady was too old. Grandmotherly, you know what I mean?"

"Any of them get jealous?"

"No, Leo had a way of talking himself out of trouble."

"Speaking of talking, did you hear what the older woman and Leo were talking about?"

"No, but I wouldn't worry about it. She didn't lay a hand on him. She seemed almost worshipful. When I got in my car, they were still standing there. I really didn't pay much attention, but I sure didn't think she could kidnap Leo."

I didn't either. But she might know where he went, or if he stayed to talk to someone else. Except I didn't bother to get a good look at her. Stupid. Stupid. I lectured guys about not really seeing older women, then I did the same thing.

Well, I would definitely look at Leo's roommate. His name was Justin, he was home when I called, and said I could come over to their place. It was about eight-thirty when I finally found his apartment complex off Dorsett and I-270, the official home of St. Louis's struggling young singles. With the money Leo pulled in, I'd have thought he'd live somewhere splendid. But Leo and Justin shared a two-bedroom apartment in a flat-roofed brick complex with an acre of asphalt parking lot. In the summer, the place must be an oven. The inside defined bachelor squalor.

Justin was an ordinary twenty-something with very short mousy-brown hair, a goatee, and a beginning beer gut. It didn't seem to bother him to live with a hunk like Leo. He was a nice enough kid, a waiter at an Italian restaurant. The hallway's focal point, as the decorators say, was a mountain bike, set off with Rollerblades and backpacks. I stepped around them, and followed Justin into a living room furnished with a pale green couch with dirty arms, two beat-up chairs, a weight bench, barbells, a state-of-the-art sound system, and big-screen TV. The coffee table was a plywood sheet on four cinder blocks. It was covered with pizza boxes, half-eaten bowls of cereal, milk glasses, and beer cans. A large black Lab snoozed on the sofa. He looked up, lazily thumped his tail, and went back to sleep. Must be exhausted from wrecking the hardwood floors. A fish tank by the window was filled with green algae.

No wonder Leo sounded restless when he talked with me. If he was thirty, I suspected this life was getting old.

"I've already told the police what I know," Justin said. "But if it will help find Jack—I mean Leo—I'll talk to you, too. I'm really worried about him. I haven't seen him since he went to work Monday. He never came home. Some nights he'd stop for dinner and get in about three, or maybe stay with someone, but he always came home by eleven A.M. He was bodybuilding and took a lot of vitamins and protein powders and shi—I mean stuff—at eleven every morning. Jack was a little nuts on the subject. That's why I think something is wrong. He wouldn't go this long without his vitamins. He said they kept him dancing."

I followed him into the kitchen to see the pill collection. My shoe soles stuck to the kitchen floor, and made slurping noises as I walked. A ten-gallon trash can sat next to the kitchen table. The sink was awash with dirty dishes and go-cups with sports logos. I was afraid to look in the pots on the stove.

Justin opened a kitchen cabinet. The shelves were loaded with vitamins and bodybuilding supplements in giant plastic bottles. Leo didn't need to lift weights. Just picking up the bottles should have given him muscles. I read some of the labels: SuperTwin High Potency Multiple Vitamins—bet that title was big with a male audience. Thermogenic Diet Fuel. Advanced Joint Support. Whey Protein Supplement. Two thousand grams of Pure Creatine Monohydrate. A box of twenty-four sports bars. "This stuff costs a fortune," Justin said. "Most of those bottles are twenty to fifty bucks each, and those sports bars are two bucks apiece. He'd never leave them."

He said Leo's black Jeep wasn't on the lot, and there was no sign of the blue gym bag with the nice green lining. His suitcase was still in the closet.

"Any clothes missing from his closet?"

"Nothing. Take a look."

Leo's bedroom had an unmade king-size waterbed, a battered dresser decorated with souvenir liquor bottles, another stereo, and a CD tower. Shirts, socks, pants, shorts, belts, towels, and bikini underwear were dropped in piles on the floor, the dresser, and the bed. Two shirts and a jockstrap hung on the CD tower. The closet door was open. Inside were thickets of empty hangers, two flashy-looking suits, and a costume under plastic. On the closet floor, under a jumble of shoes, hangers, and clothes, was a black nylon suitcase.

"How can you tell his clothes are all here?" I said.

"I can see them," Justin said, surprised I would

ask. "This probably looks like a mess, but he's got his clothes sorted into piles for clean, dirty, and dirty-but-I-can-wear-it-if-I-have-to."

I found Leo's leather jewelry box under a mildewed towel. It had a lot of chunky, cheesy stuff you find in pawnshop windows: gold chains, big rings with cloudy stones, link bracelets, cigar cases.

"Gifts from his lady friends," Justin said. "It's not my style, but nothing's missing that I can tell."

The bathroom's algae rivaled the fish tank. For some reason the toilet had a matching green tank cover, seat cover, and fitted rug, trimmed with dog hair. It was a homey touch, but the fixtures were so dirty I'd rather use a bus-station restroom. The medicine cabinet held a box of Trojans, a bunch of tubes squeezed in the middle, hair spray, theatrical makeup in manly shades of bronze, and Joe Blasco makeup brushes. The lad took his work seriously.

His eyeliner was still on the sink. That's when it finally hit me. He was dead. Had to be. I couldn't see Leo going anywhere without his eyeliner.

I tried to find a tactful way to ask, "Why would he live in this pit with what he made?" Finally, I said, "He lived simply for a man taking home twelve hundred a night."

"He saved almost every penny," Justin said. "He was hoping to retire soon. He figured he'd just about peaked, and when the Titanic act got old, he'd quit. He was getting tired of women scratching him with those long nails. They really tore him up, you know."

"I saw."

"Some of those cuts got infected. They took forever to heal," Justin said. "Women are animals."

5

I was looking for a dead man when the murder took place.

I was convinced that Leo D. Nardo was dead, his twelve hundred dollars were gone, and his sexy black Jeep was in a chop shop. But it was just possible he'd bought a plane ticket and walked out of his life. Other men had done it. Women, too. He could have taken that twelve hundred dollars and hopped a plane.

Monday morning, I took his photos out to the airport and showed them around the ticket counters. I showed them to janitors, skycaps, parking lot shuttle bus drivers, and fast-food counter clerks. Thousands of people went through the airport every day, but they didn't look like Leo D. Nardo. Someone would have remembered him.

No one had seen him. Airport security had no reports of abandoned black Jeeps in the parking lot. I was convinced that if Leo had left town, he didn't go by plane. He could have driven, but in that case, why didn't he pack any clothes or take his precious vitamins and protein supplements? He thought they kept him dancing, and that's how he earned his living.

I ate a pizza slice and a cinnamon bun at the airport—the smell of both had tantalized me all morning—and by eleven-ten I was heading back to pick up Georgia for her radiation treatment. I'd make one more visit to the Heart's Desire tonight to wrap things up and have the Leo story finished tomorrow. No problem. Barnes-Jewish Hospital had Georgia in and out of radiation onocology in thirty minutes. I was back at the *Gazette* by one-thirty.

The minute I walked into the newsroom, I knew something was up. Instead of the usual idle gossip and malicious comments, conversations were quick and decisive. Assistant city editors were issuing orders, reporters were talking purposefully on the phone, staffers were grabbing notebooks and cameras and bailing out for the parking lot. It must be a hot story. This was the time I loved newspapers best, when we actually reported the news. Newspapers were like armies—peacetime made us fat and lazy, interested only in fighting with each other. War made us lean and mean. This was war, newsroom style.

Jennifer, our newest reporter, was rushing back and forth across the newsroom, like a busy brown bird. Dart. Dart. Dart.

"What's up?" I said.

"Another doc's been shot at Moorton Hospital," she said, breathlessly. "In the Doc in the Box building. An oncologist this time. Early reports say the killer walked right into his office and shot him. That's all we know. Tina's covering the main story, Jasper's interviewing the people in the office, and I'm doing the victim profile. That's what these are for," she said, hefting a stack of thick computer printouts.

"Who's the dead doc?"

"Dr. George Brentmoor."

"When did it happen?"

"Sometime around noon. Gotta run."

Around noon. The same time as the radiation on-cology shootings. Brentmoor, the victim, sounded vaguely familiar. The best way to find out why was to check the morgue. That's the newspaper nickname for the reference department. It's accurate enough. Our dead stories are buried in the files.

A quick check of the computer showed Dr. Brent-moor and his wife, Stephanie, often starred in Babe's gossip columns. "The newsome twosome," in Babe-ese, appeared in photos at an endless number of hospital fund-raisers and parties. His wife had ex-pensively streaked blond hair, surgically tightened fa-cial skin, and a wide, stretched smile that looked like she might suddenly start screaming and never stop. She was so thin, I bet her backbone looked like a string of doorknobs.

The late doctor had the face of a fleshy third-rate Italian tenor: cleft chin, Roman nose, and thick wavy blond hair that surely was a torment to his chemo patients who were losing theirs. He looked hand-some, even noble, in his posed studio portrait, but he must have ticked off the *Gazette* photographers, be-cause their pictures of him were not pretty. In candid party photos, he had bags under his eyes, a paunchy middle, and a disfiguring sneer. He also had consider-able money and power, because Babe's coverage was adoring. This item from last Tuesday's column was typical:

"Superdoc **George Brentmoor** and his lovely wife **Stephanie** were bending elbows to benefit **Moorton Hospital** at the **Adam's Mark Hotel.** 'We're having a wonderful time. We're always happy to help the hospital,' cooed spouse Stephanie. Superdoc hubby played the strong silent type. Also present at the $200-a-pop pouring was hospital president Silas . . ."

I'd bet my paycheck that Superdoc refused to talk to Babe and the burden of making nice fell on his wife's skinny shoulders. No wonder she looked ready to scream.

I wouldn't learn anything if I stood with the other media outside the late doctor's office. The press would get the usual spokesperson statements. But I knew someone who could tell me about Dr. Brentmoor—Valerie Cannata, the red-haired chemo nurse I'd seen at the Heart's Desire. She worked at Moorton.

I left a note with city desk that I was checking out a chemo nurse who knew Brentmoor. It took me twenty minutes to drive to Moorton and park. Cop cars, evidence vans, and ambulances clogged the street between the hospital and the Doc in the Box building. I finally found a meter spot on a distant side street and hiked to the chemo ward. The hospital had spread through this pleasant residential neighborhood like cancer. Old brick homes were torn down for parking lots. Other houses were converted into medical offices. Some of the old lawns and gardens still survived, and they were so alive on this hot spring day, I could almost hear the new plants pushing through the ground and the leaves unfolding. Everything smelled green and new and sun-warmed. Then I reached the hospital. The automatic doors opened like a maw, and I stepped into cold air and the sickly smell of chemicals. If it turned my stomach, what must it do to Georgia?

I could tell it was a bad day in the chemo ward. The waiting room was full of people who looked grumpy as well as sick. The nurses were rushing around, not smiling. I asked for Valerie, and after five minutes, she came to the front desk. She looked worn and worried. Even her bouncy red hair seemed tired. "Something wrong with Georgia?" she said.

"Georgia's fine, Valerie. I wanted to ask you about the doctor who got shot this noon. I need to get an idea what he was like." The patients elaborately riffled through magazines and industriously read paperbacks, pretending not to eavesdrop.

"Francesca," she said, "this place is in an uproar, the patients are upset, and we're running an hour behind."

"It's two-twenty," I said. "I bet you haven't had lunch yet. You won't help anybody if you pass out from hunger. I'll buy."

"Deal. I'll meet you at the hospital cafeteria in fifteen minutes. But I can't stay long."

It was more like twenty minutes by the time she showed up. The cafeteria offered fried fish, fried chicken, burgers and fries, a salad bar loaded with ranch dressing, cheese and croutons, twelve kinds of cakes and pies, and an ice cream sundae bar. I wondered why hospitals always served unhealthy food. Valerie wanted fried chicken, cherry pie a la mode, and a large diet Coke. I settled for a virtuous bottle of water. I'd reached my grease quota at the airport.

I recognized chemo patients at other tables. Some were drinking white soda and picking at packages of crackers. The ones with steady stomachs were wolfing down chocolate cake and other sweet treats. Or maybe the hearty eaters were the caregivers.

"I figure you know all the chemo doctors," I said.

Valerie nodded her head yes and took a hungry bite of bird.

"I'm not going to quote you. I just want some background. What was Dr. Brentmoor like?"

"A real bastard," she said, between mouthfuls.

"A bad doctor?"

"He was okay. His five-year survival rates were as good as any oncologist's at Moorton, and maybe better than some. Some oncologists are caring and compassionate. They are special people. Then there are the Brentmoors.

"George Brentmoor had the compassion of Dr. Mengele. Last week, I had a man come by for his chemo shot. I was really worried about this guy. He was doubled over with cramps. I called Brentmoor's office and explained. I thought he'd want to see him. Instead, he told me to have the patient get Imodium A-D, an over-the-counter medicine, and have the man call in the morning if he was still in pain. To me, that's like handing a Band-Aid to someone who's hemorrhaging, but I'm only a nurse, so I didn't say anything. But I was right. His wife had to take him to the Emergency Room that night, where they gave him a prescription for pain medication. Dr. Brentmoor could have saved him the four-hour ER wait. But he didn't want to be bothered.

"I had another chemo patient, a single mom trying to hold down a job at a bank and take care of her little girl. She was having problems with nausea. She asked if he could do anything else to relieve the symptoms. You know what he told her? 'What did you expect? I told you chemo would be tough. Be glad you can still function at your job.'

"That was his attitude: 'Chemo's supposed to be tough. Don't bother me.' He had no sympathy for his patients' suffering. He didn't want to hear it. If they asked questions that made him uncomfortable, like, 'What are my chances of recovery?' he'd walk out of the room. End of consultation. It upset his patients. They thought they'd done something wrong, when it was really him.

"Patients always want to know their chances, like they're betting on a horse race. You try to give them something positive to focus on during treatment. You say, Your white blood cell count is good this week. Or, You're not losing weight. Or, These symptoms are caused by the chemotherapy, they don't mean you are getting worse.

"But you know what Brentmoor told a man who asked what his chances were? He said, 'It's in the hands of God.' The patient said, 'So why is my insurance company paying you the big bucks? I could go to a priest for free.' "

"I'm surprised Brentmoor would say that," I said. "He sounds like the kind of doctor who thinks he's God."

"He's a jerk," she said. "I should say he *was* a jerk."

"You don't seem to have many regrets that he's dead."

"Just one," she said, finishing the last of her pie. "It's too bad he didn't suffer as much as his patients."

Brrrrrr. I was thoroughly chilled, and it wasn't just the hospital air-conditioning. Even the *Gazette* felt warm and homey after Valerie's description of Dr. Brentmoor. For once, I was glad to be back at the newsroom. I could see Tina pounding the computer keys, her high pecan-colored brow furrowed in concentration. She was the reason the *Gazette* hired so few African American women: she was glamorous, smart, said exactly what she thought, and refused to sleep with management to advance her career. An uncooperative troublemaker, by Charlie's standards. I always wondered why she stayed, until I met her boyfriend. A hunk. The minute his brokerage firm transferred him out of St. Louis, she was out of here.

I didn't want to disturb her, but she waved me over to her desk. "I'm working on the Doc in the Box murder," she said.

"Is that what we're calling it?"

"Not in the *Gazette*. It's a physician slaying. But that's what everyone called the Wellhaven Medical Arts Building, and one of its docs is now in a different box—a coffin. Besides, we can't refer to one murder as a massacre," she said matter-of-factly. "I heard you were talking to a chemo nurse about Dr. Brentmoor. Find out anything useful?"

"Interesting, yes," I said. "Useful, no. The doc's heart could be used for dry ice. The man was cold. Is that your reading?"

"Amen, sister. The police were interviewing everyone in the waiting room, and they asked one patient about Dr. Brentmoor. 'I'm sorry he's dead,' the patient said, 'but you practically had to put a gun to his head to get him to take your pain seriously.' "

"Good quote. How'd you get it? Don't they keep the press away from those interviews?"

"A uniform cop told me," she said. Tina had a re-
markable record of coaxing information out of the
police and other balky sources. "Too bad the *Gazette*
won't let me use it. We don't speak ill of the dead,
especially after Babe drooled over him in his gossip
columns. So I have the hospital spokesman's canned
quote and one from his partner, Dr. Partland, ex-
pressing his 'profound regret.' The best I could get
from his patients was, 'Nobody should have to die
like that.' "

"Not exactly overcome with grief, were they? What
about his wife, Stephanie? Did she show up?"

"Rushed right over from their house in Ladue.
Snippy little blond bag of bones. But she didn't talk to
me."

"Too distraught?"

"Too busy demanding that his paycheck be cut immediately. She also wanted to know when his next
incentive check was due and how soon his death benefits would be paid."

"Sounds like Babe's 'newsome twosome' were
well-matched for coldness. How did the doctor die,
by the way?"

"The police think the killer somehow got into the
doctor's private office. He could have been a patient.
But the office's back door was not locked in the day-
time, so anyone could have slipped in. The killer
could have been dressed as a UPS delivery person.
One was seen running from the building at the time
of the shooting."

"Any description of the UPS driver?"

"One woman said he was wearing shorts, had
tanned, muscular legs, and tight buns. Never got to
his face."

"Reverse sexism. I love it."

Tina laughed and then quoted from her notes: "Dr. Brentmoor saw patients that morning until twelve-fifteen. Then he went into his office and was shot five times. A nurse heard the doctor begging for his life, then saw someone running for the fire stairs. She thought the shooter was male, but 'he' might have been a tall woman. A witness saw someone running out the fire-stairs door wearing a baseball cap, jeans, and a blue work shirt. He or she ran toward the hospital parking garage, disappearing into the heavy lunchtime traffic. That's all we know. It's not much to go on. Police are checking out reports of both suspects, the UPS man and the jeans person."

She glanced at the newsroom clock. "Gotta go, Francesca. This is due in less than an hour."

I could tell which reporters weren't working on the Brentmoor murder. They were clustered around Endora's desk. She's our society reporter. The horse-faced Endora belonged to a well-connected St. Louis family, which was how she got the *Gazette* job in the first place.

"Hey, Vierling," she called in a loud voice. Why did women who went to expensive schools always yell? "Want to join the tornado pool? We're betting on how many wire service articles about tornadoes contain the phrase, 'sounded like a freight train' for the next four weeks."

"Including tornado features?"

"No, news stories only. If there's a tie, you have to estimate the number of houses and businesses without power during the four-week period. It starts today with this AP article about a tornado that wiped out a new subdivision in Marshalltown, Iowa. The tornado hit a house when a workman was inside. He said, 'The sky turned black, and all of a sudden . . . ' "

"I heard a noise that sounded like a freight train," we chorused. We lived in Tornado Alley. People used that phrase again and again because it was absolutely accurate, but we sure got tired of the quote. I picked my numbers and put down five bucks.

It was seven o'clock before I could leave the office and head over to Illinois and the Heart's Desire. Its tacky liveliness was appealing after the hospital grimness. The secondhand smoke and stale beer smells were a healthy change from Moorton Hospital's refrigerated sickness. There weren't quite as many women in the audience, and their screams weren't as frenzied as they were for Leo, but Officer Friendly had plenty of enthusiastic fans. In fact, if I hadn't seen the crowds for Leo, I'd say he was a hit. One chubby brunette kept stuffing five-dollar bills in his G-string like it was a craft project. I watched him dance for a while. He knew the moves, and he was handsomer than Leo in a more conventional way, but he didn't have what my grandmother would call sex appeal. The wild, unpredictable streak that made a woman want to forget herself wasn't there. He really was Officer Friendly.

I didn't have any plan. I wanted to sit and watch for a while, and see if I saw anything interesting. I took a table at the back of the room and ordered club soda from a topless young man wearing only a black bow tie and Speedos. I knew this getup was supposed to be sexy, but I kept wondering if he'd get one of his chest hairs in my drink. I sucked down three club

sodas, and by break time, I was looking for a restroom. I made a wrong turn in the hall and caught a
glimpse of Officer Friendly being very friendly in the
wings with a smashing young blonde who had platinum hair down to her waist. He had his hand down
her red hip huggers and was kissing her deeply. She
had her arms around his muscular shoulders and was
enthusiastically returning the kiss. Pretty young
women were an indulgence in his business. He
should be chatting up the chubby brunette who
passed out fives like fliers for the VFW picnic. When I
came out of the restroom, the blonde was gone, and
Officer Friendly was waiting to go back onstage. I
waved to him, and he came over. "Good crowd," I
said.

"Not bad," he shrugged. "I have some fans."

"So I saw. That blonde was definitely demonstrat-
ing her appreciation."

"She was just a friend," he said, but I saw the fear.
"Gotta go."

If she was just a friend, I'd like to see him with
someone he knew well. I swilled club soda through
the last show, then waited till the crowd thinned.
Twenty minutes later, I blended in with a group of
giggling women heading for the parking lot. When
they went to their cars, I turned toward the distant
employees' lot, and stood in the shadows by the
Dumpsters. I could hear something small rustling
through the smelly ooze inside, and hoped it was a
hungry cat. But with the chemical plants belching
their unnatural yellow smoke, even that probably had
two heads.

About half an hour after the show Office Friendly
came out the backstage door, looked around to see if

anyone was watching, then ran for a blue Miata. As soon as he opened the passenger door, it took off, leaving a white rooster tail of rock dust in the parking lot. The bright security lights caught a long flash of frosty white and blood red inside the car. The platinum blonde in the red outfit was driving, and she kept her car's headlights off until they were on the highway. Officer Friendly had something to hide.

I could see the Miata was heading toward Belleville, an old German community on the East Side that was like my neighborhood in south St. Louis, only more so. More little red brick houses and more appreciation of order and sameness. There weren't too many cars on the road at that hour. I floored my Jaguar and quickly caught up with the Miata, then followed at a sedate pace behind. Soon we were on Belleville's main street, which was called Main Street, until the Miata turned off into a brick apartment complex. I watched them park, noted which door they unlocked, then went home. It was one-thirty in the morning.

The next morning I was back in my usual routine, having breakfast at Uncle Bob's. I was glad I got custody of Uncle Bob's when Lyle and I split. That's what happened when a couple broke up: they divided up their old stomping grounds, like they divvied up their other joint property. Lyle got the Central West End, where he lived, and I got the South Side, my natural territory. It wasn't as bad for us as some couples. I had one woman friend who lost a dry cleaner, a shoe repair shop, and her favorite supermarket in the divorce. The husband was no big loss, but those were irreplaceable.

I'd settled comfortably into my booth with my breakfast when a shadow loomed over me, blocking my light. Oh, god, it was Warren. I wasn't ready for Warren before I had my coffee. Warren was a paunchy fifty-five-year-old car salesman who fancied himself a ladies' man. He used to pat Marlene accidentally on the bosom and buns, until she accidentally dropped a pitcher of ice water on his head. He wore a brown polyester jacket, yellow knit shirt open to reveal silver chest hair, self-belted tan polyester pants, and mustard yellow socks with brown clocks to tie the color scheme together. He had a clunky fake Rolex, an imitation diamond ring, and an insincere smile.

"I saw Lyle yesterday," he said. Funny, my real friends never saw Lyle. Just people like Warren.

"Oh," I said cautiously.

"He was at that place you used to hang out together, O'Connell's. Looked like he was waiting for someone. I didn't see her arrive, though. I had to go." That little knife twist. Her.

"Then how did you know it was a woman he was waiting for?"

"An educated guess. A guy like Lyle won't be sitting around getting lonesome after you've thrown him out. Of course, if you're ever feeling lonesome yourself, you can always look me up." He grinned flirtatiously, showing yellow teeth.

"Warren, if I spent six months in a lighthouse, I wouldn't call you."

"You don't have to get nasty," he said. "You ain't getting any younger, Francesca. It pays to be nice, you know." But he left in a huff. I hoped he was really mad and wouldn't speak to me ever again, but I knew I'd have no such luck.

"Want me to dump this pot of decaf on him?" Marlene asked.

"I wished he'd soak his head," I said. "What a jerk."

"Get anywhere with the dancer story?" she said, pouring me another cup. I told her how it was going, then mentioned that Georgia's doctor was a partner with the murdered Dr. Brentmoor.

" 'Better Sell' Brentmoor," she said. "I'm surprised someone didn't shoot him long ago."

"You knew him?"

"I knew about him. A lot of ER nurses eat here. One of his colon cancer patients was brought to the Emergency Room one afternoon with a possible bowel blockage. The ER doctor called Brentmoor in for a consultation—he was in his office at the Doc in the Box building. The patient was writhing in pain, and the ER was waiting for Brentmoor's opinion on the X rays, when he looked at the clock, saw it was three forty-five, and said he had to make an emergency phone call. He grabbed his cell phone and went into an empty consultation room. One of the nurses needed some supplies in that room, and heard what the big emergency was. He was calling his broker. 'The market's still dropping?' the great healer said. 'Better sell.'

"After that, he was known in the ER as Better Sell Brentmoor."

"Jeez," I said, "no wonder his patients didn't want to talk to the police."

Marlene went off with the coffeepot to top off diners' cups, and came back from her rounds excited. "Something's going on in the back room," she said. "I think it may be the Doc in the Box case. A bunch of police brass are back there, all guys, who think they're so sharp they'll cut themselves if they rub their hands together."

"If they were really sharp, they'd tip you," I said.

"Oh, I'm just a dumb waitress," she said. "What do I know?"

Marlene knew everything that went on at Uncle Bob's and a lot that happened in City Hall. The back room was semiprivate, and a lot of city skulduggery went on there. The men who used it generally tipped Marlene as if each dollar was stripped off their hide, and ordered her around like they were little kings. Marlene got her revenge by reporting their conversations to me.

"I'm really busy today," she said. "I can't hang around back there and listen."

"Think I'll use the back bathroom," I said.

"It was open last time I checked," she said. "Lock the door, and I'll put up the sign. And make sure the boys in the back room don't see you going in there."

I walked down the back hall next to the kitchen where the waitresses and dishwashers sneaked cigarettes and caught a glimpse of the knotty-pine paneled back room. Two younger-looking men were listening to a fit silver-haired type as if he was promising them eternal salvation. The younger men had that short-haired scrubbed-clean look of very good yes-men. I didn't know them, but I knew the older guy. He was Major Gideon Davis, high-ranking brass in the St. Louis Police Department. Davis was the first person to get his mug on camera whenever there was a high-profile case, and he often served as a police spokesman. If the case was solved, he never gave credit to the detectives who did the work, but somehow managed to imply that he cracked the case himself, without actually saying that. The three sat at a long table covered with paper placemats, coffee cups, and legal pads, deep in conversation. No one looked up.

I slid quietly into the back bathroom and locked the door. I heard a clunk on the outside. Marlene had hung the Out of Order sign on the doorknob. I kicked off my shoes. If I stood on the toilet seat, which had a tendency to wobble, I could hear some of their conversation through the vent near the ceiling. I held on to the top of the scratched beige metal divider with one hand, and put my other hand flat against the tile wall, and listened at the vent. I caught ". . . the hospital lawyers are going to refuse us . . . mumble . . . we have to make a formal request anyway . . . mumble . . . be denied access to patient records . . . ask our in-house counsel to file an appeal in circuit court . . ."

There was more talk about strategy and precedent and court cases. The court cases were cited by the slick young assistants, who liked to show how smart they were. My feet were killing me and I was having a hard time staying balanced on the wobbly seat. The strong cherry-scented disinfectant did not mask the restroom smells. Also, I had to use the bathroom, but I didn't want to miss anything major while the police brass were talking. God, they were still talking. I heard, "The police couldn't see them without the patients' written permission . . . mumble, mumble . . . we'll probably lose . . . hospital will refuse us . . . a matter of life and death . . . Missouri Attorney General . . . grave bodily harm . . ."

They batted these same phrases around like a cat playing with a paper ball and said something about a precedent which I couldn't quite decipher. But I thought I'd heard enough to figure out what was going on. Police investigators wanted access to the late doctors' patient records, but the hospital lawyers refused. The law protected confidential medical records, the hospital claimed, and the police couldn't see them without the patients' written permission. The police were protesting this decision. They were going to ask their in-house attorneys to file an appeal in circuit court. This was a story, if I ever got out of the bathroom.

At last, I heard a chair scrape back and someone try the doorknob. Then more chairs were scraping. The police brass were leaving, and none too soon. I waited long enough for them to pay the bill, then put on my shoes, used the john, and left, flushed with success.

"Hi, Francesca," said Mayhew, waving me over to his table. "Come join me for breakfast."

"Sure. I'll just have coffee, though. I have to get back to the office. I'm not hungry."

"Since when?" he said, shoveling in a huge forkful of bacon. That man looked good even with his mouth full. He was wearing a navy sport coat with gold buttons and a gold wedding ring. I concentrated on the wedding ring, reminding myself that he had little kids. Marlene poured us both fresh cups and he gulped his down. He asked what I was working on, and I told him about Leo D. Nardo's disappearance. Unlike Marlene, he didn't take the missing dancer seriously. "Probably shacked up with some customer," he said.

"Are you still working on the Moorton Hospital murders?" I asked.

"Yeah. We've done a lot of interviews: all the hospital staffers on duty that day, the security people, the victims' family, friends, former roommates. I'm beat."

I didn't have to ask if there were any leads. He sounded too down. "Get anything on the tip hotline?"

"It's clogged with calls," he said. "More than three hundred. Most are useless. The killer is their neighbor, their brother-in-law, or someone they saw at the 7-Eleven."

"Did you find the UPS driver who was running from the scene, the one with the tanned legs and tight buns?"

"How'd you know about him?" He looked surprised.

"I have my sources," I said. If I told him it was Tina, I'd lose any sense of mystery.

"He turned out to be a real UPS driver," Mayhew said. "Heard the sirens and ran to get his truck out of a tow-away zone."

"I wonder how they ID'd him—by his tanned legs or tight buns?"

Mayhew laughed, which meant he wasn't going to tell me. I waited until he took another bite and then said, "I hear your in-house attorneys are going to go to court so the police can see the confidential patient medical files."

He stopped chewing. "How the hell did you find that out?" he said. "Marlene doing your work for you again?"

"I hear things," I said, truthfully. "You think the killer is a disgruntled patient, don't you?"

"We suspect he *might* be," Mayhew said, carefully.

"And we're not even sure it's a he. I'd like to know where this leak is coming from."

"You know I can't reveal anything about an ongoing investigation," I said, just to yank his chain. It worked.

"Francesca," he said, seriously, "tell me you're not doing anything on the Moorton Hospital murders."

"Why not? At this point, the police have about as much information as I do," I said.

"Don't even go there," he said. "You almost got killed and sued last time you investigated a murder."

"Me? Interfere with a police investigation? Wouldn't think of it. I'm going to concentrate on the case of the disappearing dancer."

I was, too. As soon as I wrote the story about the police wanting to examine the patients' private medical records. I enjoyed calling Major Gideon Davis when I got to the office. He blustered a bit and threatened to fire the person or persons responsible for leaking confidential information to the press. I almost told him where I got it, just to see if he'd fire himself. Then he calmed down and decided to put the best face on things. He said it wasn't a big deal because they were going to hold a press conference tomorrow anyway. He confirmed that the hospital attorneys had denied the police access to the patient records and the police in-house attorneys were going to file suit in circuit court. Then he actually gave me a decent quote:

"We do not believe these were professional hits or random killings," Gideon said. "We believe the killer knew the victims, and knew his or her way around the building. One theory we're working on is that the killer may be the relative of a deceased patient who used the radiation oncology facilities or a patient whose life expectancy has been shortened by some procedure in that department. A look at patient records would help us determine the feasibility of this theory."

By the time I finished the story and took Georgia for her treatment, it was almost twelve-thirty and I was ready to work on Leo's story again. I stopped by the main library and checked a crisscross directory, a nifty book that listed people by phone number and address. If you had the address, you could find the name and phone number. If you had the phone number, you could find the name and address. The directory told me who Officer Friendly's mysterious platinum blonde was.

Next, I drove to Belleville to the brick apartment complex. A rather sharp-nosed neighbor confirmed my suspicions. I now knew enough to ruin Officer Friendly's exotic dancing career. I marched over to his front door and knocked boldly, for a blackmailer. One P.M. was a late start even for a slug like me, but it was early for a stripper. A bleary-eyed Officer Friendly opened the door in a not-so-exotic blue terry bathrobe.

I peeked in the door and saw signs of the blonde— one red spike heel flung off by the kitchen and an abandoned gold bracelet on the coffee table. In one corner was a box of toys. A little boy with white blond hair was roaring around the kitchen on a brightly colored plastic tricycle.

"I need to talk to you," I said.

"I'd love to, but I'm busy," Officer Friendly said,

starting to shove the door closed in an unfriendly manner.

"You tell me about your wife, or I'll tell everyone else," I said.

He turned white, then reluctantly let me inside. The little boy toddled up and presented me with a toy truck. It was slimy with saliva.

"You're married and this is your little boy," I said.

"Jazmin is just a friend I'm staying with," he said, eyes darting frantically.

"You're lying. She's your wife. That's your wedding picture on the wall over the couch."

He went from frantic to defiant. "Okay, we're married. So what?"

"So it could ruin you if it got out. Do you think those women will drive to the Heart's Desire to watch Ward Cleaver take off his clothes? They can see a naked family man at home for free."

"Please, don't tell my boss. I have a family to support."

"Then tell me everything you know about Leo D. Nardo."

"There's nothing to tell," he said. "He likes the ladies and they like him, and he hopes one day someone will like him so much she'll take care of him permanently."

"That can't be all there is to him."

"It is. Please, you have to believe me."

I remembered the building crowds last night, and the chubby brunette eager to fill his G-string with fives. "You wanted to be a star. You had him killed."

"No! How can you say that?" Officer Friendly looked so horrified I thought he'd pass out, right in front of me.

"Then you helped him disappear."

"No. I swear I didn't. I'd never do that. You got to believe me. I liked things the way they were when I was the warm-up act. I was making nice money, with no pressure. Jazmin works at a bank during the day, and I watch Tyler, then work in the evenings. I never wanted to be a headliner. Now Steve gets on my case if the gate's too small and drink receipts are too low, like it's all my fault if the women aren't buying booze. I don't know what happened to Leo, and I'd do anything to bring him back."

"Then tell me who he dated. Men? Women? Customers?"

"No men. He's definitely straight. He never dates one girl, I mean lady, I mean customer, very long. The older ones like to give him presents, and he likes to take them. But he wasn't with anyone the night he disappeared. I would have told you. I saw him talking to an old lady in the parking lot, and that's all I saw. I swear it. Then I went straight home."

By this time, the little boy was crying, and Officer Friendly was on the verge of tears. I left. I hated to see a grown man cry. I felt like a louse, making wild accusations to stir him up.

No pain, no gain, I told myself. That was a concept Leo would understand. I had enough now to write a hell of a story about his disappearance. I'd also keep asking questions around Moorton Hospital. My life was about to get really interesting. I'd stirred up two hornets' nests at once. I couldn't wait to see what would happen next.

6

Nothing happened.

My story about Leo D. Nardo ran, but it didn't solve the mystery of his disappearance. No one saw him after he left the Heart's Desire—no one who would admit it, anyway. His killer, if there was one, didn't want to discuss it. I'd hoped the gray-haired woman seen talking to him in the parking lot would call. But she didn't.

Plenty of Leo's fans called, though. They wanted to talk about the times they'd seen him dancing. They described his active abs and gorgeous glutes in graphic detail. It was like being trapped in a sorority of heavy-breathers. Jeez, no wonder Leo wanted to get away from his life. I was afraid he got his wish, too. I tried not to think about the strangely innocent man with the wicked body lying in a shallow grave.

I kept asking questions at Moorton Hospital, but I got nowhere there, either. I talked with all the chemo nurses. I tracked down several of Dr. Brentmoor's patients, and everybody I could find who went to radiation oncology in the week before the killings. We regulars recognized each other, so it was easy to start a conversation. Georgia belonged to the club. It wasn't exclusive—more than one out of three Americans has cancer—but the initiation is hard. Once you've heard those words, "You have cancer," you never look at life the same way. You're a different person, and so is everyone who cares about you. That's why patients talked to me when they wouldn't talk to the police. I was an associate member of the club, thanks to Georgia. I heard countless examples of Dr. Brentmoor's uncaring arrogance and radiation oncology's criminal rudeness. But no one saw anything that would lead to murder, or heard anyone making death threats.

I was frustrated at the dead ends. But there was one good result. Sometimes I didn't think about Lyle for a whole day. A whole half day, anyway. Then I would see something, any little thing—a man who looked like him from the back, or whose hair curled over his forehead like Lyle's, and the loneliness would hit me like a punch to the gut. It sounds terrible, but I was glad Georgia's illness distracted me.

When I took to brooding too much, I went to Uncle Bob's. I got my first lead there. Along with my skimpy breakfast, Marlene served up a generous side of gossip. She poured herself a cup and sat down in my booth.

"I'm on break now," she said, "and I have some news you can use. A customer who's a nurse at Moorton told me that Dr. Better Sell Brentmoor was running around on his wife with a nurse."

"Now there's a real surprise," I said. "I bet half the doctors at the hospital are cheating on their wives with nurses."

"I bet your estimate is low," she said. "But my source says Brentmoor got the nurse pregnant."

"No surprise there, either. My friend Jinny Peterson was a family planning counselor at a women's clinic, and she used to see way too many pregnant nurses, and the father was often a doctor. You'd think if anyone would know where babies come from, it would be doctors and nurses. But you'd be surprised how many nurses came in for abortions. They really believed the doctor would leave his wife and marry them."

"Brentmoor was going to leave his wife and marry her," Marlene said.

I think my mouth dropped open. "You're joking."

"Not according to this nurse. She says Stephanie the wife was on her way out, and the nurse—her name is Heather—was on her way in."

"She must have been a knockout," I said.

Marlene shrugged. "Not really, not what I heard. She was not as classy as the current Mrs. Brentmoor, but she was a lot younger and curvier."

"Maybe with a nice settlement, the current Mrs. Brentmoor would be happier without him. He sounded like a real jerk."

"He was. But Heather told my nurse that Brentmoor was 'really going to rub his wife's nose in it.' She wouldn't get a penny. He'd hired Hal Hawthorn. Know who he is?"

"Sure. The big Clayton divorce lawyer."

"The big mean divorce lawyer. The kind who declares war on the spouse and strips her of everything. Mrs. Brentmoor would have come home from lunch at the Woman's Exchange one day real soon and found the electricity cut off, her charge cards canceled, and her checking account cleaned out. And that would be just for starters. Before she knew it, she'd be selling real estate to pay the rent, like every other fortyish West County divorcée."

"Sounds like Dr. Brentmoor died at exactly the right time."

"And you know," she said, "it couldn't happen to a nicer person."

I thanked Marlene and tipped her well, which wasn't difficult when my entire breakfast came to three dollars and seventeen cents.

All the way downtown, I thought about what Marlene had told me. Was Brentmoor really planning to dump his wife for Nurse Heather? Her information was usually accurate, but I needed more confirmation. Unfortunately, I knew who I'd have to talk to, and I dreaded it. This was exactly the sort of thing Babe, our gossip columnist, would know.

A lot of *Gazette* reporters treated Babe as a joke. I thought he was the symbol of everything wrong with the paper. He was on the take in lots of sleazy little ways. The *Gazette* had a policy that reporters couldn't accept gifts or free meals, but Babe ate free at the best restaurants in town nearly every night. Restaurant owners had to swallow tabs of two hundred dollars or more, because Babe brought his friends. He never tipped. Bars and restaurants that played his game were touted as "society watering holes" in Babe's column. Places that didn't got snotty little digs. Every day, tribute arrived at his desk: flowers, candy, gift certificates. Store owners gave him "discounts" on jewelry and clothes. The *Gazette* management knew what he was doing and permitted it because they used his inside gossip, too. Just like I was about to do. I guess that made me as bad as them, but at least I felt guilty about it.

Babe was on the phone when I got to his desk. The person he was talking to must not have been important, because Babe was rude and abrupt. "Listen, I don't have time to take that down. If you want to see your item in my column, fax me the information." He hung up the phone without saying good-bye.

"Stupid bitch!" he said. "Do I look like a secretary?"

"Certainly not," I said truthfully. Babe didn't look like anything normal or useful. He was tall, pale, and cadaverously thin. Babe was a creature of the night and low light. The morning sun revealed his blotched and pouchy face, and the broken veins on his nose.

"I saw you lost a column regular to the Doc in the Box killer," I said. "Dr. Brentmoor."

Babe looked solemn. "He was a truly great man. A terrible loss for the hospital and the city. Terrible."

"What about his wife Stephanie?"

"That bitch." It was Babe's favorite word for women who were not important. I knew immediately Stephanie's stock had fallen dramatically. "The only thing she ever did was run after me to get her name in my column. 'Babe, please come to our party Saturday night. Charlie your managing editor will be there,' he said in a singsong voice. 'Babe, please come to the benefit. John Goodman will be there.' Babe this and Babe that. And those dresses! Oh, my god, the money she spent on clothes, and she still looked like an overdressed ragpicker. Those short skirts and knobby knees. I wonder how Brentmoor stood her."

Babe paused to deliver his payload. "He was going to dump her, you know, and I couldn't wait to see what Hal Hawthorn was going to do to her." Babe looked gleeful at Stephanie's downfall. "She was living in a house in Ladue that cost a million and a half dollars—and she spent another half million decorating it. She told me that, and I knew her decorator. When Hawthorn finished with her, she'd be lucky to afford a one-bedroom dump in Florissant." Florissant, a blue-collar suburb out by the airport, was social Siberia to Babe. "She's just lucky her husband died. Especially since that nurse he was going to marry was pregnant. Pregnant. Can you imagine?"

"What will happen to the nurse?" I asked.

"She's screwed. Dumb bitch." Babe's eyes glowed with hatred just for a second and then went dead again. I'd glimpsed the loathing he must feel for the people he wrote about. If Brentmoor had married the nurse, she would have been a new star in Babe's column, someone else he'd have to suck up to for silly one-paragraph items. But that hadn't happened. She no longer existed in his world.

I wanted to disinfect my entire body after my encounter with Babe, but I had what I needed: two sources confirming the information. Time for the next step. I called the new widow, Stephanie Brentmoor, and told her I wanted to write about her late husband. Stephanie naturally assumed I wanted to do a tribute, and I didn't say anything to persuade her otherwise. She was eager to talk to me. "I'm not playing tennis today," she said. "But I have a luncheon at the club, so perhaps you could come over this afternoon at one-thirty? I live on Upper McKnight Road. Do you have any idea where that is located?" She could have added, "you peasant."

"Yes," I said. "But I have another engagement this

afternoon. I couldn't make it before two." I didn't tell her my other engagement was taking Georgia for radiation treatment. Let Stephanie think my social calendar was crowded with glamorous events.

Stephanie Brentmoor lived in Ladue, my least favorite part of St. Louis. Lyle used to say I had a grudge against the place because the inhabitants were so rich, but that wasn't true. They weren't exactly on welfare in Town and Country, but I didn't hate that suburb. I objected to Ladue's old money arrogance. A few rich white guys from Ladue ran the city, and didn't give a damn about anyone but their own in-crowd.

Upper McKnight was between Upper Ladue Road and Upper Barnes Road. There was no lower anything in Ladue. Twisty and tree shaded, it was a tame Disney woods of baby deer and bunny rabbits. I caught snowdrifts of white dogwood through the green leaves and brilliant patches of hot pink azaleas and exotic flowers I couldn't name. Upper McKnight was in what passed for a mixed neighborhood in Ladue: the old money WASPs had to tolerate living alongside new money and a few Jewish people. The only brown people I saw here were wearing uniforms.

The Brentmoor house, like its neighbors an eighth of a mile away, was a colonial-style white stone with green shutters. I rang the doorbell. A coffee-colored housekeeper in a white polyester uniform answered the door, said Mrs. Brentmoor would see me in the den, and she would take me there. I got to see some of the half-million-dollar decorating on the way. The place looked like a Ralph Lauren showroom. He was the perfect choice for the unsure new rich. It was difficult to commit any sins of bad taste with Ralph, but Stephanie and her decorator skirted close to the line. In fact, they skirted, swagged, looped, draped, and tasseled the line. I would have been satisfied with the tassel concession alone. There were tassels on little gold ornamental keys in little marquetry tables, tassels on cushions, curtains, and shade pulls.

The tassels stopped at the den, which looked like an expensive English men's club in forest green and burgundy leather, except everything was brand new. The bookcase had Danielle Steel and LaVyrle Spencer hardbacks on the lower shelves. I was pretty sure the upper shelves had been filled by the decorator. I couldn't see a Danielle Steel fan reading leather-bound versions of Dickens and Eugene Field. One whole wall was devoted to photos of Dr. and Mrs. Brentmoor posed with conservative celebrities: Charlton Heston at an NRA fund-raiser, Henry Kissinger at a children's home benefit. I'd covered that shindig, and I knew the cocktail party and photo with Henry cost an extra thousand dollars. I wondered what the Reagan and Bush photos went for. In each one, Stephanie had perfect hair, high-priced clothes, and that ready-to-scream smile.

She looked much more relaxed in person. I wondered if that had to do with the late doctor's timely death, which saved her income and social position. Her blond hair was perfect and she was thin enough to be mistaken for a closetful of coat hangers. But she had unusual gray eyes that never showed well in the photos. She was about five-nine, but looked taller. Stephanie made her entrance after I'd had just enough time to be impressed with her possessions. She took her place on a shiny new leather sofa covered with hobnails and plaid pillows.

Her well-tailored beige pants, long-sleeved beige silk shirt, and pearls looked like an illustration for "How to Dress Like Old Money." Stephanie had everything down right, but something was missing—the careless arrogance, perhaps. Under Stephanie's silk I thought I sensed something tough and scrappy. She'd fought hard to get here and she'd fight harder to stay.

"I'm sorry we've never met, but I just love your managing editor, Charlie, and his new wife, Nadia. I see them at so many events. He's such a hoot," she said, letting me know she hobnobbed with the *Gazette* management and I didn't.

"Parties are Babe's territory and thank goodness," I said. "I'm not a party person." So much for establishing a rapport with my subject.

The housekeeper brought in coffee, and things settled down. Stephanie went into full gracious mode. I threw her some softball questions about her life and family. They had two sons, "both in college now, so my carpooling days are over. I nearly went mad trying to coordinate all their sports and school activities." George Junior was going to be a doctor like his father. The Brentmoors had been married twenty-five years. She had been an elementary school teacher when they met. After their marriage, she taught for a few years, then became a full-time homemaker. She chaired the hospital fund-raiser and loved helping the less fortunate. She didn't strike me as grieving, but she said the right things.

I asked her about the awful day Dr. Brentmoor was killed. I wanted to find out if she had an alibi. She wanted to retell the whole dramatic story. "I was at a Junior League luncheon, we had Peter Raven from the Missouri Botanical Garden speaking—you know Peter, don't you?—and we were just being served our salads when I got the terrible news and went rushing to my husband's side, but it was too late," she said. She managed to look sad, although she didn't cry. She also didn't mention the part about demanding his paycheck over his dead body. I wondered what else she was leaving out.

We went on like that for a half hour, and then when I'd asked all the polite questions, I started in on the impolite ones. It's an old journalist's trick to save the worst for last. That way if you're thrown out, you still have most of your interview.

"Mrs. Brentmoor, I am really sorry about your husband's death, but I must ask you to help me put some rumors to rest. I understand that your husband was having a . . . relationship . . . with a nurse at the hospital, and she was having a child and he was planning to marry her." And dump you and divorce you and leave you without a penny.

Stephanie's gray eyes turned to granite, and any graciousness was gone. "Let's get one thing straight, Francesca. I am Mrs. George Brentmoor, the widow of Dr. Brentmoor. Period. If you print anything—and I mean anything—to the contrary I'll sue you and that fishwrap you write for."

"I can certainly ask questions on subjects that people are discussing," I said. I wasn't intimidated by her.

"There was no divorce," she said. "No papers were ever filed. And if that blond bimbo says it's his kid, she better have a DNA test to prove it, because she probably slept with every doctor at the hospital. Got it?"

I got it, and I got out of there. I had a certain

grudging admiration for Stephanie. She was as tough as a two-dollar sirloin.

Could she have murdered her philandering husband? I wouldn't put it past her. But how did her husband's murder tie into the other killings? Had she killed him and made it look like a Doc in the Box killing? Would she murder four innocent people as a cover for the killing she wanted? It had been done before. And Stephanie was cold-blooded enough, that was for sure.

But how did she do it? Could she be the tall woman the nurse saw leaving the building? Stephanie wasn't anywhere near as tall as me, but some people thought five-nine was tall for a woman. The average American man is five-ten, and I've dated most of them. The average woman is five-three. By my standards that wasn't average, that was shrimp city. Stephanie had a good six inches on the average woman. She was tall.

Maybe she was smart, too, and got someone to do her dirty work for her. She could have hired a killer, the way she hired someone to clean her pool and mow her lawn.

All the way back to the office I kept running this theory through my mind. Stephanie seemed the type, and lord knows she had a motive. But the opportunity, that's where my theory tripped up every time. Rich ladies didn't just go to the Ladue Marketplace and pick up a killer-to-go. If she had a boyfriend, the police would have tumbled to it by now. They always looked for things like that. Besides, Babe would have told me. He picked up dirt like a Hoover. He knew when every Ladue woman screwed her yard boy, and he would have spread the word. No, I didn't think

Stephanie had talked a lover into killing her husband. So how did she get rid of the man, when she had hundreds of Junior League lunchers to swear she was eating lettuce when he was eating lead? Was she really that crafty? Or was she innocent? I wasn't sure my interview with her had accomplished anything.

"Just what did you think you were doing, Francesca, badgering an innocent widow?" Charlie was literally spitting, he was so furious. The minute I walked into the *Gazette,* I'd been sent to his office.

Stephanie, may her facelift sag like a cheap suit, had called Charlie and turned on the waterworks. She said I'd come to her house of mourning and made horrible, horrible accusations about her poor dead husband, attacking his character when he couldn't defend himself, and now I was going to print these awful accusations in the *Gazette* and ruin his reputation, and she would never be able to hold up her head again. Charlie was furious. He felt I'd embarrassed him in front of his society buddies. I could tell how mad he was by checking his bald spot. It turned red when he was angry. Now it was a dark blood color. That meant the Bald-O-Meter was off the charts.

"I did not make any accusations," I said, but I sounded defensive. "All I did was ask her a few questions. The woman may be involved in the Doc in the Box murders."

"That's ridiculous. She belongs to the Petroleum Club. You had no business asking her questions about her husband's so-called girlfriend. The man's dead. What difference does it make? You have no business making that poor woman cry. I have assured

Mrs. Brentmoor that you will not write anything derogatory about her husband. And you will not write another word for the *Gazette* until you write that woman an apology."

"An apology!" I was outraged. "I have to apologize for doing my job?"

"You have to apologize if you want to *keep* your job," Charlie said. "And I expect it on my desk today."

On the way out of Charlie's office I ran into Georgia standing in the hall, looking small and fierce. "I'll see you in my office immediately," she said, and I could see the smirking staff behind her.

"You're in trouble big-time," she said, when I got in her office and she shut the door. "The only way I can save you is to make it look like I'm chewing you out. Stephanie Brentmoor wants your head, and since she's Charlie's asshole society buddy, he just might hand it to her. This is no time for you to get on your high horse. What does he want you to do?"

"Write an apology! Or he'll fire me. I can't believe this. I'll quit first before I kowtow to that face-lifted phony."

"Shut up and count yourself lucky," she said. "We've got an out on this one that can satisfy even your delicate conscience, and we're going to take it. You'll tell her that you are very sorry that you upset her."

"I will not!" I said.

"You will too. Pick up your pen and start writing what I dictate. 'Dear Mrs. Brentmoor, I am very sorry that you were upset . . .' That way you're not apologizing for anything you did. It's the truth. She is upset and you're sorry. You don't have to say why you're sorry—you're sorry she's landed you in the soup. She'll consider it an apology. You'll be off the hook."

She was right, of course. I wrote the letter and gave it to Charlie, who read it as if he'd scored a deep moral victory. Evidently, its subtlety escaped him, too. Putting one over on Charlie should have made me happy, but I felt oddly cheated. It was no fun if he didn't know he'd been had.

That was the old Georgia, ordering me around, scheming to beat Charlie. God, I was glad to see her again. Sometimes I was afraid that Georgia was gone for good. She came back when I needed her, but only briefly. Outwitting Charlie yesterday seemed to have used up all her energy. Georgia wasn't feeling well today. She didn't say anything, but I could tell. Her skin had that yellow, sagging look, and she had dark smudges under her eyes. She moved carefully, because her breasts hurt from the radiation. Her hair had fallen out right on schedule but she had to tell me the first time she wore her new wig. It looked so much like her own hair, I couldn't tell.

Her moods swung from optimism ("A few more treatments, and this will be over.") to despair ("I'm enduring all this pain and I'm going to die anyway. It's cruel to make me suffer for nothing."), sometimes in the same day. I was running out of ways to cheer her up. I felt worn and tired and angry at her because I couldn't help her. Secretly, I had the same fears she did. But I never said them out loud. That would make them true.

Instead, I repeated what the chemo nurses told us: Her white blood cell count was good, her weight had stabilized, and her symptoms were fairly mild, considering. "Easy for you to say," Georgia would growl on a good day, "you aren't keeping barf bags in your desk."

"Yeah, but think of all the exercise you're getting, sprinting for the john," I'd say.

Georgia was past the halfway point with her radiation treatment, and the struggle was starting to show. Going back to the murder scene for treatment was getting her down, too. I tried to get all her treatment at the highly efficient Barnes-Jewish Hospital, but her insurance company wouldn't hear of it. She had to go back to Moorton. The radiation oncology department had reopened after a coat of paint and new carpeting in the waiting room. The back rooms had tile floors, and Georgia said they cleaned up fine. On hot afternoons, I swore I could smell the blood, but I never said anything to Georgia. It was hard enough for her to go back there. It took all her courage to open that department door the first time. It took all mine, too.

The hospital had a security guard right in the room, but I still jumped at every sound and looked up anxiously whenever the door opened. The department had a whole new staff now. The new receptionist, a thin woman with long gray hair, was nervous but extremely polite. The doctor and the radiation therapist were professional, sympathetic, and a little distant. Georgia said this was exactly what she wanted, but it was a hell of a way to change the staff.

After today's radiation treatment, we had one more stop to make, a quick trip to chemo to straighten out some paperwork. She had a long day coming up later this week, radiation and chemo both. I hoped she'd be feeling better than she was now. A sickly older woman came to the reception desk while we sat in the waiting room. She was a regular, the woman in the white turban I'd seen in the radiation oncology department the day before the murders. Today was not a good day for Mrs. Turban. Her eyes were vague and she looked shaky and confused. "It's not there," she told the receptionist. "The cab's not there."

"It *is* there," the chemo receptionist said, firmly. "I just called it for you. The cab is waiting by the front entrance. It's the second time it's come back for you. It won't come a third time."

"I looked and I didn't see it," Mrs. Turban insisted, but she was so sick she could hardly focus on anything.

"Okay, I'll take you there," the receptionist said, and called, "Rebecca, watch the phones for a minute, will you? I'll be right back." Then she gently took Mrs. Turban by the arm and steered her out the door.

"Wow, that was nice," I said. I wondered how these women could be so kind after all they saw. They were nicer than the oncology doctors I'd encountered, yet they spent more time with cancer patients. Maybe it was because nurses made a lot less money. Maybe their profession attracted fewer greedheads.

"They're so sweet here," Georgia said. "If the Doc in the Box killer hurt my chemo nurses I don't think I could bear it." She began to cry, then wiped her eyes. "I don't know what's wrong with me."

I patted her hand and promised myself to keep looking for the murderer, and not just because I wanted the story.

7

My resolution to solve the murders made no difference to the killer. There was another Doc in the Box murder the next day.

The third killing was puzzling. This victim was an internist in private practice. His office was on Chippewa in south St. Louis, miles from the hospital and the Doc in the Box building. Tina gave me the details when she came back to the office. This murder must have been a harrowing story to cover. Tina normally looked like Whitney Houston with a notebook. But now her cocoa-brown suit was wrinkled and one stocking was laddered. "Lord, what a scene," she said. "You never saw such crying and carrying on: patients, nurses, even the mailman was in tears."

"They were genuinely sorry he was dead?" I said.

"Definitely. Big difference from the others. Dr. Dell Jolley was well-liked."

"That was his name—Dr. Jolley?"

"Yep. Big old Santa Claus of a fellow. All he needed was a white beard. His patients were crazy about him, his nurse broke down and cried, and his wife of forty years had to be sedated from shock. I hope I don't have to go through too many more of those scenes for a while."

"That's a switch," I said. "Folks practically cheered when the other people were shot. That's what was so weird about these murders. Usually, when some nut walks into a building and starts shooting, he takes out a bunch of nice harmless people. It's such a waste. I've always wanted to give the killer a list of people who should be shot."

"Francesca!" Tina said, sounding genuinely shocked.

"Well, it's true. If I gave him a list of *Gazette* editors to kill, he'd be performing a public service. Up until Dr. Jolley, this killer seemed to shoot people who deserved it."

"You are too much," she said, but I thought she meant that literally. She started reading her notes, possibly to change the subject.

"Police say the shooter hid in Jolley's private office and shot the doctor when he went back to his desk at lunchtime to return phone calls."

"Another noon shooting," I said. "That's three. But why would he kill the first receptionist and not the others?"

"Don't know," she said. "No one knows how the shooter got past the receptionist, either. The door to the examination area opened with a buzz lock, but the receptionist says she let in only patients with scheduled appointments. This was a busy day for the doctor, but the patients were all regulars. There is a back exit, and that door has an alarm, but it's not turned on until after hours, so it's possible someone slipped in that way."

"Do the police still suspect the killer was a disgruntled patient?"

"Yeah. But I'm not sure why. This doctor seemed popular with his patients."

"So who wanted Dr. Jolley dead?"

"Answer that question," Tina said, turning back to her computer keyboard, "and you'll have a prizewinning story."

I wanted that prize. I wanted it like a lover. Or in place of the lover I'd lost. This would truly be a consolation prize. If I won a major award, I'd have respect and freedom. But I wouldn't win anything sitting here. I wracked my brains trying to think who I knew who'd know Dr. Jolley. Probably not Valerie. Chemo nurses usually dealt with oncologists, not internists. But St. Louis was the world's biggest small town. There had to be someone. Then I thought of the person. It was so obvious. My neighbor, Janet Smith. She knew everyone on the South Side. She'd know Dr. Jolley. I called her and got lucky. She was home.

"Hey," she said. Her voice sounded a little off, like she had a cold. "You must have read my mind. I've been thinking about calling you. I saw this sign at the supermarket at Hampton Village. It said, 'WIN A RIDE IN A POLICE CAR!' I thought that sounded kind of neat, so I went over for a closer look. 'Shoplift here and you win a ride,' it said. It was an antishoplifting ad. Don't you love it?"

That's what kept my column going—people like Janet. Sometimes I got a column. Other times, I just got a laugh. Either way, I was grateful.

"Suits our neighborhood better than a sanctimonious lecture," I said. "Now I've got a question for you. Did you know Dr. Jolley?"

"Know him?" she said. "He's been my GP for over twenty years. I heard on the news that he got shot. I've been crying ever since." That explained her voice. She didn't have a cold. She'd been weeping for Dr. Jolley, like all his other patients.

"How would you describe him?"

"A real old-fashioned family doctor. Kinda short, with a stethoscope sticking out of his pocket. He always wore a long white coat, the way doctors did when we were kids. It crackled with starch and had his name embroidered in blue over the pocket. He had this little squinty twinkle in his eye that made you feel good. He's the type of doctor who always touches your hand, or pats your shoulder, even when he's bawling you out for not losing a million pounds."

I noticed she kept switching tenses, the way you do when you've just learned someone has died.

"So he was a good doctor?" I said.

"He had the nicest smile." I heard the hesitation.

"Janet, I'm not going to blacken his reputation in the *Gazette*. I'm just trying to get a feel for what the man was like. You had some reservations about him, didn't you?"

"Not about him," she waffled. "Not as a person. He was always there for me. But sometimes he doesn't— didn't—hear everything I was saying. It led to mistakes. He prescribed a medication that reacted badly with something else I was taking. I blamed myself for not making it clearer to him, but I didn't used to have to do that. Dr. Jolley was getting old and he didn't always pay attention like he should. I loved him, I really did. But I was starting to think I needed a younger doctor. I just didn't know how to break the news to him.

"Now," she said with a sigh, "I guess I won't have to."

Dr. Jolley wasn't cruel or arrogant like the other shooting victims. But he made a dumb mistake with Janet. I wondered if it meant anything. Even the best doctors, like the best reporters, made mistakes. Would his waiting room be so crowded if he slipped up too often? It was information to file away, like the shoplifting sign Janet saw at the supermarket. Maybe I could use it later.

That night, I went for a walk in my neighborhood. There was a new Thai takeout place on South Grand, which used to be a Vietnamese carryout, and before that a hot wing joint. The walls were still painted yellow from the wing days. Some Thailand travel posters had been added. The menu was a single stained sheet of white paper with the dishes neatly typed. I ordered SPICIE PEANUT NOODLE (Mild or Hot). "I'd like it hot," I said.

The tiny Asian woman behind the counter said in halting English, "Hot for you, or hot for me?"

I ordered hot for sissy Americans, and it still stripped my sinuses and made my mouth feel like it had been rubbed in ground glass and chili peppers.

"Hot for you, or hot for me?" Now there was an interesting distinction. That meal was probably mild by Thai standards. I was a foot taller than the Asian woman, but I was brought low by a couple of peppers. Twelve inches taller . . . I would be tall to her. Well, I'd be tall to most people. But would Stephanie be tall to her? Would a man of five-nine be tall to her? He'd be short for me. "Tall for you, or tall for me?" I wondered.

A nurse in Dr. Brentmoor's office had seen a man, or maybe a tall woman, leaving the scene of the shooting. What was tall for her? I'm sure she told the police, but I didn't know.

I stopped by the Wellhaven Medical Arts Building that morning and asked for the nurse. She worked for one of Brentmoor's partners now. She wasn't quite as short as the Asian woman, but if she was five-five she was pushing it. Her name was Karen and she said she'd talk to me because she was a big fan of my column.

"I've got your column about diets on my refrigerator," Karen said.

"The place of honor in any house," I said.

"I've already told this to the police," she said, looking worried. "I really didn't see much. It was more like an impression of a person running, if you know what I mean. I don't even know if it was a man or a woman. I think the person was wearing a baseball cap, but I don't know if they had short hair, or long hair shoved under the cap. I guess I'm pretty useless."

"No, no, not at all," I said. "I'm mostly trying to get an idea of how tall this person was."

"I'm no good at guessing heights," Karen said, despairingly.

"Where would the person be on me?" I said.

Without hesitation, Karen reached up and touched the middle of my ear. About five-nine. Tall for you. Short for me. Exactly right for Stephanie Brentmoor.

• • •

I had another idea. Dr. Jolley may have been making mistakes with other patients besides Janet Smith. If so, there was someone who would know about doctors' mistakes, my pathologist friend, Cutup Katie. She worked at the city medical examiner's office. She saw a lot of doctors' errors—on a slab at the morgue. I left my number on her beeper and she called right back. I knew she recognized my number, because she started in without any preamble: "If you're asking about the Doc in the Box murders, I can't talk right now. Call me tomorrow." Before I could say anything, she hung up.

That was Katie. She didn't mince words. I checked the newsroom clock. It was almost time to leave for Georgia's double-barreled day at the hospital. Chemo and radiation. As I packed up my portable computer and the notes for the column I was working on, I thought what a drag this was getting to be, then felt ashamed. If I was tired of hospitals, how did Georgia feel?

She was in a funny, optimistic mood today. She breezed through the radiation treatment and seemed cheerful about her chemotherapy, even though she'd be hooked up to an IV drip for a couple of hours. She didn't even complain about the long wait. The chemo waiting room was just as down-at-heels as the old radiation oncology waiting room, but it didn't seem that way. The chemo folks did their best, adding live plants, cartoons ripped from magazines, and baskets of hard candy. Hard candy kills the terrible sulphur and bleach chemical taste some chemo patients get.

Every chair was filled. I glanced around at the crowd. If they weren't in the chemo waiting room, I'd never guess some of them had cancer. Like that thirtyish man sitting across from me. He was bald as an egg, and wearing a Cardinals baseball cap. If I saw him on the street, I'd figure he was in style—lots of young guys shaved their heads these days, and thanks to Mark McGwire half the city wore Cardinals caps. On second thought, he was a bit too skinny to be healthy. But the tall, broad-shouldered woman next to him looked fashionably thin. The cancer diet. How effective. She reached to pick up her briefcase and I saw a bicep bulge. Did she work out? The only way I could tell she was a chemo patient was that her eyelashes were missing and she'd carefully drawn on dark eyebrows. I suspected her curly dark hair was a wig, but it was hard to tell. Women's wigs were so much better than men's. No wonder the skinny guy with the Cardinals cap decided to stay bald.

There was no doubt the woman in the next seat was sick. She looked wasted and old beyond her years. Her head was wrapped in a bright blue print scarf that seemed to drain all the color from her sallow face. I wondered how old she really was—forty? sixty? I couldn't tell if the handsome, healthy blond man pushing her wheelchair was her son or her husband, but he seemed to care about her very much. Next to them was a couple who seemed to be father and daughter. They had the same nose and chin. I couldn't figure out which one was the patient. They both seemed sickly. My robust good health seemed almost shameful beside them.

Valerie came out for a minute to say hi. I asked her, "Did you know the doctor who got shot?"

"Dr. Jolley? No, never met him."

"How do you think the killer's getting into these places?"

"Beats me," Valerie said. "I'll tell you this, because it's no secret. We tightened our security after radiation oncology. Hired more guards. Put cameras at all the exits. Made sure all delivery people showed IDs and signed in at the desk. Locked all entrances except the main one after seven P.M. Didn't do any good. The killer walked into the Wellhaven building the next week and shot Dr. Brentmoor."

"So how do you think the shooter's getting in?"

Valerie shrugged. "For all I know, you're doing it. You could be using Georgia here as a cover to get in these doctors' offices."

"But she never went to Dr. Jolley," I said seriously. Valerie laughed, and so did other waiting room patients.

"I'll come back for Georgia in about ten minutes," she said.

"Nice interview technique," Georgia muttered. "Why not use a rubber hose next time?"

"You don't think I'm a good reporter?" I said, suddenly sounding defensive.

"I think you're way too good for the *Gazette*," she said firmly. "I don't understand why you stay."

"Fine talk from management. It's simple. I like my job."

"You could work for any paper in the country."

"Not as a columnist. We're white elephants these days. You know that. Papers don't want us anymore. The only reason the *Gazette* keeps me is that readers would go ballistic if they got rid of me. At another paper I could be a reporter, but I'd never have the freedom I do here."

"What freedom? Charlie's always on your ass."

"Not if I solve these killings," I said.

She snorted. "Why not buy lottery tickets instead? If you win the thirty-eight-million-dollar Powerball, you could buy the *Gazette*."

"First thing I'd do is fire you," I said. Several patients laughed, and I realized we'd been entertaining the waiting room with our conversation. I was relieved when Valerie called Georgia in for chemo.

The treatment rooms had bare white walls, white tile floors, and two big blue recliners for the patients. The nurses and caregivers sat on spindly metal-legged chairs with thinly padded gray seats. A TV bolted to the wall played a soap opera no one watched. Valerie set up Georgia's IV drip and left.

At first Georgia and I shared the treatment room with a wan thirty-something woman who had dark circles under her eyes. But then Valerie came in and said, "I'm really sorry, Judy, but your white blood cell count isn't high enough. You can't take chemo this week."

"But I have to," Judy pleaded. "I missed last week, too."

Valerie shook her head. "It's not a good idea. I'll call your doctor, but I expect he'll confirm this decision."

Judy waited for the doctor to call back. We could hear other nurses in the break room, singing happy birthday to someone. Judy began to cry silently. I wondered if she was crying because she feared she wouldn't have another birthday. A few minutes later, Valerie came back and gently told Judy her doctor definitely said no. Judy picked up her book and purse and walked out, her shoulders slumped in defeat. The only thing worse than taking chemo was not taking it.

"Jesus," Georgia said. "The things we see here."

We had the small, bare room to ourselves now. The big recliner seemed to overwhelm Georgia. She shivered slightly in the refrigerated air. I got up, went to a cabinet, and found a thin hospital blanket. Georgia pulled it up around her and said, "Thanks, Francesca. You've done a lot of favors for me. Now I want you to do one more. Call Lyle. Quit being so goddamn stubborn."

Tears welled in my eyes, but I wouldn't cry. "I can't do that. This is something we can't work out. I don't want to marry. He does."

"What's wrong with marrying Lyle?" she said.

I laughed bitterly. "How can you say that, knowing what happened to my parents?"

"Your parents had a booze problem, plus a few dozen other problems. I've never seen you drink anything but club soda."

"There's hardly a happy marriage at the *Gazette*. Look how Charlie and his pals cheat on their wives."

"You really think Lyle would be like Charlie?" she asked, incredulous.

"No. I don't. I just haven't seen any happy marriages."

"If it doesn't work out, you can always divorce."

"Divorce isn't the answer. Look at Marlene and her ex. She spends more time thinking about that man now that they're divorced. She has to haul him into court to collect every dollar of child support. Marriage may not last, but divorce is forever."

I sat there, defiant and hurting, waiting for her next snappy comment. Instead, she hit back with the one thing I can't stand—sympathy. "Is there anyone else, Francesca?" she said softly. "Is there another man? Or are you just restless? You dated Lyle a long time. Maybe you need to check out the competition."

I shook my head. There was no one else.

"I didn't think so," she said. "Then look around here. Quit spending your days around computers and cancer wards. Life is short, too short for stupid stubbornness. You love that man. He loves you. What difference does a piece of paper make? You're married to him, anyway."

"I don't want to be a fool," I said.

"You already are," she said, angrily. We sat in silence until Valerie came back and disconnected Georgia's IV.

The next day, Georgia was not at the office. I called her home, but no one answered. I checked with her secretary. "There you are. I was just going to call you," she said. "Georgia called in with a touch of the flu, but she says it's nothing to worry about. She wanted me to tell you that she was skipping her radiation treatment today, but not to worry."

There was a lot of flu going around this spring, but I was still worried. Flu could wreck her white blood cell count. After work, I stopped by Kopperman's deli for chicken soup. I'd been raised Catholic, but I believed in the healing power of chicken soup from Jewish delis, especially when they used lots of dill.

I had a key to Georgia's penthouse. She'd given me one when I started driving her. I rang the doorbell and knocked loudly, for good measure. When no one answered, I let myself in and put the chicken soup on the kitchen counter. I found Georgia in bed, weak and sweating, racked with pain. She was wearing a jaunty pink turban that only made her look sicker.

Her hands scrabbled at the sheets as the pain hit her
in waves.

"What's wrong?" I asked.

"I don't know," she said, and then doubled up in
another spasm. "I have terrible cramps. I can't even
sit up. I called my oncologist this morning, but the
bastard was too busy to get back to me. His assistant
called at five and said the doctor on call would phone
me. He hasn't yet."

I looked at her bedside clock. "It's after seven.
You've been lying here suffering all day. That's outra-
geous. What's that doctor's number?"

I called the number and half an hour later, the doctor finally called back. He said to take Georgia to the
Emergency Room, and he'd fax his orders to the ER
staff. Georgia didn't want an ambulance. I helped her
dress and half-carried her to the car. At the Emergency Room, the knife-and-gun club was out in full
force. A woman had slashed her boyfriend across the
face and genitals, and he needed eighty-five stitches.
A drug dealer had a gunshot wound to the chest.
There was a two-car accident on Lindell, and the
bloody human wreckage was brought in. Georgia and
I spent the whole time sitting on molded plastic
chairs. Overhead, a TV mindlessly blared away. I was
sure they had TV in hell.

It was almost midnight when the medics got
around to Georgia, and I'd been fuming the whole
time. The doctor hadn't faxed his orders. Finally,
Bruce, the male nurse, a kindhearted fellow, called
the doctor directly. "I don't believe this," Bruce said,
and slammed the phone down. "The doctor's emergency number is a recording! I had to keep pushing

buttons and hitting the pound key to get to his answering service. I got lost and now I have to start over." Exasperated, he went through the routine again and finally said, "This is an emergency. I'm calling from Moorton Hospital . . ."

I looked over and saw Georgia huddled in an uncomfortable chair. She looked cold. Why were hospitals such refrigerators? I found a blanket in a supply closet and wrapped her in it. Twenty minutes later, she was taken to a cubicle, where the doctor on duty said she'd probably had a bad reaction to her pain pills. He put her on an IV and left her there for a while, then sent her to X-ray to check for a possible bowel obstruction, then brought her back and took some blood tests, then left her alone some more. Sometime during the next two hours, her cramps went away, and she fell into a restful sleep on the gurney. I felt achy and stiff from sitting on the hard plastic chair at her side. At two-thirty A.M. the doctor pronounced Georgia fit to go home.

"You must stop at a drugstore on the way home," he told me, "for her new medicine." I asked if he could give us samples, but the doctor said he couldn't. "There's an all-night pharmacy right up the road."

Georgia was sleeping when I parked the car at the pharmacy, and I didn't wake her. I went into the vast, empty drugstore. It was one of those places that sold ice cream and lawn furniture, cameras and clothes and cosmetics. The pharmacy was way in the back. The pharmacist was a young Hispanic woman with long dark hair and creamy skin and a name tag that said Rosie.

"That will be fourteen seventy-five," she said, as

she handed me Georgia's prescription. I handed her a twenty.

With that, the lights went out. The big store turned into a black cave. Then the emergency lights flickered on, providing an almost useless brownish light. The bright counter displays and seductive products were now threatening obstructions, dark with shadows.

I would have to pick my way carefully to the parking lot. I had to get out to Georgia. What would she think, waking up alone in a pitch-black parking lot? Where would she go for help? There was a Chinese restaurant on one side and a bagel shop on the other, both closed for the night. We were surrounded by a vast empty parking lot. We were absolutely isolated. I understood at last those news stories about how five or six people in a store were shot by a single gunman. That's when I heard the angry voices up front.

"It's a holdup!" Rosie the pharmacist said fiercely. I froze. She grabbed my arm and pulled me into a storeroom. Rosie bolted the door from the inside and whispered urgently, "Get over there in the corner, behind those boxes. If he shoots through the door, you have a better chance of surviving." I wondered if the last thing I'd see on earth would be a giant carton of Charmin bathroom tissue.

We could hear a man talking and the sound of a struggle. It was hard to tell, but he seemed to be dragging the manager through the store to the back. He was coming our way. No. Please god, no.

"Where's the tall one?" he kept asking. "I want the tall one." The manager kept protesting there was no one tall here. She was telling the truth. The pharmacist was about five-two. The manager was even shorter. The only tall one in the store was . . . me.

Was the gunman after me? Why? That made no sense. There must be another store employee.

Rosie and I heard the holdup man demanding once more, "Where is the tall one? I said I want her," then the cracking sound of a hard slap.

I made a move, but Rosie pushed me back down behind the Charmin boxes with surprising strength and whispered, "You cannot help her. You can only get yourself killed."

I waited for the gunshot. Instead, there was the blessed sound of sirens, then footsteps running out the back door. The gunman was gone.

"It's okay," the manager said, knocking on the storeroom door. "The police are here."

Rosie cautiously opened the door. I followed her out, weak-kneed and wobbly. Red-and-white police lights were strobing through the semidarkness. I could see Anitra, the manager, rubbing her face where the gunman had hit her. She was a small dark woman with high cheekbones and beautiful bronze braids pulled into a chignon. Her cheek looked swollen, but she didn't seem to be hurt otherwise. Rosie wrapped Anitra in a blanket and gave her hot coffee, but Anitra couldn't stop shivering. Rosie took her shaking hands. She said they were cold and clammy. The coffee cup didn't seem to warm them up.

Anitra could tell the police nothing except that her assailant was a white male, "kinda tall," but compared to Anitra, everyone was. He wore a navy knit ski mask with red trim, so she couldn't see his face and neck. But she knew he was white because she saw his hands. She didn't know how old he was. Maybe twenty. Or thirty. Even forty or fifty. He had on jeans and some kind of long-sleeved shirt but she was too scared to notice what color and the store was so dark she couldn't see it, anyway.

She knew one thing for sure. "He had a big gun and he shoved it right in my face, but he never asked for the money in the register. He kept asking for the tall one, and when I said there weren't any tall people here he hit me. He said I was lying and started dragging me toward the back. I thought I was dead."

Anitra had one more comment before she started shaking again and the paramedics arrived to treat her for shock. "He was weird," she said firmly. That really narrowed down the suspects, especially when you're talking about people out at three A.M.

I was worried about Georgia, sitting alone on the parking lot. I found a police officer named Mullanphy and he went out there with me. Georgia was sound asleep. We woke her up.

She was the one who'd called the police. "I woke up when the store lights suddenly went off and used my cell phone to call 911. Then I dropped off again. Chemo does that," she said. "Sorry."

Sorry? She'd saved us all.

The police asked if I thought the gunman was after me. I didn't know. I didn't think so. If he wanted me, wouldn't he say, "Where's Francesca?" I was a columnist, a local celebrity. He was probably one of those looneys you encounter in any big city.

The cops weren't so sure. They thought I could be the tall one. They asked me who I'd offended recently. No one except Charlie, and he'd rather kill my column than me. Had I been working on any controversial stories? Well, there was the missing stripper and my Doc in the Box inquiries. But Leo D. Nardo was still missing, and the killer was still loose, so I was hardly a threat.

The police weren't so sure. They were concerned about my safety. Did I live alone? they asked. Was there anyone I could stay with tonight? No, I said. I wanted to go home, to my own bed. I was perfectly safe. If the gunman knew where I lived, he wouldn't be following me into all-night drugstores—if it was even me he was following. The police cautioned me to take extra care. They asked again if I was sure I didn't want to stay with someone.

I wasn't going to do that, but I was still shaken. Officer Mullanphy offered to radio ahead and have someone check out my flat, but I said I'd be fine. Besides, I had to take Georgia home. She said I could spend the night with her, what was left of it, anyway. But I wanted to go home. How could staying at Georgia's provide any safety, when she was so weak and sick? If the guy really was after me, I'd just be a danger to her. I'd stay with her if I thought I could help her, but she only wanted to sleep. I could go to a hotel, but I'd written too many stories about hotel rapes and break-ins to feel safe there.

I told the police I was better off in my own place, in my own neighborhood, where everyone knew me. I said the ever vigilant South Siders were better than any security service. The neighbors would watch my flat and call the police if they saw anything out of line.

I couldn't tell the police the real reason I wanted to go home. I had nowhere else to go. My family was dead. Tina was my closest friend at work, but I didn't feel I could turn up on her doorstep at four-thirty in the morning. My other choice was to ask Lyle for help. I'd rather die.

It was after five by the time I got Georgia in her bed and headed for mine. I parked under a street-light. The moon was still bright, the sky was blue-black, and the zoysia grass was wet with dew. I wished I hadn't refused the cop's help to look around my flat for me. But then I saw my neighbors two doors down had their kitchen light on. The warm, gold glow in their curtained window was reassuring. Cindy and Joe left for work at six-thirty. If anything went wrong, they were within shouting distance.

Still, I spent extra time checking my front and back doors before I went in. There was no sign any-one had disturbed them. I carefully opened the front door, flipped on the light, and climbed the long, nar-row inside stairs, wishing I'd used a brighter bulb. I stood cautiously at the top and looked around the living room, then walked through the kitchen, bed-room, and dining room. I checked all the closets and the bathroom and opened the shower door.

Next I checked all the windows to make sure they were locked. Then I found the canister of pepper spray and put it on my bedside table next to the phone.

For good measure, I stacked my grandmother's noisiest pots and pie pans in front of the doors—the South Side burglar alarm—and put a kitchen chair on its side at the top of the steps. If I needed to leave in a hurry, I'd probably fall over it and kill myself, but I felt safer.

8

The phone was ringing.

I reached for it, knocking off the pepper spray and overturning my bedside clock. I felt like I'd been asleep for about two minutes. Who was calling at this hour?

It was the day-shift pharmacist. Rosie had left instructions to call me about the five dollars and twenty-five cents change from my twenty I'd left behind last night. Too bad Rosie didn't tell him to call at a decent hour on a Saturday morning.

"What should I do with your money?" he asked in a whiny voice. Nobody should hand me a straight line like that. Especially not a whiny man. So I told him exactly where he could stick the five dollars and twenty-five cents.

"And change it to quarters first," I added, as I slammed down the phone. I'd feel guilty about this later. It felt good now.

I crawled under the bed to find the pepper spray, then righted the bedside clock. It was seven thirty-six. Then I went back to bed and tried to go back to sleep. It didn't work. I kept replaying the events of last night in my head. Was someone really after me? Why? Because of my search for Leo, or the Doc in the Box story? I couldn't tell which one was going nowhere faster. The whole thing had to be a mistake, but that wasn't any comfort. People get killed for mistakes, too.

After half an hour of useless speculation, I gave up, got up and got dressed. I went out on the back balcony, a grand name for a slightly sagging porch with no exit. It was a brilliant spring morning, and the new leaves on my maple tree were a heartbreaking lime green. A squirrel skittered in the branches. I could see a neighbor's big old lilac bush in bloom by her back fence, heavy with sweet-smelling purple flowers. She'd also planted her ash pit with purple and yellow pansies. Years ago, South Siders burned trash in concrete ash pits back by the garage, until the city outlawed it. But we can turn anything into a decorative planter, from an old truck tire to a toilet.

These homey scenes didn't reassure me. I still felt jittery. The police thought someone with a gun was after me and I didn't know why. I hated guns and would never use one, but I needed protection, and I wasn't about to hire a bodyguard. What was I going to do?

Get a grip, that's what.

I went back inside and hauled the chair away from the top of the stairs, feeling pretty silly. What kind of protection was a chair? Then I started carrying the pots and pans I'd stacked in front of the doors back upstairs and put them away. I had a Dutch oven, three dented aluminum sauce pans, and a cast-iron skillet, and I still had to go back for a stack of muffin tins and pie plates. Did I really carry all this stuff downstairs at five-thirty A.M.? This had to stop. I refused to be spooked. There was no way that guy in the drugstore was looking for me. I wasn't the only tall person in St. Louis. Probably just another city crazy. I wasn't going to hang around the house and worry about it. Even if it was a Saturday, I was going to do some work. It was the only way to handle this. I grabbed my briefcase, took the pepper spray off my bedside table, and carried it in one hand. It wouldn't hurt to be a little careful.

I opened the front door cautiously and heard an odd scraping sound. There on my doormat was a pile of needles and clear plastic tubing, a surrealistic pincushion trimmed in red. The pile was about three feet across and a foot high. I bent down for a closer look, careful not to touch it. That's when I saw what the red trim was, and felt my stomach lurch. The tubing had blood in it, dark red and unreal. That meant it was used, and so, I guessed, were the needles. Someone had left a pile of dangerous medical waste on my doorstep, and I'd nearly stepped on it. A slip of plain white paper was stuck on one needle. Printed in blue ballpoint were four words, "Quit asking stupid questions."

Hands shaking, I shut and locked the door, and called 911. Then I sat on the couch and waited for the police, pepper spray clutched in my hand.

After the strange gunman last night, the police officers took this doorstep surprise seriously. They sent for an evidence van, and the tech gingerly removed the bloody pincushion present and my doormat. I'd be really embarrassed if that worn-out thing was ever used in a courtroom. Exhibit A: Francesca doesn't have time to go to Kmart for a new mat. The tech fingerprinted my front door, and took my fingerprints to exclude them. He said they'd also try to get fingerprints off the needles and tubes.

The police beeped Mayhew, and he showed up. He wanted to know what stupid questions I'd been asking, but I didn't know. Too stupid, I guess.

I told him I'd been working on the stripper story and he guessed I'd been poking around in the Doc in the Box matter, but I said I'd had no success with either. He said I must be more successful than I thought—I'd upset someone. He wanted the names of the last four or five people I'd interviewed. I refused. Officer Friendly had enough problems without a real police officer bothering him. I didn't want Mayhew talking to my other interviews, either. I wasn't going to upset my sources by siccing the cops on them.

"At least move in with someone for a while," Mayhew said. "The killer knows where you live."

"No point," I said. "If he can find my home, he can find out where I've moved. All he has to do is follow me there."

"I can't help you if you're going to be stupid," he said.

"Like my questions," I snapped.

"Please, Francesca," he said, softer this time. "Please listen to me. Move out for a few days. What's the big deal?"

I didn't want to get anyone else involved in my troubles. And I didn't have anywhere to go. But I didn't say that. Instead I said, "I'm not leaving."

Besides, I had a bodyguard. Mrs. Indelicato was fluttering in the background, a steel-haired guardian angel, wringing her hands and talking about the neighborhood going downhill. She'd watch my place better than a platoon of Pinkertons, and she had the ideal post in the confectionary downstairs. She'd see everyone who approached through her plate-glass window, and she could hear anyone on my porch. God help the mail carrier if Mrs. I heard him before she saw him.

That took care of home security. I'd take my pepper spray with me for protection. It was after nine by the time the police left and Mrs. I was sufficiently reassured that I'd be okay. Then I headed over to Uncle Bob's for breakfast. I told myself it was for information, but I really went there for comfort. Uncle Bob's was the only family I had. I was secretly pleased when Marlene greeted me with, "What's happened now? You look like the last day of a hard winter."

I told her the whole bizarre story while she kept me in decaf coffee and after a while I began to feel better.

"It has to be the Doc in the Box story that has this person upset," I said. "What do needles and tubes have to do with a missing stripper? They use them at the hospital for chemotherapy."

"Makes sense to me," she said. "I remember those tubes and that awful inch or so of blood that accumulates in the IV from when my mother was going for chemo. The nurse always throws the tubes and needle into the biohazard bin, and often it's overflowing at the end of the day. Anyone could grab a handful, provided they weren't afraid to handle hazardous waste."

"But why would they go after me? I don't know anything."

"He—or she—thinks you do," Marlene said.

"Great. Now I have to convince someone I don't know that I don't know anything."

"Either that," she said, "or you could solve it."

Before I left Uncle Bob's, I called Georgia's house to see how she was. No one answered. Was she sick again? Was today going to be a repeat of yesterday? I called the office to see if she'd checked in. Instead, Georgia herself answered her phone.

"You're at work? You feel okay?" I said, anxiously.

"I'm fine, and I'll be even better if you're not fussing over me like some old biddy." Ah, abuse. The sound of good health. We made a date for radiation Monday.

Then I got out my pepper spray, and Marlene escorted me to my car while Tom the cook watched out the back kitchen window. There was no one lurking on the lot, but I still felt nervous and exposed, even with Marlene and Tom watching. I wondered how long I'd have to keep feeling afraid. I had to solve this and get my life back.

The Family section was deserted on Saturday. I planned to get a lot done with no one around to bother me. After I read the weird wire service features. And piddled around on the Internet. And e-mailed jokes to my fifty closest friends. At three o'clock, I called the Heart's Desire strip joint. Steve the manager said there was still no word on Leo. Steve was clearly suffering down to the roots of his dyed blond hair. "The police aren't taking this seriously," he said. "I know Leo is dead. I just know it."

I knew it, too. "I'm sure they'll find him," I lied soothingly.

"They'll find his body. Maybe," he said. "But none of my ladies will want to look at it."

Bodies. That reminded me I was supposed to call Cutup Katie and see if she'd talk to me about the Doc in the Box killings. We played telephone tag for most of the afternoon. I reached her about four P.M. and set up an interview for Monday at the morgue. I left the office an hour later, having accomplished little besides a few phone calls. I felt nervous and jittery. I jumped at every strange sound, and on the walk to my car, I nearly pepper-sprayed an empty paper cup rolling down the street.

9

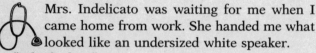 Mrs. Indelicato was waiting for me when I came home from work. She handed me what looked like an undersized white speaker.

"What's this?"

"A baby monitor. The batteries are new. Mrs. Geimer loaned it to me."

"Mrs. Geimer is eighty-six. Why does she have a baby monitor?" I said.

"For when her great-grandson Brian visits," she said. "I talked to Mrs. Geimer today. She will watch your backyard. I will watch the front. You need to put this in your room. Then I can hear if this crazy person breaks in and attacks you in the middle of the night. My bedroom is right under yours."

"You want me to use a baby monitor?"

Mrs. I's mouth hardened like a line in concrete. "Everyone uses them," she said. "Mr. Heinrich keeps one in his garage. His garage has not been broken into since he installed it. Mrs. Geimer has a monitor in a planter on her front porch. She heard two boys— fourteen years old, mind you—stealing radios out of cars. She called the police and they caught them. She also heard the Hendersons arguing about her mother coming to visit, and Miss Jerold propositioning the meter reader. Imagine. Asked him flat out!"

"My lord, is the whole neighborhood wired for sound?"

"It works and it's cheap," Mrs. I said, and that was the last word.

South Siders are naturally nosy, but I didn't realize the eavesdropping had gone electronic. Some people resented this prying into their personal lives, but not me. I didn't have a personal life, not since I broke up with Lyle. Mrs. I could plant microphones under my mattress and broadcast to the whole street.

Having arranged the twenty-four-hour security setup, Mrs. Indelicato now extracted her price. "Schnucks' has a sale on geraniums and some nice petunias," she said.

South Sidese, like Chinese, depends on voice inflection for its meaning. This was a command. It was time for the annual sacrifice of the flowering plants, which was the South Side version of throwing a virgin into the volcano. Every spring, we bought innocent plants—always geraniums and petunias—and put them in concrete pots on the brick porches to roast in the St. Louis summer. By August, they looked like they'd been hit with a blowtorch. It didn't matter that they'd die a horrible death in the hell breath of summer. A proper South Sider put out flowers in the spring. Mrs. I's neighborhood pride must be appeased. I would buy the doomed blooms.

Mrs. I and her starched shirtwaist moved stiffly back into the store. I could tell she was preparing more arguments in case I rebelled, but I was secretly amused. I'd been spending too much time in the world of missing strippers, murderers, and wealthy women who wanted their wandering husbands dead. I needed more time with normal people who put out petunias in the spring.

I checked my answering machine at work one more time, and was glad I did. A couple named Bill and Irene had invited me to their fiftieth wedding anniversary Monday. They were going to renew their vows at the place where Bill had proposed more than half a century ago—the Whispering Arch in Union Station. Then there would be a reception in the station hotel's Grand Hall. They apologized for inviting me on the spur of the moment, but their daughter thought this might make a column.

Oh yes, I said, grateful to be back in the real world. I called Bill and Irene and told them I'd be glad to attend. Irene said the ceremony would take place at the Whispering Arch at noon. Her oldest daughter had hired a photographer, and I could use some of those pictures if I needed them. Better and better. It was hard to get a photographer on short notice at the chronically understaffed *Gazette*. The ceremony's timing was just right, too. I'd see Bill and Irene, then go talk to Katie at the medical examiner's at one-thirty.

I slept well that night, or as well as anyone can sleep with a canister of pepper spray at her side and a baby monitor capturing every snore. When I woke up, the sun was shining and the birds were singing, and my fears of three A.M. gunmen and stalkers who left bloody surprises on my doorstep seemed ridiculous. So what if someone left a pile of needles and IV tubing on my doorstep? It was probably some nut irritated by a story I did months ago. "Quit asking stupid questions" wasn't much of a threat. I asked a lot of stupid questions. I couldn't keep track of them all.

But I wished I was smart enough to get some answers this time. I didn't know who was killing the doctors and medical personnel, and didn't know how to find out. I didn't know what happened to Leo D. Nardo, but I did know each day he was gone, there was less chance of finding him alive. I wondered if I'd ever see him alive again.

I knew one other thing: I was going to return to the normal world. I went to Uncle Bob's for my usual breakfast. It would be crowded with churchgoing families on Sunday, and literally crawling with kids, but that was good. I needed to be with people who did wholesome, everyday things. This time, I left the pepper spray in my purse. I did park my Jaguar, Ralph, in the front of the lot between two big-doored cars, so I'd be only a short run from the front door. I'd still rather risk a ding on his door than get trapped in the lonely edges of the back lot.

That's why I wasn't as alert as I should have been. I was still thinking about the missing stripper, wondering where he was. What I saw in the main dining room left me stunned as steer in a slaughterhouse. I just stood there stupidly. Leo D. Nardo was in a corner booth, looking happy and handsome in an expensive navy suit and power tie. A distinguished silver-haired woman with a merry smile and a well-styled gray pantsuit was next to him. Nearly empty plates of pancakes were in front of them. "Hey, Francesca," Leo said, waving to me, "come over here. We just got back in town an hour ago. Meet my new wife, Nancy."

I stared. Wife? She had to be seventy if she was a day.

"Pick up your jaw, sweetie," Nancy said. "I'm old, but I'm not dead."

I wasn't ready to make nice with Nancy. I was still mad at Leo. "Where have you been?" I said. "We thought you were kidnaped. Murdered. The police are looking for you in two states. And you didn't even have the courtesy to call."

Leo kept silent. Nancy dismissed my concerns with a wave of her hand. She was clearly in charge.

"It was very spur of the moment," she said. "I'd been pursuing him for months, and when I finally got Jack to say yes on the parking lot, I wasn't taking any chances that he'd change his mind on me. It took me a while, but I found the argument that convinced him. I said if he'd marry me, he'd only have to perform for one woman every night, and I'd take care of him better than that strip club ever did. We could travel and see the world."

"We're very happy," Jack said, looking into her eyes and smiling. I think he was. Nancy looked rich enough so he'd never have to work again. That rock on her finger could buy a two-family flat on the South Side. Her watch cost more than an Uncle Bob's waitress made in a year.

"Excuse me," she said, "I've been drinking coffee all morning," and headed for the restroom.

I was still angry and let Leo know it. "We've all been worried sick. We thought you were dead. Your roommate was frantic. Your fans have been in mourning. Your boss filed a missing person's report."

"Ex-boss," he said. "I'll call him as soon as the club opens, I promise. I'm retiring. Leo is no more. I'm

Jack now for good. Nancy persuaded me to run away with her and get married. We sailed from New York to Southampton on the *QE2* and took the Concorde back. She's an heiress to a manufacturing fortune, you know. She talked me into it on the parking lot that very night, and I just up and went away with her. It's the most impulsive thing I've ever done."

"Why didn't you call someone and say you were safe?"

"We didn't think people would be so worried. And we wanted this time to ourselves."

"Why didn't anyone see you at the St. Louis airport?"

"Because we drove my car to Chicago and flew to New York from there." He was studying his syrupy plate now. Something funny was going on. I let my voice get hard.

"Level with me, Leo. There's more going on than you two wanting time together. Why did you keep your marriage secret for so long?"

Leo fluttered his long eyelashes. I was immune to his charm. I fixed him with a glare. He squirmed. Finally he said, "Okay, I guess I owe you that much, after all the trouble I caused. But please don't put it in the paper. Nancy didn't want her children to find out we ran off together right away. She thought they'd pitch a fit and try to stop her. I'm . . . well, I'm ten years younger than her son. Her daughter is a lawyer and Nancy was afraid she'd try to have the marriage annulled and get power of attorney. So we stayed for a while in Europe until things settled down. Nancy's lawyers have the situation firmly in control, and I signed a prenuptial—or I guess it's a postnuptial—agreement. Anyway, the money I get comes from a trust that belonged to Nancy's mother, so it won't cut into her kids' inheritance, but I'm fixed for life."

"I still don't understand how you could up and leave like that. What about your clothes? You didn't pack a bag. You didn't take your vitamins." I sounded like an accusing mother.

"She bought me new clothes. I didn't want the old ones anymore. I dressed like a stripper. That awful purple muscle shirt." He shuddered delicately and shot his medium-starch cuffs. The cufflinks looked like Cartier.

"We were married in port by a judge, before the ship sailed. So romantic.

"Don't be angry, Francesca. You know why I did this? Because of you. You made me think about my life, with all your questions about my future. I realized I didn't have one. I finally saw things the way they really were. All those women screaming and scratching me every night." He winced, and I could see those long, bloody scrapes once again. "Those scratches hurt. One slip of those nails, and a man could lose everything. I didn't want to dance anymore so women could claw me until I bleed. Nancy made me an offer and I went with her on impulse and I haven't regretted it. Not one minute. I'm very happy."

He smiled so sweetly, I had to forgive him.

"I won't write about the trouble with Nancy's kids for now," I said sternly, "since you say it's been worked out. The first sign that a lawsuit's been filed, though, and the deal's off. And I have to let my readers know you're alive and well."

"Of course," he said. "I'll be glad to tell the world about my bride."

He gave me his new phone number. Nancy came back to the table, sat down, and gave his knee a proprietary pat. I noticed that her unpolished nails were very short.

So much for my lurid imagination. Leo wasn't murdered. He was married, and he'd married well. If it wasn't true love, at least the partners in this match were getting what they wanted. I'd imagined all sorts of horrible fates for him, but Leo was just a normal, healthy, young gold digger. No gunmen were after me, and the needles on the porch were just that—someone needling me.

The newlyweds decided to finally face the world, or at least Nancy's family. They paid their bill and left. I found an empty booth, just as Marlene came over to me.

"Wow," she said. "Who's your friend? I'd like to start my morning with that, even if he was guarded by his mother."

"That was his wife," I said.

"She rich?" Marlene said shrewdly.

"Very. That's how she married him. That's the former Leo D. Nardo, the missing stripper. The one I thought was dead."

"Wish I could come back from the dead as well as he did. Speaking of dead, get a load of Mayhew. Doesn't he look like the living dead?"

He did, except a fashion plate like Mayhew normally wouldn't be caught dead in the outfit he was wearing this morning. His dark brown jacket hiked up in the back, his blue shirt was wrinkled, his black pants needed pressing, his shoes were brown and his socks powder blue. He looked like he just got off the overnight bus from Omaha. The dark circles under his eyes added to this illusion. He slid into the other seat in my booth and reached for the coffee Marlene poured him like a drowning man grabbing for a life preserver.

"You look like particular hell," Marlene said. "Is the case going that badly?"

"We finally may have a break," he said. "We still cannot get into the doctors' records, but we may get a look at the health insurance records. We can see if any procedures were denied and what kind of treatment the insurance is paying for. It may tell us something. It's a step forward, but it's going to take so damn long to sift through those records and evaluate the information." He gulped more coffee, rather noisily.

"I know patient privacy is important, but isn't there a law that medical records have to be revealed if there's an emergency?" I asked.

"You're talking about the Tarasoff case in California. It won't help us for a lot of reasons. First, it concerned shrinks. It said mental health professionals have a duty to warn potential victims of violence if a patient threatens an identifiable individual. But these doctors aren't shrinks, and no one's made any threats to the victims. We don't know if there will even be any more victims. So Tarasoff doesn't do us any good."

"Do you still think the killer is a disgruntled patient?" I asked. "Brentmoor died just in the nick of time for his wife. He was going to dump her and marry a pregnant nurse."

"We know about the wife," Mayhew said. "If every doctor's wife killed her unfaithful husband, half the docs at Moorton would be dead."

"Anyway, it's a good start," said the unhappily divorced Marlene. She seemed cheered by the thought of dead philandering husbands. She plunked down a bowl of oatmeal in front of Mayhew, a man who'd never been too faithful, either.

By ten-thirty Monday morning I was on my way to Union Station, a sturdy stone castle in the middle of downtown St. Louis. I loved this old building with its arches, turrets, and tall clock tower. The rundown old railroad station had been redeveloped into a hotel and shopping mall, but the Whispering Arch remained unchanged. It was right on the Grand Staircase to the station's hotel. The ornate marble arch was framed by gold curlicues and set with a blazing jewel of a stained glass window. The arch was an accident of architecture, an absolutely pure semicircle. If the architects had set out to create one, they couldn't have. The arch's secret was supposed to have been discovered during construction, when a workman dropped a hammer on one side of the arch, and a painter heard him on the other side, forty feet away. What the workman said was lost to history, and perhaps it's just as well. But his discovery has been the delight of lovers, tourists, and curious kids for more than a hundred years. This is where Bill proposed to Irene.

Irene and Bill stood under the arch with their minister. They were a tiny couple, hardly more than five-two. Irene's huge white orchid corsage looked big as a cabbage on her shoulder. Bill wore a boutonniere in his best blue suit, and a fat, puffy tie that was years out of date.

This was nice, I thought, taking my place behind a

cluster of grandchildren. This was ordinary in the best sense. The hotel had roped off the staircase during the short ceremony. Bill and Irene repeated their vows. Then she walked to one side of the arch, and he went to the other. He whispered something and she giggled like a young girl. Everyone applauded, and the crowd trooped upstairs to the reception in the Grand Hall. Bill and Irene looked even smaller in that enormous, elegant room.

As I watched the couple, I knew my first impression was wrong. Bill and Irene were not ordinary. They were extraordinary. They'd been married fifty years and they were still in love. They held hands and looked at each other as if they were the only people in the room. Even with three bossy daughters issuing orders and eight grandchildren tugging at their clothes, calling "Grandma, look!" and "Grandpa, watch!"

Irene was eager to tell me their story. "I met Bill when my family was traveling to Chicago. My father bought a newspaper at the tobacco shop. Bill was a clerk there. It was love at first sight. My father was a successful lawyer, and we often took the train to Chicago. Bill asked me out, but my parents didn't like me to see him. They wanted me to marry someone who had prospects, a lawyer or a doctor. We couldn't meet very often, but whenever I came to the station we'd go to the Whispering Arch to talk. That's where Bill first told me he loved me. Six months later he proposed there and I said yes, even though he had no money. My parents opposed the marriage. They thought I could do better. But I knew there was no one better than Bill. When Bill was promoted to shop manager, we eloped. I thought I'd never hear the end of it. My

parents didn't speak to us until after our first child
was born.

"Bill was determined to make something of himself. We scrimped and saved and he went to night
school, and then he got a good job in sales. Twenty
years ago, he bought the company. But I always knew
he would do well," she said, patting his hand.

"You were very brave to take such a chance," I said.

"If you don't take chances, you don't live," she said.

Her words were like an ice pick in my heart. This
little old woman with the fluffy white hair was braver
than I could ever be. She'd built her whole life on a
proposal whispered into an architectural impossibil-
ity. I was too cowardly to marry. I told myself that
times were different and women were expected to
marry when Irene was young. But I knew she was
right: if you don't take chances, you'll never live.

"Have you ever tried the Whispering Arch?" she
said.

"Never."

"You must. It won't be the same with an old lady
whispering in your ear, but at least you'll hear how it
works. Come on, I'll show you. I'll be right back, Bill,"
she said.

She moved with a surprising girlish grace, as if
she'd gone back in time to the days of her romance.
She skipped lightly down the marble steps of the
Grand Staircase. On the landing, the arch's gold
curlicues glowed like liquid fire.

"You stand there," she said, pointing to a shallow
marble recess in the wall, like the secret entrance to a
mummy's tomb. "Now, put your ear to the marble. I'll
go to the other side. Wait and you'll hear me."

I pressed my ear to the air-conditioned marble and

waited. Nothing happened. About three minutes later Irene came back with a big smile on her face. "Did you hear me? Did you hear what I said?"

I shook my head and she seemed so disappointed I wished I'd lied and said yes. I wanted it to work for her sake. "We'll try it again," she said. "Sometimes it takes time for your ears to adjust. It's noisy in here. There are lots of people today."

I dutifully put my ear to the marble again. Two seconds later, I heard a whisper loud and clear. It was a malevolent hiss: "Die, bitch, die!"

That was not Irene. I stepped out of the recess and looked around. Irene was still picking her way through a sudden burst of people going up and down the marble staircase. I saw two African American kids in matching Tommy Hilfiger shirts take off running down the stairs, laughing. They pushed aside a big dishwater blonde, who glared at them, and nearly knocked down a thin man with brown curly hair. They skidded around a frail woman in a wheelchair, and the blond man pushing it yelled, "Hey, watch it!" I was about to take off after them, when a high school tour of about twenty kids with forty backpacks came up the steps. There was no way I'd get through that.

Then it hit me. I could hear it again in my mind, that soft, insinuating, evil whisper: "Die, bitch, die!" I was frightened, more frightened than I'd been when I found the bloody IV tubes on my doorstep, more frightened than when the gunman was looking for the tall one. I tried to tell myself it was a kid's prank, but that didn't stop the clutching in my stomach. I looked around frantically. The two kids I'd seen running down the steps were gone.

A few minutes later, Irene came back to my side of

the Whispering Arch, her corsage bouncing jauntily. "Did you hear it this time?" she asked.

"Definitely," I said. "I got the message loud and clear."

So much for normal life. I wasn't cut out for it. Irene got promises of love at the Whispering Arch. I got death threats. I didn't belong in the world of ordinary people. I managed to say good-bye to Bill and Irene. Then I left to meet Katie at the morgue. When someone whispers "Die, bitch, die!" in your ear, you definitely don't want to go to the medical examiner's office. The morgue was a grim reminder of all the things that could go wrong, and all the threats that became real.

Katie's office always spooked me, because it looked so normal but it wasn't. Katie never had anything obvious like a severed head in a jar. But I knew I'd see something strange. I checked it warily. There were framed diplomas and honors, a bookcase with fat, serious books, and a box of d-Con on the third shelf.

"You have rats?"

"No," Katie said, with that little grin, and I knew I'd stumbled on the strangeness. "That box killed a man, but he didn't commit suicide. He was a retired farmer who moved in with his city sister. He had to take a blood thinner called warfarin. You probably know it by the trade name of Coumadin. He knew that's what rat poison is—the warfarin thins the rats' blood and they bleed to death. He used it to kill rats in the barn. He didn't want to pay the prescription co-payment, so he calculated his body weight versus a rat's and took d-Con instead."

"And killed himself," I said.

"No. He did fine for ten years. Took it along with his Metamucil. Then he lost twenty pounds. That's what killed him. He forgot to recalculate for his weight loss. The man was too cheap to live."

Katie knew about farmers and their habits. She was a country girl, who drove a pickup and kept a loaded shotgun in her bedroom. Nearly shot her boyfriend one night when he came sneaking in the door to surprise her.

"So what do you want to know about the Doc in the Box killings?" she asked.

"What can you tell me?"

"You're not going to print this, right?"

"Not unless I check with you first. It's strictly background."

"Good. My ass is grass if you use it without permission. All the victims were killed with a thirty-eight. The killer's a decent shot, but he's not a pro. He put between two and five shots in the victim at fairly close range. Most of the shots are in the chest area, where they tear up the heart and lungs and major arteries. Some are in the head. The guy is using hollow points, which means he shoots to kill. Hollow points do a lot of internal damage. A thirty-eight is fairly easy to conceal. Somehow, he's getting in the doctors' private offices and nobody notices him or sees that he's carrying. The shooter might even be a retired cop."

"Do you think the killer is a man?"

"Not necessarily. You have a female shooter in mind?"

"Brentmoor was cheating on his wife with a nurse and he was about to dump her," I said. "Stephanie's pretty cold-blooded. Do you think she could have killed him?"

Katie snorted. "A rich Ladue lady packing a thirty-eight? No way. It would mess up her manicure."

"How did you know she lived in Ladue?"

"Because I know the type of woman who'd marry a doctor like Brentmoor. They're all blond, weigh ninety-eighty pounds, and don't have the muscle mass of a gerbil."

"That's her, all right."

"A skinny-assed doctor's wife who knows nothing about guns is not going to use a thirty-eight. She'd get a little sissy twenty-five, maybe, or a twenty-two."

"Maybe Stephanie used a thirty-eight so Brentmoor's shooting would look like a man did it."

"The shootings were all done by the same person," Katie said.

"Maybe she killed the other four people to cover up her husband's death."

This time Katie's snort nearly took out her sinuses. It was followed by a raucous laugh. "You really think a blond ditz could orchestrate five murders?"

"She's not stupid or disorganized," I said. "She's carpooled two kids and chaired hospital benefits. She's organized and hard as nails. Five killings would be easier than one hospital benefit and she wouldn't have to write any thank-you notes."

"She's not a serial killer," Katie said. "You saw how much blood there was with the radiation oncology murders. Could you see this woman ruining three separate outfits?"

She had me there. That was an awful lot of Ralph

Lauren to ruin. Besides, Stephanie did have an air-tight alibi. "Maybe she hired someone," I said, trotting out my hired gun theory one more time.

"Where? Could you see her in a redneck bar? Or reading *Soldier of Fortune* magazine?"

"Okay, you're starting to convince me."

And a plan was slowly forming. I knew Katie moonlighted at Moorton Hospital, working in the ER to pay off her student loans. I also knew the police couldn't get into the patient records. All they could do for now was depend on anonymous tips. Even if they got a look at the health insurance files, there would be hundreds of patient records to sort through. I thought I could cut some corners and get the information quicker from Katie. But I had to back into this slowly.

"Can you get patient records at a hospital?" I said.

"If I have privileges there," she said.

"What records are in the hospital computer?"

"Face sheets—that's insurance information, next of kin, home addresses, stuff like that—and lab results and surgical pathology reports. If I need more information, I can call the medical records room and have them send me the records. Why?"

I didn't answer that question right away. Instead I went back to the murders. "I'm trying to make these murders fit together, but I can't quite. It seems there's a pattern, and then there isn't. The first time, the killer shot the receptionist, the doctor, and the radiation therapist. After that, just the doctor was shot, even if the receptionist was sitting in the same office. And the victims' occupations are all over the place. The dead include the entire radiation oncology department, an oncologist, and then a plain old family doctor. What's going on? That's a wide range of doctors."

But as I said that, I realized Georgia had all these doctors and more. Her internist referred her to an oncologist, and after surgery she went to radiation oncology.

"Oh, my god," I said. "The killer has cancer."

"Or someone in his family has cancer," Katie said, "and he's killing doctors for revenge.

"But let's say it's an angry cancer patient, offing his doctors. The internist is the one who has to refer him to the oncologist. For some reason, the oncologist screwed up, or the killer thinks he screwed up, so he kills the internist *and* the oncologist. Then he'd have to go to radiation oncology for treatment, and they didn't cure him, so he kills them, too."

"Worse. They're rude and coldhearted," I added. "They may have insulted the killer while they treated him. I've been in that department with Georgia. I wanted them dead, too."

"I know they're bad," Katie said. "That department is notorious. We've all complained about it."

"That's a terrific theory, Katie," I said, hoping she would think this was her idea. "And you work at the hospital. You have access to the records the police don't. You can help me find the killer. The key is right in the computer."

"Are you kidding?" Katie said. "No way. First, it's a violation of patient privacy. I could lose my license. Second, I'd have to go through the records of literally hundreds of patients. It would take weeks, even months." But Katie didn't sound all that outraged at my request, so I kept arguing.

"It would be a violation if the cops went through

those records. But you're a doctor. You could look, and not tell me anything except the names of the people you think are suspects."

"So I'd violate the rights of a handful of people instead of hundreds," she said.

"The folks getting shot are having their rights violated, too."

"Look, Francesca, even if I wanted to do that, and I'm not sure I do, there are too many records to go through right now. One person couldn't do this work. You'd need an army. We need to know what kind of cancer the killer has. Then I can narrow it down."

"How are we going to find that out?" I asked.

"Wait for the next murder," she said.

10

Dr. Hale Tachman spent the last morning of his life trying to commit adultery, according to a nurse. She told police the doctor kept coming back to the filing area and flirting with the new bleached blond secretary. Two days ago he'd yelled at the same secretary for a typo in a letter. But yesterday she'd been shimmying around in a skirt that looked painted on, in the nurse's opinion, and the doctor had a change of heart, or something. He spent a lot of time watching her bend down for the V-Z files. Today, he'd come in all spruced up and the nurse heard him ask the secretary to lunch at the Channing Hotel, which everyone at Moorton Hospital knew was tantamount to asking her to sleep with him.

Unfortunately, the nurse didn't hear the answer. A patient hit the emergency call button in the bathroom and needed immediate attention, but the nurse noticed the doctor was going around whistling all morning.

The secretary told police that of course she refused Dr. Tachman's invitation. He was a married man with two little children. And besides, she added, why were the police listening to that nurse? It was common knowledge that she'd had an affair with Dr. Tachman last summer and he'd dumped her. The nurse was just jealous.

Dr. Tachman was a gastroenterologist. When he wasn't hitting on the staff, he gave sigmoidoscopies at Moorton, using a long, flexible tube with a tiny light to examine patients' colons. It was a primitive and painful procedure compared to a colonoscopy, and people dreaded it. They dreaded it more when Tachman worked on them. He was always in a hurry, and preferred to use the rigid sigmoidoscope, instead of the flexible one. The rigid sig was faster, but he couldn't see as much of the colon with it, which meant he could miss a "right-sided" tumor. This never worried Tachman, and his patients didn't know there were different kinds of sigmoidoscopes. They did know he was preoccupied, impatient, and unnecessarily rough, and complaints were made to the head of the gastroenterology department. Today, he was rushed, as usual. He finished his last scheduled morning procedure at eleven forty-five.

Dr. Tachman never made it to lunch, with or without the secretary. He was shot when he stopped in his private office to pick up his jacket around eleven-fifty. Dr. Tachman's office was at the end of a long corridor, right by the exit to the stairs. He'd complained about this office ever since he'd been assigned it. He wanted one that was bigger and not so isolated.

The doctor was right to complain. Police believed the killer simply stepped out of the exit door, shot the doctor four times as he paused to unlock his office, then ran back down the stairs and out on some other floor, where he blended with the crowd that was always at the hospital. No one saw the killer and the new staircase security camera was malfunctioning that day. Once again, the Doc in the Box killer got away.

I heard all the details from Tina when I got back to the newsroom. Tina was on the Doc in the Box team and covered this murder, too.

Katie had told me less than half an hour ago that we'd have to wait until the next murder to figure out what kind of cancer the killer had. Another doc was dead—a gastroenterologist—so now we'd know, and know quickly. That is, if Katie and the police were correct. I still wasn't ruling out the doctor's wife or, after Tachman and his antics, maybe a consortium of wives, as the killer. But I immediately beeped Katie. Ten minutes later she called back.

"We didn't have to wait long," I told her. "There's been another Doc in the Box killing."

"Who did he bump off?" she asked.

"Dr. Hale Tachman. A gastroenterologist. Did you know him?"

"Yes. He was an asshole," she said. "No wonder he specialized in looking at them. Takes one to know one."

"We have our next dead doctor. Now can you tell me what kind of cancer the killer has?"

"I can't talk," she said. "Want to meet for dinner?"

"Sure. Name the place."

"Blueberry Hill. Seven o'clock."

I had to spend the afternoon at radiation oncology with Georgia. She had a later appointment today, because Charlie had called a long morning meeting she couldn't miss. She was in a good mood. The doctor's reports were excellent, her white blood cell count was good, she'd quit losing weight, and she had more energy.

I recognized some of the regulars. Mrs. Turban was looking better today, more alert. I saw a new couple, a man in his fifties, waiting with his wife, who was about the same age. She was wearing a perky blue hat to cover her chemo baldness, and looked very pretty. As she sat down, he gave her bottom a little pat. She smiled at him. He smiled back. I felt terribly alone, and thought of Lyle, then pushed that thought away.

"God dammit, give him a call," said Georgia, who had a spooky way of reading my mind. I shook my head. I just hoped I could talk Katie into going through the hospital files tonight. I was actually looking forward to being awake most of the night looking at medical records. I'd rather go through old files than old memories of Lyle.

After the hospital, I stopped at Kopperman's deli and picked up some bagels and chicken soup for Georgia's dinner. Then I took her home. I got to Blueberry Hill ten minutes late. Katie was already sitting in a booth and had ordered a beer.

Blueberry Hill was in University City, an older suburb of St. Louis around Washington University. It had a delightful collection of boomer toys and memorabilia: gorgeous glowing old jukeboxes, Howdy Doody dolls, Beatles toys. Rock-n-roll legend Chuck Berry still did his famous duck walk once a month in the downstairs Duck Room, named in his honor. Even the bathroom walls were entertaining. My favorites included: "I'm so broke I can't pay attention" and "Gravity: It's not just a good idea—it's the law!"

Blueberry Hill also had a fast, efficient staff, cold beer, and a juicy burger.

As soon as I sat down, a waiter with an earring took our orders. Katie wanted a plain burger, medium rare, and a small salad instead of fries. I figured my fat cells would get extra credit just sitting next to a salad, so I ordered the cheddar burger with double fries. I had a long night ahead of me and needed the fuel. So did Katie, but she didn't know it yet.

The latest Doc in the Box victim had arrived at the morgue, Katie said, but she probably wouldn't do the autopsy. Her boss liked to do the celebrities.

"Do you know the kind of cancer now?" I asked.

"I have a pretty good idea," she said. "I think the odds are it's colon cancer. There are a couple of others a gastroenterologist would be looking for, but colon cancer is the most common. It's one of the big killers, right up there with breast and lung cancers. Colon cancer is more likely to hit men. Breast cancer generally goes for women."

"So we're looking for a man?"

"Probably. But women get it, too."

That was the problem with good doctors. They never gave you a straight yes or no answer.

The waiter brought our food, and I waited until the plates were on the table before I started talking. "Now that you've narrowed it down, you can check the patient records for likely suspects, right?"

"Wrong," she said. "I can get fired and lose my license. Unauthorized use of patient files is illegal and a breach of medical ethics."

"Come on, Katie. I've spent too much time around hospitals. Those records are not sacred, and the staff gossips like a small-town sewing circle. Anyway, who's going to know? You think I'm going to tell? If anyone asks me where I got the lead, I can say I overheard a patient talking. Everyone knows I practically live at Moorton these days."

"No," she said. "It's too dangerous."

"It's more dangerous not to find this killer. He's got a grudge against Moorton. You work there in the ER. Maybe you treated him. How do you know he won't come after you?"

"Because I keep a shotgun loaded with doubleought buckshot in my bedroom," she said, and bit fiercely into her burger.

"He won't be in your bedroom. He'll shoot you at the hospital, where they frown on doctors toting shotguns. Even if you are carrying a gun, you'll be dead before you can get it. Look what happened to Tachman. A gun wouldn't have helped him. He was ambushed outside his office."

We both chewed in silence for a while. I hoped that would persuade her. It didn't.

Katie said, "What makes you think I'll find anything? The information you need may not be in the hospital computer. Or we might miss something important. Unless you are at the Palace on Ballas—St. John's Mercy to you—hospital computers are always hopelessly out of date and slow. This is especially true at Moorton Hospital. I was on the computer committee there. Did I ever tell you about that? No? I guess I was too frustrated to discuss it."

Great. Now she had technical as well as ethical reasons not to do it.

"You have way too much faith in hospital computer records," she said, digging into a pile of lettuce like she enjoyed it. "The buying is always done by a committee, so the system is out of date before it starts."

"Why? The committee is too slow?"

"And stupid," she said. "The committee I was on was run by guys in suits who spent hours discussing a subject they didn't know anything about. They had no computer experience and there wasn't a medical degree in the bunch. They were going to buy this big optical disk 'jukebox' to store data, but at the time there was no technology available to *read* this data. Nobody but me thought this was strange.

"I felt like I was telling the emperor he was nekkid. I stood up at this meeting and said, 'Now let me get this straight . . . you want to spend two hundred grand for something to store data, but we have no way to easily retrieve this data, and we have no guarantee anyone will invent a way to readily retrieve this data?'

" 'Yes,' said the guys in suits.

" 'Why?' I said.

" 'Because we *need* to store it. It's a Joint Commission requirement,' they said.

" 'But if you can't get to it, what good is it?'

" 'That's not the point,' the suits said. 'We're not required to be able to retrieve it. The regs only specify that we store it.' "

I was impressed. "That's awesome stupidity. They could be *Gazette* management."

"The only good thing about the whole experience was that it gave me an intimate knowledge of the Moorton computer system," Katie said. "We won't have to spend all night at the hospital checking the records."

Did she say "we" and "checking the records"? She

was going to do it. She was going to search the medical records for me.

"Nowadays most people can work from their home
computer late at night using a modem and a dial-up
number. I bet you do that with the *Gazette*."

I nodded, but didn't interrupt. Keep talking, Katie,
I thought. Talk yourself into this. I can't do it without
you.

"I do that all the time when I'm on call. I'll get a
late-night call from the hospital and look up the patient's lab results from home. I have to. Half the time
the residents calling me don't have a clue what the
results are because they've been up all night and
they're dead tired.

"I can check most of the hospital records from my
home. I'll narrow down the candidates to a manage-
able number, maybe ten or twelve. Then we'll have to
go back to the hospital and get those records pulled.
That's the good news. The bad news is my dog Willis
likes to sit on my feet when I work at home, and that
makes my feet asleep."

"What can I get to keep you and your feet awake?
Coffee? Soda? Junk food?"

Katie finished her beer, and said, "Copious
amounts of Diet Mountain Dew and coffee. No junk
food. If I'm staying awake all night I have to avoid
carbohydrates like the plague, or I'll get a big rush of
energy and then a big crash. My late-night snacks of
choice are meat, cheese, and scrambled eggs with hot
sauce. I like omelets, too, but I suspect you can't
make omelets, can you?"

"I could, but you could patch tires with them. I
scramble eggs pretty good, though."

"That's your job, then. You can scramble me some

eggs in a few hours, and throw in lots of ham, bacon, and cheese. I'll need some beef jerky in between. I love to eat beef jerky."

"Done," I said. "When do we start?"

"Right now. I don't have too bad a schedule tomorrow, and you'll hound me until it's done. Follow me home, so you can find my house. You can get the snacks later."

I paid while she ducked into the john to check out the latest philosophy. She came out laughing. "There's a new one on the wall that fits our situation," she said. "It says, 'To err is human, but to really screw up you need a computer.'"

I followed her pickup to an old white farmhouse off Manchester Road, surrounded by big shade trees and old-fashioned flowers like bridal wreath, lilac, and iris. Willis greeted us at the door, a big friendly gray-brown mutt with a lot of terrier in his genetic past. There was a great deal of tail-wagging and ear-scratching, then Katie poured out his dinner.

While Willis ate and Katie made coffee, I wandered through the house. It had four rooms originally, two on each floor. The big comfortable living room had a fieldstone fireplace. Other rooms had been added on over the years in a rambling style. The most recent addition was Katie's, a new kitchen with cherrywood cabinets, a cooking island, and lots of sharp knives I hoped Katie didn't bring home from work.

Willis and I followed Katie into a small home office. He sat on Katie's feet. I moved a pile of papers and sat on a small beige sofa. Katie fired up the computer.

"Let me see if I can even get in tonight," she said. "The system could be down."

It wasn't. When I left for the supermarket, Katie was punching keys and Willis had fallen asleep on her feet. At the store I bought cheddar cheese, bacon, and a big ham steak for Katie, a loaf of sunflower seed bread, a dozen eggs, a dozen packs of beef jerky, and two chilled twelve-packs of Diet Mountain Dew. I planned to carbo-load, so I picked up pretzels, onion-and-sour-cream dip, and Oreo cookies for myself.

Back at Katie's house, I put the food away, popped an iced Dew, and set a stack of beef jerky packs by Katie's computer. Then I brought out my own laptop, sat on the couch, and started writing the column about Irene and Bill that was due tomorrow afternoon. The Oreos, dip, and Dew powered a huge energy surge, and I had my column written by midnight, when Katie put in a request for scrambled eggs with plenty of ham, bacon, and cheese. I turned out a tasty plate for the two of us, with green onions on top and hot sauce on the side. Katie ignored the loaf of toast I fixed, so I ate that, too.

Then she returned to work, with determination and another Dew. Katie regarded a computer as a balky donkey that had to be beaten, threatened, and cursed frequently to move. She loudly cursed the hospital computer's slowness and stubbornness. Her standard method of extracting information was to type in the commands, then during the long wait that followed, she'd flick the screen with her finger and snarl, "Cough it up, bitch" or "Spit it out, asshole." Katie's computer could be either sex. Once, she thumped the terminal hard on top and yelled, "Come on!" The whole hospital system must have crashed, and I thought our quest was canceled for the night.

We drank Mountain Dew and stared glumly at the screen and the SYSTEM ERROR messages. Katie had been ready to print a big file when the whole thing died, and now she wondered if her illegal search had been discovered.

Suddenly, the computer came back on and began spitting out the information, slowly, reluctantly, whining, grinding, and complaining. Katie was searching for colon cancer patients who had all the dead doctors. Then she looked for some problem they had that cried out for vengeance. About one A.M., I crashed on the couch, awakened periodically by Katie's snarls and threats, plus an occasional thump. At two-thirty A.M., she woke me up and announced that she'd narrowed the killer down to twelve possible candidates, and now we had to look at the hard copy files. She called the hospital's patient records room for the complete medical records for all twelve. Katie was remarkably alert, but so hopped up on caffeine she talked practically nonstop. I could hardly move. The couch was about as comfortable as a slab of concrete, and my back and neck ached. I stumbled out to my car. Katie packed a thermos of coffee and took a handful of beef jerky. She drove her pickup, and I followed in Ralph. I was so bleary-eyed I could hardly see. The road was a blur and the streetlights had rings around them.

We entered the hospital by an employee entrance in the back of the building. "You wait here in this room. I don't want anyone to see me wandering around here with a newspaper columnist," Katie said, shoving me into an office the size of a shower stall. There was barely room for a half-size desk and chair.

She closed the door and I wondered how long it would take me to develop claustrophobia. Perversely, now that I was off the road, I was wide awake. There was nothing to read in the room but a memo for the hospital blood drive and "Moorton Musings," the incredibly dull in-house magazine for patients, which featured photos of the administration sucking up to rich donors. This was an old issue. It showed a grinning Dr. Brentmoor at a party with his almost ex-wife, a lot of thin well-dressed women, and fat well-dressed men. I was reading the special bequests at the back when Katie returned with a huge pile of well-stuffed files.

"That medical records chick is a Nazi," Katie said. "She thinks all patients' medical records are her personal property. You'd think I'd asked to borrow her car. She wouldn't give me anything until I signed off on all my old delinquent charts. And she wants these back before she gets off work at six, or else. They're all a bunch of burned-out doctor-haters."

She parked her rump on the desk and said, "There are twelve patient files here. I think I can weed out some."

"Can I help?" I asked.

"How?" she said. "You don't know what you're looking for and you can't read the doctors' writing."

I spent the next hour in a chair designed by the Spanish Inquisition, listening to Katie mutter to herself. "In. Definitely. That one's out. No. Maybe. Maybe. No, can't be him. Wrong doctor." Then the file would go in the reject pile, and she'd start muttering again. She poured herself coffee and pawed through files. Meanwhile, I was deep into "Moorton

Musings," which was about as exciting as the *Gazette* editorial page. I read the message from Moorton's CEO, an article about the dedication of the Herbert Snernford lobby in Building D, and the entire list of Moorton Angels in the magazine. Dr. and Mrs. Brentmoor were on that list, too.

"Okay," Katie said. "I think I've got it down to three people. Let's go through the list:

"The first one is a twenty-seven-year-old man who died of colon cancer recently. He was unmarried, no children, worked as an engineer up until his death. He's past wanting revenge, but I wondered if his father, a widower with no other children, might want vengeance against the people who killed his only son. From reading his records, it looks like it took almost two years to diagnose his cancer. The doctor probably didn't think someone so young could get it. They put him through some tough treatment, but the guy died anyway. The father might be bitter enough over the loss of his only son to kill his doctors.

"The next candidate is a forty-five-year-old woman with inoperable colon cancer. A very sad case. She's married and has two kids in middle school. She'll never live to see them grow up. Her white blood cell count is too low and she can no longer tolerate chemotherapy."

Katie shook her head. "Another stupid diagnosis. The woman had a questionable sigmoidoscopy, so her family doctor, lovable old Dr. Jolley, ordered a CT with contrast. It came back with some very iffy results, but the doctor delayed giving her those results for several months."

"What does that mean?"

"Reading between the lines, I'd guess the doctor stuck the report in a drawer or buried it on his desk and forgot about it. She had a very fast-growing cancer, and by then it was too late to remove it. The surgeon performed a colostomy to make her more comfortable, and tried to shrink the tumor with chemo and radiation, but that didn't work. The cancer might have been fatal anyway, but with that delay in treatment she's going to die for sure."

I forgot about my aching back and sore neck and being stuck in this small uncomfortable room. All I could think of were these poor people, condemned to death by someone's carelessness.

"That's an awful story," I said. "I'd want to kill the doctors who did that to me."

Katie had one more file to show me.

"This is the last case, a thirty-year-old man operated on for colon cancer. His initial results looked good, but fourteen months after his operation, they found more cancer."

"Did it come back?"

"Can't tell. It was probably in there in a teeny, tiny microscopic amount, and then later . . . poof! Could have been something the doctors didn't catch the first go-around, could be something new. But it showed up first in his liver, and then in his colon again. I saw the poor bastard's path report. Not a chance he'll make it. He's discontinued radiation but still takes chemo. It probably keeps him going. I saw something else, too. About six months ago, he requested that copies of his medical records be sent to a lawyer."

"What's that mean?"

"He's thinking about a lawsuit. He's someone who definitely wants revenge.

"There are some other possible candidates for our killer, but none of them have stories as dramatic as these. I'd say the chances are good that one of these three is the killer. They all had Dr. Jolley for an internist. They all had a sigmoidoscopy at Moorton. They all went to the same oncologist, the late Dr. Brentmoor. They were all treated in the hospital's radiation oncology department. And they all have reason to be furious. Colon cancer is a very curable cancer, if it's caught early. If I had to get a tumor, it's one of the ones I'd want. Provided it was small. And not in the lymph nodes. To die of it would piss me off, too."

"Do any of these people fit the description of the killer?"

"Well, we don't know what the dead guy's father looks like. The woman was fairly tall—five feet nine and one hundred fifty pounds when she was diagnosed, according to her chart. Her weight's dropped to one twenty now. Her hair's light brown.

"The guy is about five-eight and he was on the heavy side, about one eighty-nine. He's down to one forty-two now."

"Hair color?"

"Dark brown."

"Who do you think is the killer's next target?"

"He's running out of people he can kill," Katie said. "Unless he—or she—has a grudge against some other specialist, I'd say it's going to be either the surgeon who performed the colostomy, or the chemotherapy nurses. And from what I know, it's unlikely this person would kill the chemo nurses. They're decent at Moorton. There's a slight chance it could be the surgical pathologist. The patient might think the path blew the call. Of course, it would take a pretty knowledgeable patient to know about surgical pathologists.

"I think it's probably got to be the surgeon. Everyone hates surgeons. I'd like to off a few myself."

Then Katie the Qualifier reappeared. "Well, urologists are usually decent. And ear, nose, and throat surgeons tend to be nice, but your average surgeon is a real prima donna. Surgeons are just glorified mechanics—cutters, we call them—but try telling them that."

Katie stretched and stood up. "Listen, do we really have to stop this guy? I think he's doing a good job so far. He's gotten rid of a lot of jerks at this hospital. That radiation oncology department needed cleaning out."

"The hospital could have just fired them, you know."

"Awfully difficult these days when there's no actual malpractice," Katie said. "You'd need tons of paperwork. The deceased oncologist had the compassion of a prison guard, and you already know my opinion of the doc who did the sigmoidoscopies. I'd be inclined to let the killer go awhile more."

Katie's conversation was making me uneasy. This went beyond path room humor. I hoped it was a caffeine overdose. "You are joking, right?"

"Well, yeah, I guess so," she said, shoving papers into files.

"Anyway, what about the murdered internist, Dr. Jolley? The police interviewed his patients in the waiting room and everyone said he was a nice guy."

"Dead men tell no tales," said Katie. "He made a stupid mistake with that woman. And I autopsied two of his other mistakes. One was a twenty-eight-year-old mother of twins. There are whispers of pending lawsuits. Nothing's gone public yet, but I've heard the rumors. Dr. Jolley had a great bedside manner, but he was careless. That kind of thing is hard to prove. The guy's not a drunk or an out-and-out incompetent who cut off the wrong leg, and doctors hate testifying against each other. We all think, when one of our own does something stupid, 'There but for the grace of God . . .' It would have taken a long time and a lot of rumors to bring Dr. Jolley down. This killer got rid of Dr. Jolley for us, and we don't have to feel guilty."

I stared at her. But then I thought about all the incompetent reporters who were still working. What did we do to stop them? Nothing. We had our own code in the media. Maybe our mistakes didn't kill people, but we could make them miserable.

"What do you think we should do next?" I asked her.

"We? Unless you got a mouse in your pocket, there is no more we. Now it's up to you. I'll give you the patients' addresses, next of kin, home and work numbers. That's all. I'm finished. You won't see any of these files. At least I'll be able to say under oath that I never showed them to anyone. They'll go back to the records room before we leave, or my life isn't worth living. The medical-records Nazi will hunt me down like a dog.

"You have to check alibis for the three names," she said. "Two of the three patients have the same surgeon, and all three went for chemo at Moorton.

"It's your move next. I've done what I could."

My move. Just the thought made me sick. If I failed, more people would die. I tried not to think of the bloody scene in radiation oncology, the blood on the walls and floors and . . .

"We don't know when he'll kill again," I said. "There's no pattern I can see. There were four days between the radiation oncology murders and Dr. Brentmoor's death. Two days between Brentmoor and Dr. Jolley's murder. Five days between the killings of Jolley and Dr. Tachman. How much time between Tachman and the next one? It looks like five days at the most, two at the least."

"It could be quick," Katie said. "If this is a terminal cancer patient, he may be running out of time. The killer could decide a violent death is the way to go, and take a lot of people with him, and he could do it in the next few days. And don't forget—he could just as easily be a she. Women can handle guns just as well as men. I certainly can."

"You said the three cancer patients have been worked on by two surgeons. What are those doctors like?"

"The young man had Dr. Gilbert Harpar. He's okay. Not really good. Not really bad. Not a doctor I'd want treating me. I could see him making some fatal screwup. I'd check out his patient first. Dr. Theodore Boltz did the other two patients. He's damn good. If I was operated on, I'd want him to do it."

"Sounds like a decent human."

"I wouldn't go that far," Katie said. "He's still a surgeon.

"Look, I can't say Boltz never made a mistake. Every doctor does. But it's more likely, from what I know of Boltz, he said something stupid to the killer and ticked him off. And if that's what happened, this situation is turning really scary."

"Why?"

"Because we all say stupid things, especially in a hospital where we're all under stress. If he starts killing people for mouthing off, everyone in this hospital is under a death sentence."

11

The sound of breaking glass woke me up.

Suddenly, I was alert. I could feel my heart pounding. Was it the gunman? Where was he trying to get in? I listened carefully. I didn't hear anyone on the steps, or trying the doors.

I grabbed the pepper spray off the bedside table, ran to the bedroom window, and lifted one blind slat with a fingernail in classic South Side spy style.

It was morning, the sun was shining, and a scrawny blond kid was standing in the alley with a baseball bat. His head hung down, and he seemed paralyzed with fear. I saw a broken side window in a garage six doors up. I could hear a gravelly male voice yelling that he was calling the cops if the kid didn't pay for a new window. A shriller female voice added that she'd call his mother if he didn't come up with the money, and don't try to get out of it, buster, because she knew where he lived on Giles.

I put the blind slat down. So much for my burglar. What time was it? Eight after eight. I'd had three hours' sleep after my all-nighter with the medical records. My back was stiff. My neck was sore. I felt

groggy, nervous, edgy. I'd had a death threat, hazardous waste dumped on my doorstep, and a crazy man
with a gun might be looking for me. Since the death
threat, I didn't even go to the bathroom without pepper spray in my hand. I took a shower with it sitting
on the window ledge. I'd seen *Psycho* and I knew
what happened in showers.

I hated living like this, always waiting for something bad to happen. My two security guards, Mrs.
Geimer and Mrs. Indelicato, reported that they'd seen
no one near my place, but I still went around locking
windows and testing doors. I jumped at every noise in
the alley and every car door slam on the street.

I had two goals:

(1) Find the killer and save the doctors.
(2) Find the killer and save my flagging career.

Not necessarily in that order.

In the meantime, my regular work kept intruding.
At eight-fifteen, I got a call from Irene. She was sorry
to call me so early at home, but she'd just talked with
the photographer. He was having trouble with his de-
veloping equipment, and their Whispering Arch
photos wouldn't be ready early today as she had
promised. She knew I was counting on those photos.
Sorry.

I was sorry, too. I needed a column today and it
had to have a photo. I'd written the story of Irene and
Bill's ceremony. It was ready to go, except for the
photos. Now I needed another column with photos
and I needed it fast. My deadline was noon today for
tomorrow's paper. I couldn't do anything about the
Doc in the Box killer until I had a column. My mind

was mush after last night. Maybe I could figure out what to do over breakfast at Uncle Bob's. I gathered up my briefcase and pepper spray, then wracked my brains for ideas all the way over. Nothing occurred to me. I was desperate. I'd have to check the slush pile when I got to the office, a sorry collection of ideas that weren't good enough for a column unless I was really desperate. Desperate was here.

The solution to my problems smiled at me when I walked in the door. "Have I got a column for you," Marlene said, showing me to a booth.

"You do?"

I felt the first faint stirrings of hope through the fatigue. Of course, it might not be a column. Lots of people told me interesting stories, but for one reason or another I couldn't make them into a column.

"Let me tell you about Jamal. High school kid. Works back in the kitchen as a dishwasher. Nice kid. Lives with his grandmother, makes A's and B's and is on the baseball team."

My newly hatched hope was starting to die. No column so far.

"One of the houses right behind us is owned by an eighty-year-old widow. A couple of months ago, a careless driver going down the alley took out a section of her back fence. She never had it replaced, and it left her backyard wide open. She had some old boards and junk out by her garage, and people started adding to the pile, using her yard as a dumping ground. They left a rusty bicycle, an old mattress and box springs, even a couch.

"The neighbors complained and she got cited by the city inspector. Jamal looked out the kitchen window and saw her arguing with the guy. The inspector told her the junk was attracting rats and she had seven days to remove it or she'd have to go to court and pay a fine. She said she didn't put it there and she shouldn't have to pay to haul it way. After the inspector left, she was standing in the yard crying. Jamal ran out to see if the old lady was okay. She told him the whole story and said she didn't have the money to have the trash hauled away.

"You know what Jamal did? He got some of the kids from the baseball team, borrowed his uncle's pickup truck, and the whole bunch hauled away the trash, then cut her lawn and put the busted fence section back up. Then with his own money, Jamal bought two geraniums for her porch. Wasn't that sweet?"

It was. It was a column, too. Jamal was a tall lanky kid with a smooth brown face. He had that peculiar long torsoed, loose-limbed body you saw on some pro baseball players. They look uncoordinated, until you see them moving on the field. Jamal was embarrassed to be caught doing good. He mumbled and said he didn't do anything, but when he realized he and his baseball buds would get their picture in the paper wearing their uniforms, he finally owned up and admitted his good deed. He said we could take their picture during practice after school. For once, I was able to get a *Gazette* photographer.

Saved once again by Uncle Bob's. This story would practically write itself. I knocked on the widow's door. She was eager to confirm the story and couldn't say enough good things about Jamal and his friends. I could have the story written by eleven o'clock.

Could have, but didn't. Everything conspired against me that day. Wendy the Whiner, my editor, called a sudden mandatory morning meeting, where she told us Charlie was unhappy with the number of typos in our Family section. The copy desk blamed the writers. The writers blamed the copy desk. Nothing was accomplished, and an hour was wasted. My phone rang constantly, mostly calls from lonely old guys who just wanted to yak. It took forever to pry them off the phone.

The only good thing was that today started Georgia's week off in the chemo-radiation cycle. I didn't have to take her to the hospital for treatment for a whole week. Otherwise, the day was a bust. It was after noon before I could finish my column and get out of the office, and I wondered if another doctor was dying in his office, even now.

Katie had given me the home and business phone numbers of her three suspects, plus their addresses. I started with the easy one first: Harry Handlein, the father whose only son had died of colon cancer. He was a widower, aged fifty-seven, and his son Brian had never married. Brian had been engaged at the time of his diagnosis, but the wedding never took place and he'd had no children. Katie wondered if the father would be bitter enough over the loss of his only son to kill.

The hospital records showed the father worked in security at the Travelers Rest, one of the nicer hotels around the airport. That meant he probably carried a gun. I could check easily enough. I had an in at the hotel. A guy I went to the high school prom with worked days as a supervisor in security at the Travelers Rest. St. Louis was like that. I could probably find some connection to the other two patients, too, if I looked hard enough.

Joe and I went steady for a while, then split up the summer after high school graduation. He married a few years later, but we stayed friends. I knew he had two little girls. He proudly showed me their pictures whenever I ran into him. It was one-thirty when I got out to the hotel and found Joe's office. A secretary said he was still at lunch. I waited in a chair outside his locked door. The hotel lobby had deep carpets, sofas you could sink into, and big expensive flower arrangements, but the plush touches stopped when you got into the working part of the hotel. The walls back here were scuffed by encounters with cleaning and serving carts. The floors were ugly gray tile. The fluorescent lights glared. I fell asleep anyway, and only woke up when I heard Joe's footsteps coming around the corner. I hoped he didn't hear me snoring.

He unlocked his door and I followed him into his office, which was dusty and cluttered. The only decorations, on a pair of battered file cabinets, were framed photos of Joe's wife and daughters. I took a chair. He offered coffee. We spent a little time making small talk and quietly checking each other out to see if we'd aged much since our last meeting. I was relieved to see that Joe looked fine. He still had his blond curly hair. He'd gained about thirty pounds since high school, but it looked good on him. Joe was too skinny when I dated him. Joe had evidently decided I didn't look too bad either, and we both relaxed. We could keep on kidding ourselves that we weren't getting any older.

"So, to what do I owe the honor of this visit?" he said.

"I want to ask you about someone who works with you. Harry Handlein."

"Why?" Joe said, warily. "Is there a problem with Harry?" Interesting. He said it as if he was expecting bad news.

"Not that I know of," I answered truthfully. "I wanted to talk to him about his son. The one who just died of cancer."

"Now there's a sad case," Joe said, shaking his head. This seemed to be a subject he felt safe talking about. "That poor bastard. What he's been through for the last five years. First, they couldn't figure out what his boy had. Then they found out, put him through an operation and all that awful treatment, and he died anyway. I tell you, it just wasn't right what that man went through."

"How'd he take his son's death?"

"About like you'd expect. Not good. It's a terrible thing to lose your child," he said, and looked at the framed pictures of his little girls, as if to reassure himself they were safe.

"I told him to take some time off, and he's taking two months' leave. But I'm worried about him. I guess that's why I reacted so strangely when you asked about Harry. I was expecting bad news. He told me he was going to spend some time in the woods. I didn't think he should be holed up alone in the middle of nowhere. That cabin doesn't even have a phone. I can't call and check how he's doing.

"Harry was bitter when his son died. Very bitter. Blamed everybody. Blamed the doctor for not diagnosing the cancer sooner. Blamed the surgeon for not getting all of it. Blamed the chemo and radiation doctors for not curing the kid. But most of all, Harry blamed himself. Kept saying he should have insisted that his son see a specialist sooner. As I understand it, the kid had to have a referral from his family doctor to see a specialist, and the doctor wouldn't give one. Instead, he made him try this remedy and that. I think the doctor was one of those quacks who didn't like to risk cutting into his HMO bonus by referring patients.

"Anyway, when Harry found out his kid had cancer, he never forgave himself. Harry said he should have just given the kid two hundred bucks to go see a specialist. He could have afforded it. But he didn't. Now Harry can't forgive himself. That's what scares me. I'm afraid he's going to kill himself. That's happened to too many retired cops. They ate their gun."

"Cop?" The news hit me hard, like a punch in the gut. "Harry was a police officer?"

"Sure. Detective. Third district. I thought you knew that. Put in his twenty and took a job with us. Most of our staff are ex-cops. They're good. They recognize the kind of problem people we attract here at the hotel—drug dealers, con men, hookers working the businessmen out of the bar. We don't mind a few working girls, if they're discreet. But you get too many of the wrong kind, and it lowers the tone. Also, you can't have the girls taking guests' wallets and such. Your ex-cop knows how to handle these things. Harry was very good at his job."

Joe laughed, a little embarrassed. "I guess you never expected a graduate of Chaminade High to talk that way, did you?" he said.

"Might have gone out with more if they did," I said. "What does Harry look like?"

"Like an old-style ex-cop. Buys his suits on sale at Penney's. Keeps his shoes shined. Wears his hair short. It used to be brown, but it's mostly gray now.

He's average height, average-looking, fairly thin except for a bit of a belly. Brown eyes. Harry looks like one more South Sider until you get a good look at those eyes. They're shrewd and very scary."

He glanced at his watch. I stood up to go. "Thanks for your help, Joe. I mean it."

"You're welcome," he said. "Any time." I'd feel silly shaking hands with someone with whom I'd steamed up the windows of his father's car, and I guess he felt the same, because he did something that was between a shrug and a bow, and I returned it.

I found my way out. But I wasn't thinking about Joe and how cute he looked on prom night. I was thinking about Harry. The ex-cop. Who surely had a thirty-eight and knew how to use it. Who also had a grudge against doctors. And hadn't been seen for almost two months. Long before the Doc in the Box killings started.

Katie's next candidate was Bill Ruddlestein, a mechanic for the Bi-State buses. Bill was thirty, divorced, and had one boy aged ten. Bill had maybe six months to live, according to Katie. I tracked down his supervisor at Bi-State. He said Bill had been out on sick leave for the last three weeks, and he didn't expect him back anytime soon. He was really sick, poor guy.

I saved my worst question for last. The supervisor gave me a strange look when I asked him, but he did answer it.

"Guns? Bill likes to deer hunt, so I suppose he has a hunting rifle, and probably something for home protection, too. Bill isn't one of those gun-control nuts."

Bill's house was in Affton, a southern suburb with my favorite business: Seven Holy Founders Credit Union. Now there was a name that inspired confidence. Bill lived in a neat brick bungalow off Gravois that was showing signs of recent neglect. The paint on the trim was still good, but the yard was weedy and spotted with windblown trash. The mail box was crammed with letters and the porch piled with yellowing newspapers. I figured no one was home, but I rang the doorbell anyway, then peeked in the garage window. That brought out his next-door neighbor, a woman with a frizzy gray home perm and a long nose that I bet she poked in her neighbor's business. Her name was Agnes, she said, and she hadn't seen Bill in a while, but the last time she did, "He looked just terrible. He's such a nice young man, with a good sense of humor. Loves his cartoons, he does. Especially Warner Bros. 'Agnes,' he'd say, 'get with it. Disney is for wimps. The real connoisseurs like Warner Bros. They've got a crazy streak you won't find in the Mouse. You need to get crazy, Agnes.'

"Bill's a great kidder, or he was before he got so sick. He has long black eyelashes a girl would kill for, and lots of curly dark hair. He still has the hair, but now his clothes hang on him. They're flapping in the breeze. The poor man must have lost thirty or forty pounds. He's too skinny now. It makes him seem taller."

Agnes was plump and short. Tall for you, or tall for me? I thought and asked her, "How big is Bill?"

"Not as big as you," she said. "I mean, not as tall. And a little heavyset. At least he used to be. Poor man. I don't think he weighs much more than I do anymore." I didn't have the nerve to ask what Agnes weighed. That would be a shocking question on the South Side for a woman her age.

Bill was divorced, Agnes said. His ex-wife and son lived in Florida. "They used to have joint custody, but when Bill got too sick she took the boy and moved home to her parents in Tampa. Said she could raise Billy Junior better with their help. Bill didn't fight it. I don't think he's in Florida now, though. They don't get along too good. I think Bill might have gone home to his mother in Michigan, but he didn't leave me a phone number and ask me to take in the mail and papers like he usually does before he goes away, so I don't know for sure."

I didn't, either. Did Bill go home to mother? Or stick around to murder? He had good reasons to do both. He could be hiding out in a cheap motel somewhere. He could be the Doc in the Box killer.

Katie's third candidate was Faye Smithman, the mother who would never see her two children grow up. I stopped to use the pay phone at Phil's BBQ on Gravois. I called Faye's office, but no one answered. It was after five, and everyone must be gone for the day. No one answered at her home, either. I'd try again in the morning. While I was there, I picked up Phil's pork steak plate with baked beans and potato salad for dinner. And people wondered why I didn't have a cell phone. If I made those calls from my car, I would have been so busy talking I'd have driven right by Phil's. That would have been a great loss. Gotta take time to smell the barbecue smoke.

On the way home I bought two red geraniums at the supermarket and plunked them in pots on my porch to make Mrs. Indelicato happy. I picked the rattiest ones at the store, so I wouldn't feel so bad when they died. They were doomed anyway.

Back at home, I found a phone message from Irene. The Whispering Arch pictures were almost ready. Her daughter would drop them by my office first thing tomorrow morning. Yes! Finally, something was going right. I was a day ahead on my columns. I could use the extra time for the Doc in the Box stories. Tomorrow was going to be a good day. I could feel it.

But tonight was bad. I dreamed of Lyle. We were holding hands and walking in Tower Grove Park, my favorite place, and I was so happy. It was a sunny day and we were talking and laughing and he kissed me in front of the fake Roman ruins by the pond where generations of St. Louis brides had had their wedding pictures taken. Then he was doing more than kissing me, and in the odd logic of dreams all the people went away and it was just the two of us and I was on the grass moaning with pleasure. But the phone was ringing, and I had to answer it or something bad would happen. Lyle said he'd wait. I couldn't find the phone, but it stopped ringing. When I came back to the ruins, he was gone. The sunshine was gone, too. Now the park was vast and cold and lonely and dark. I looked everywhere for him but I couldn't find him. I wandered through the dark, and stumbled over tree branches, and shivered in the cold. I knew he was gone, but I was so lost I couldn't find my way out. I was so alone, I could hardly go on.

I was awakened by the sound of a shower running. Then I heard thunder. My head cleared and I realized it was a rainstorm, a dark steady downpour that threatened to last the whole day. Fat drops hit the windowpanes, small waterfalls gushed from down-spouts, cars left fishtails of water as they plowed through the semiflooded streets. My feet were soaked by the time I walked to the car. I quit trying to juggle a briefcase, an umbrella, and the pepper spray and tossed the spray into my briefcase. If the killer wanted to shoot me today, he'd put me out of my misery.

Before I left my place, I'd called Faye Smithman's office at NationsBank. A man said she was on leave. Good for Faye. If my days were numbered, I couldn't see spending them at the *Gazette*. Next I called her home and asked if Faye was there.

"Why do you want to know?" a woman asked cautiously.

"I just wanted to know how she's doing."

"Terrible," the woman said, bursting into tears. She was Connie, Faye's sister-in-law, and she was watching the kids. Connie lowered her voice, presumably so the kids wouldn't hear, and said Faye was in a coma at Suburban General Hospital and not expected to recover and wasn't it just awful? I agreed. She said that poor Faye had been in a coma for the last week.

In a coma. At another hospital. Katie wouldn't have seen that information on her record at Moorton. Faye couldn't have committed the last two Doc in the Box murders. I was about to cross her off the list when I thought of something and called Katie.

"Our third candidate, the woman, has been in a coma for a week," I said.

"Can't beat that for an alibi," Katie said.

"True. But what about her family? Does she have any relative who would murder for revenge?"

"Let me check the face sheet printouts again," Katie said. "They should have next of kin."

There was the sound of paper rustling, and then she said, "Both parents deceased . . . no sibs . . . two kids, but they're in middle school. Besides, they were in school when the murders were committed . . . holy shit!"

"What? What did you find?"

"It's right here on this form. Husband. Occupation. Owns Cal's Cash for Loans Gun and Pawnshop on Delmar. The guy sells guns."

So that's where I was headed on a rainy morning—to a pawnshop in one of the less desirable sections of Delmar. I should be glad for the rain. It increased the chances that my car would still be there when I left the pawnshop.

The trip took twice as long as usual. There seemed to be dozens of little fender benders slowing down traffic. Finally I found the pawnshop, parked, popped the face off my radio-tape player and stuck it in my briefcase, so it was worthless for thieves. I didn't want it turning up at the pawnshop.

All the shops on the block had either bars or metal roll-down shutters. Cal's Cash for Loans was in a row with a tae kwon do studio, a chicken wing and chop suey joint, and a check cashing shop—all the businesses that thrive on poverty. The pawnshop looked like a cross between a jewelry shop, a hardware store, and a stereo center. There were glass cases of 10-karat gold jewelry—rings, chains, and big hoop earrings. There were shelves of VCRs, stereos, speakers, cordless drills, and socket wrenches.

Ron the manager said Cal the owner was not there. "When will he be back?" I asked.

"You ain't gonna cause him any trouble?" he said. "The man's got enough problems. Are you sure this isn't something I can't handle for him?"

"No, no, I just want to ask him about his wife, and she's not even in the business," I said. Ron relaxed.

"Faye's a nice lady," he said. "Cal hasn't been around much for the last few weeks. His wife's sick in the hospital. In fact, she's not expected to live. I'm trying to keep the place together. Cal's falling apart. He practically lives at the hospital these days."

Oh, boy. I needed a description of this distraught husband fast.

"Maybe I could track him down at the hospital," I said. "Cal's a little fat bald guy, right? About sixty?"

"You got the right pawnshop, lady?" Ron the manager asked. "Cal's in his late forties, medium height, on the thin side, with a full head of blond hair, although it's been getting grayer since Faye got sick."

Cal definitely sounded like a killer candidate.

"You're right, I must be thinking of some other guy," I said. "Don't bother Cal. He's got enough to worry about."

I got out of there before Ron had time to think about these goofy questions. I now had three men who sounded like good Doc in the Box material: all desperate, distraught, or bitter. All had guns, plenty of motive and nobody really knew where they were. Maybe if I talked with Katie again we could narrow them down to one or two likely suspects.

I found a pay phone at a gas station in a safer neighborhood and stood in the rain, dropping change in the phone and swearing I was going to get a cell phone. I did that a lot on rainy days. But I hated the idea that the *Gazette* could reach me in my car.

I called the office first to see if Bill and Irene's pictures had arrived. Scarlette the department secretary actually answered the phone for a change. "You better get in here, Francesca," she said, delighted to be the bearer of bad news. "Wendy's looking for you. You're in big trouble. That kid you wrote about today is a gang member!"

"*What!* You're joking."

"No, I'm not. I got the call first. Some lady saw the picture and said he was in a gang."

"How does she know?"

"I'm not sure. But she was positive. She demanded to talk to the editor, so I transferred her to Wendy. Now the whole place is in an uproar. You better get right in here."

Gang member? Jamal? I couldn't believe it. I called Marlene at Uncle Bob's.

"That can't be," she said. "They have the wrong person. Jamal's been working here since his sophomore year. He's a good kid."

"This woman called the paper and insisted."

"She's wrong. When is Jamal going to have time for a gang, between school, his job, and baseball? Gang members don't work in a hot kitchen for minimum wage. The kid's an A student. I'm positive he never had anything to do with gangs."

I hung up the phone and headed for my car. This was trouble. Wendy was terrified of any controversy, and would sell me out in a minute. Worse, she'd destroy Jamal while she was at it. A little bit of the wrong kind of publicity, and a promising kid could wind up washing dishes for the rest of his life. I stepped on the gas, dodged two more accidents, took side streets and back alleys, and got to the *Gazette* in record time.

All the spots were taken at the closest *Gazette* lot, so I parked the car in the far lot and trudged two blocks to the office. I stood on the street corner in the pouring rain, waiting for the light to change, worried sick and soaked to the skin. A truck went around the corner, rolled through a dirty puddle the size of a small pond, and splashed me with oily water. My misery was complete.

At least until I got inside. I stopped in the john and tried to scrub some of the oil and mud off my legs. My hair was frizzed, my suit was soaked. So much for dress for success. My shoes squished water when I walked. I squished to the Family department. Wendy was waiting for me. She looked worse than I did, but drier. Her suit today appeared to be cut from old T-shirt material, bunched and wadded at her thick waist. She had a run in her pantyhose and a chip on her shoulder.

"Francesca," she whined, "you've caused nothing but trouble again. Charlie wants to see you in his office immediately."

She waddled importantly through the newsroom. I trailed behind her, leaving wet footprints.

Charlie looked like a weasel in a striped suit. His eyes were redder than usual, giving him a feral expression. He said nothing for two full minutes, hoping to get me to talk first. When I didn't, he handed me a copy of today's feature section and said, "We've had complaints about your story, Francesca. You haven't done your homework. You've written a piece glorifying a gang member."

"Jamal is not a gang member," I said.

"He is. Mrs. Glorietta Altec called this morning and told us. She also told all her friends and neighbors. The phone has been ringing all morning with readers complaining about that photo. How many calls have you received, Wendy?"

"Thirty-two," she said, with satisfaction. She knew each one was a nail in my coffin. For good measure, she added, "They were very upset."

"Does Mrs. Altec know Jamal?" I asked.

"Of course not!" Charlie said, sounding shocked. "She's an account executive who lives in Webster Groves."

I groaned. The only gangs Mrs. Altec was likely to encounter were *Brady Bunch* reruns.

"Then how does this woman in Webster Groves know that a city kid is a gang member?"

"She looked at his hands," Charlie said.

"His hands?" Was there a ring or a tattoo or something? What was I missing? I looked at the photo, but only saw a bunch of teenage boys horsing around for the camera. It was a cute picture.

"He's making secret gang signals with his hands," Wendy said.

"Oh, for Pete's sake," I said. "He's a kid goofing off with his friends."

"He is not," she said. "He's signaling the other gang members. He's using the *Gazette* to conduct gang business."

"How the hell would a woman in Webster Groves know about secret gang signals?" I said.

"She recognized them from the police department booklet, 'Sixteen Signs of Gang Activity,'" Charlie said. "Also her husband Brandon volunteers for a program that teaches life skills to inner city youth."

"And that makes him a gang expert?" I said.

"He is knowledgeable about those things," Charlie said seriously. "It is imperative that we apologize to our readers as soon as possible. We should also do a follow-up article on how to spot gang signals."

I could feel the fury rising in me. "And brand an innocent kid a gang member. Jamal is an A student. He has a steady job. If he could make five hundred dollars a week selling crack, why is he working for minimum wage washing dishes in a hot kitchen?"

"He's fooled you," Wendy said. "He's a gangbanger in disguise."

"The kid must be a master of disguise," I said. "I'd never guess he was in a gang. His cover is perfect. Jamal is the only gang member in town with dishpan hands."

"He doesn't even have a Christian name," Wendy burst out.

I began to have some idea what was wrong. "Let me see that picture again," I said. I studied it for a moment.

"I know what's wrong," I said. "Jamal and all his friends are black. If those were a bunch of white kids horsing around in a photo, no one would look twice at their hands. But because they are black kids, they must be gang members. Instead of telling Mrs. Altec that Jamal is a model student, you agreed with her, and now you're prepared to ruin that young man's reputation. I hope you do print a story saying that Jamal is a gang member. Then the kid can sue you for damaging his good name. I can just imagine how a city jury will see this photo."

The jury was likely to be mostly black, and they'd had a lifetime of Mrs. Altecs. They'd award him heavy damages at the *Gazette*'s expense. Jamal would never wash another dish.

Charlie looked like a trapped weasel now. His little red eyes shifted back and forth between me and Wendy. I checked the Bald-O-Meter on top of his head. It was hot pink. He was angry, but this time he couldn't take it out on me, and he knew it.

"Go back to your desk, Francesca," Charlie said, trying to recover his dignity. "Wendy and I would like to discuss this further."

I knew the subject would be quickly dropped. I'd said the magic word: lawsuit. The *Gazette* was terrified of a jury of its peers. It would be composed of readers the staff had ignored, insulted, and transferred into phone hell.

As I left, I noticed I'd left a little puddle where my skirt dripped on Charlie's carpet. My shoes still squished out wet footprints. I'd dry out eventually. Charlie and Wendy would always be all wet.

12

Eleven forty-three.

I wondered if another doctor was dead.

Seventeen more minutes and I'd know for sure.

The Doc in the Box killer liked to murder at noontime. Tachman was the earliest. He died around eleven-fifty. Brentmoor was the latest. He was shot at twelve-fifteen. That meant today's doctor had maybe half an hour at most. Then he would die.

Eleven forty-seven.

Maybe more than one doctor would die. The killer wiped out the whole radiation oncology department.

Eleven forty-nine.

He'd killed three people the first time. The whole staff was there but the waiting room was empty. Almost empty. For some reason, he overlooked Georgia. Maybe my theory was right—he was killing out of revenge. He had no quarrel with her, and she never saw him, so he let her live. Now he only killed doctors, one at a time. Time.

Eleven fifty-two.

I watched the red second hand make another

sweep around the newsroom clock. The black minute hand moved forward one more notch.

Eleven fifty-three.

It reminded me of the lecture we got in second grade from Sister Mary Delphina. She had our class watch the minute hand make a full sixty-second sweep, then said, "You are now one minute closer to your death." She touched off an epidemic of nightmares and bed-wetting with that one sentence. I never looked at a clock face the same way again.

Eleven fifty-nine.

Did the murdered doctors know why they died? Did they recognize their killer? In the last moment of their lives, did they know their carelessness and greed had condemned someone to a slow, painful death? Did they feel a twinge of remorse in their final terror? Or did they die knowing they were innocent—and their killer was wrong?

I wondered which fate was worse.

Twelve-oh-four.

The doctor would be dead by now. Maybe. In a few more minutes, we'd hear the activity on the newsroom scanner, the urgent calls for ambulances, the coded phrases that said this was a major emergency.

Twelve-thirteen.

Two more minutes. That was the outer limit of his killing time. Killing time. That's what I was doing. I was killing time. He was killing doctors.

Twelve-fifteen. It was over. I'd know soon if another doctor was dead. Were other doctors in the city looking at their clocks like I was? Avoiding their offices until after the noon hour? I doubted it. There were the usual outcries about the killings, demands for more police protection and security, talk about gun control. But so far as I could tell hanging around the hospital, the doctors seemed to think these shootings happened to other people. No one would kill them. They were safe in their invincible arrogance.

At twelve-thirty I began to relax. At one o'clock, I felt much better. I was fairly sure no doctors had died today. By one-thirty in the afternoon, I knew the city's doctors were safe for another day. I would have heard about any murder by now at the *Gazette*. There were no reports of shootings. I checked with the newsroom clerk monitoring the scanners once more to make sure. Nothing. I had at least twenty-four hours before the Doc in the Box killer murdered again. I had a chance to save the next victim. Under that noble monument of a phrase crawled the greedy worm of ambition. Save the victim—who was I kidding? I was doing this for myself. I wanted to win a major prize. I wanted better assignments, and if I bought them at the risk of a human life, so be it.

Katie thought the killer would go after surgeons next. Bill the bus mechanic and Cal's dying wife both had the same surgeon, Dr. Boltz. Harry's son had been operated on by a different surgeon, Dr. Harpar. Three patients, two doctors.

I figured the best thing for me to do was hang around the most likely doctor's waiting room and try to spot the killer. If I saw him, there would be plenty of security in the doctors' building. Many doctors' offices, especially if the physicians had privileges at Moorton, had beefed up their security. I'd simply inform an armed guard, who'd have the guy quietly removed. I'd let the pros with the guns handle the tough stuff. I wasn't about to tackle a gun-toting killer when all I had was pepper spray.

But I couldn't be in both places at once tomorrow. Which doctor would he kill? I felt like I was playing a bizarre game of Russian roulette. Maybe Cutup Katie could help me choose the best one. I called her at the morgue.

"Had lunch yet?" I said.

"Haven't had a chance to get away. I've got work piled everywhere." I hoped she was talking about paperwork. "We'll have to make it quick, though. I have to get back. Unless you want to eat here." I could almost hear her grin. Katie knew I dreaded the morgue, and did everything to avoid it.

"How about if I take you to lunch on my magnificent *Gazette* expense account?" I said.

"A lunch those cheapskates will pay for? Where are we going? McDonald's?"

"I was thinking of some place right on the Mississippi River. Unpretentious, but with a spectacular view."

"Sounds good to me," Katie said.

"Fine. I'll pick you up in fifteen minutes."

She was waiting outside the building, a thin, wiry figure in a tailored navy suit. The rain had stopped, but the saunalike atmosphere and roiling gray clouds promised more later. Even the normally chipper Katie looked a little frizzed and soggy from the recent downpours. She climbed quickly into my car and said, "Where are you taking me?"

"It's a surprise," I said as we headed toward the Riverfront. I found a parking spot on the cobblestone levee, almost under the Gateway Arch. The Mississippi River looked like a churning sea of mud, but the water was still low enough I could park on the levee. Sometimes after a hard rain, the furious brown river rose so fast it engulfed the cars parked there.

Katie surveyed the brightly colored riverboats bobbing at anchor. Some were excursion boats, others were for gambling. "So where are we eating? A spectacular view doesn't usually go along with anything in the *Gazette* budget." Then she saw the boat at the far end.

"Oh, shit, you've suckered me, haven't you?"

"I've delivered as promised. An unpretentious spot on the river, terrific view, fast service, and prices even the *Gazette* won't balk at. Besides, this place is unique."

"It's a fucking McDonald's," she said.

"It's a floating McDonald's," I said, laughing. It was a barge topped with an imitation Victorian riverboat, like a white cardboard pastry. The size of its golden arches was mandated by law so they wouldn't outshine our own six-hundred-and-thirty-foot silver Arch. The rain had kept the tourist crowds down, and we quickly got our food and ate at a table on deck. I not only paid, I dried the seats with a hunk of paper napkins.

"Listen, I'll take you somewhere decent next time," I said. "I promise. I just couldn't resist."

"You'll sacrifice anything for a joke," Katie grumbled. "Even my stomach."

"In that case, why is Miss I'll Have a Salad Instead of Fries eating a Big Mac?"

"Everything in moderation. Even virtue," Katie said. I eyed her Big Mac and extra-large fries enviously. My plain burger and side salad looked sadly skimpy. But I had other things to worry about besides food.

"I've done some checking," I said. "All three of the candidates you picked look good for the murder. I checked them out, then ran their names through the newspaper files. Nothing bad on any of them. The bus mechanic wasn't in the paper at all. Cal the pawnshop owner was quoted in a *Gazette* story, but it was a friendly feature about yuppies using pawnshops after the stock market went belly up. Cal told the interviewer that they were pawning five-hundred-dollar Dunhill briefcases and laptop computers. The ex-cop got a commendation for bravery fifteen years ago, when he was still on the force. That's all. I can't eliminate any of them. They're all equally good suspects. They have two surgeons between them. You still believe the surgeon is the next target?"

"I do. But I'm not making any guarantees," Katie said. "I just think he's the most likely target." She looked worried and earnest, even with a tiny fleck of special sauce on her lip.

"Let's say you're right. When do you think he's going to kill again? He's taken between two and five days between murders. There were no murders today, so he's not speeding up. Tomorrow is the fourth day after the Tachman killing. If he's still operating on the same schedule, he'll kill again either tomorrow or the next day. Does that make sense to you?"

"It does," she said. "But he may decide to wait longer for some reason we don't know. Then again, he may stop completely. If he's killing for revenge, maybe he's already nailed everyone he thinks deserved to die. If he's a terminal cancer patient, he may be too sick to continue."

"And if he has a dying wife, he may be spending all his time at her bedside," I said. "Cal's wife is in a coma and not expected to live. He could be waiting until she dies for the final revenge."

"There you go," she said. "That's another reason."

"The one I can't figure out is the ex-cop. Harry's boss says he's unreachable. There's no phone in his cabin. So is Harry waiting for something in particular, or just sitting in the woods, drinking himself to death? Maybe there's some anniversary or something that's important to him. When did his son die, Katie?"

"I don't know. I can check. But if I have to get that information from the medical records Nazi, you really owe me."

"Another lunch," I said. "One that's not on the expense account."

"Deal," she said.

"Which of the two doctors do you think he'll go after?"

"I'd say Harpar," Katie said. "Maybe. If you think the person is murdering because of medical mistakes, then Harpar is more likely to be the surgeon who'd screw up. If you want a doc who'll tick off someone by saying the wrong thing, Boltz is your man."

"What would you do now if you were in my shoes?" I asked.

"Go to the police with what you know. Have them put extra security on both surgeons."

"Wouldn't work," I said. "I'd sound like a complete nut. Anyway, how could I tell them where I came up with my information? And who would believe me?

Mayhew is always telling me to stay out of police business. He'd just lecture me on my half-baked theories. You remember how he carried on last time. I couldn't find him now, anyway. Marlene says he hasn't been in Uncle Bob's in days. He's working long hours on these Doc in the Box murders, and it's getting to him. Last time I saw him, he looked like death warmed over."

Katie dredged a french fry thoughtfully through some ketchup. "Well, in that case, I'd hang around one doctor's office and warn the other."

"All day?"

"At least until twelve-thirty. There haven't been any shootings later than that. You can bring your laptop and write."

"But what if nothing happens tomorrow? This could go on for weeks," I whined.

"It could," Katie said, "but I don't think it will. They've increased security at all the Moorton Hospital buildings, and that's where Boltz has his office. He's probably the safer of the two. I'm sure the police have figured out the same pattern you have and warned them. Harpar has an office in some ritzy section of West County, so he's not going to alarm his rich patients with too many rent-a-cops and security cameras. He'd be more at risk. I'd hang out at Harpar's office for a few days, and warn Boltz with a phone call. It's all you can do."

The river seemed to be rising while we talked, and I wondered if it was time to move my car. We watched a big sycamore tree with a scrap of pink cloth caught in its roots rush by. Then the rain started again, big fat drops. We dropped our trash in a can and ran for the car.

An hour later, Katie called me at work. "You hit it right," she said. "The ex-cop's son died a year ago Saturday. If the grieving father is going to do anything, my guess is it will be in the next two days."

What about the grieving husband? I checked the hospital to see how Faye Smithman was doing. The person in patient information said, "I'm sorry, but Mrs. Smithman is no longer at the hospital."

No longer at the hospital? What did that mean? Did Faye recover enough to go home? Was she transferred to a hospice? Or was she dead? I hated to call her home, so I called the pawnshop instead. I got this recording: "We are closed until Monday due to a death in the family. Thanks to all our friends and customers for their sympathy and understanding."

Faye was dead. Cal the pawnbroker and Harry the ex-cop both had serious reasons to want revenge. Cal's grief was new and raw. Harry was facing the first anniversary of the death of his only son. And what about Bill? How much time did this terminal patient have left? Was it too late for him to get revenge?

I called Dr. Boltz's office to warn him. His staff treated me like a cross between a blackmailer and a candidate for a jacket with wraparound sleeves. I wished I hadn't used my real name when I made the call.

Dr. Boltz's first name was Theodore, and even his own mother never called him Ted. I'd never met the man, but Valerie had pointed him out to me in the halls at Moorton. He looked like a prototype for a human being, with his long head, large nose, big ears, thin arms and legs. Nothing was quite in proportion, as if he were made from spare parts. His hands, though, were superb: slender and sensitive. Hands like that might give a woman interesting thoughts about Dr. Boltz. Until she saw the sneer on his face. Boltz regarded ordinary humans as inferiors. Ordinary humans preferred to deal with him only under full anesthesia.

I'd spoken on the phone with his receptionist, Sandy, who'd transferred my call to his assistant, Kristine, who brushed me off when I told her Boltz's life might be in danger. "We will inform security," she said coldly.

"You might want to check your records for disgruntled patients and their families. Pay special attention to anyone who threatened to sue Dr. Boltz, or anyone who claimed their wife's or son's death was Dr. Boltz's fault." That was as close as I could go. I couldn't name Bill, Cal, or Harry, or it would be slander.

My delicate hints were wasted. Kristine went from cold to downright frosty. "Dr. Boltz is a highly skilled surgeon who has never been sued," she said. "His patients and their families are very satisfied. Moorton Hospital has excellent security, which has recently been increased. We have received an alert from the St. Louis Police Department. Dr. Boltz does not need help from a . . . newspaper columnist." She said the word "columnist" as if my profession was something disgusting. Maybe she was right. Then Kristine said Dr. Boltz would consider legal action if he were exposed to "unwarranted media attention." She implied that I was doing this for the publicity. Maybe I should just let him get shot. Some people are mighty hard to save.

But Katie said he was a gifted surgeon. I couldn't

let him die, no matter how unpleasant he was. His death would be a terrible waste. There was a real possibility that Boltz was on the Doc in the Box death list, and if so, time was running out for the good doctor. Well, I'd warned him. It was the best I could do.

The next morning dawned dark and humid, another dismal day of rain. I packed up my pepper spray, umbrella, and laptop and prepared to spend the morning at Dr. Harpar's office on Woods Mill Road. The office was a forty-minute drive from downtown on a good day, and this was not a good day. A relentless rain stripped flowers off stems, turned puddles into lakes, and morning traffic slowdowns into angry, horn-honking snarls. It took over an hour to reach Harpar's ugly, expensive office building. The dash through the downpour on the parking lot left me thoroughly soaked. I shook out my wet umbrella, dropped the pepper spray in my pocket, and looked for a place to settle in for the morning. It was nine-oh-three. I had no idea what Harpar looked like, but at nine-ten a fortyish white-coated doctor with beautifully graying dark hair entered through a side door. He looked like an actor playing a doctor. I could almost hear him saying, "Nine out of ten doctors recommend . . ." I hoped this guy was Harpar. He was definitely worth saving.

Harpar was in practice with two other colorectal surgeons, Drs. Cobbleman and Harg. Their waiting room was painted a dreary powder blue. Rows of square, stiff chairs were upholstered in the same fabric. The walls were decorated with generic boat paintings. I wondered where doctors got all this mediocre art. Was there a Warehouse of Waiting Room Paintings? I could almost hear the salesman: "We have some nice flowers here, doctor, nothing too Georgia O'Keeffe, if you know what I mean. Then there's your sailing ships. Ships probably aren't suitable for waiting rooms with pregnant women, but they convey a very manly, very in-charge feel for a surgeon. Nice investments, too."

Most of the patients this morning were small, frail, and elderly. They didn't look anything like the descriptions of Harry, Bill, or Cal, our three potential Doc in the Box killers, and I was grateful for that. I was looking for three men who were absolutely average: average height, average looks, average age between thirty and fifty. Weight a little on the lean side. Try picking those faces out of a crowd. All I had to go on was that Bill the bus mechanic had curly dark hair and long eyelashes. Cal the pawnbroker had thick blond hair, and Harry looked like a graying South Sider with steely eyes. But by the time I saw those eyes or Bill's long girlish eyelashes, it would be too late.

Just in case they recognized me from my picture in the paper, I'd crammed all my hair under a scarf turban. That might look strange in most offices, but it helped me blend into a place that catered to cancer patients. In a turban, I was a new woman—one I didn't much like the looks of. Usually, my round German face was slimmed by long straight hair. The unflattering turban made my face look like a potato. Ah, well, I didn't want to be recognized. My best friend wouldn't know me in this getup.

The Rockford Files was on the wall-mounted TV. *The Rockford Files* was always on in a waiting room somewhere. James Garner would live forever in doctors' offices. I took a seat with my back to the television, so I could watch the nurses calling patients in for their appointments, and started typing on my laptop. The morning crawled painfully forward, like a wounded animal. Rain pounded the windows. Scores of wet patients arrived and departed, but none of them looked even vaguely like Harry, Bill, or Cal. Harry was the one I was really watching for, since this was his son's doctor, but I kept an eye out for the other two, just in case. You never knew how St. Louisans were connected.

Two nurses were calling patients' names. One was a brunette, petite and serious. Her name tag said Kim. The other was a lanky blonde named Lucy who liked to joke with people. It was a little after eleven when I heard the blond Lucy say to a man, "No, no, you have Kim and me mixed up. It's because we look so much alike. I'm Dr. Cobbleman's nurse. Kim works for Dr. Harg."

I felt a rising stab of panic. Which one worked for Dr. Harpar? Wasn't this his office? I closed my laptop, went to the receptionist's window, and rang the bell. I glanced down at the sign-in sheets. There were long lists of names for Cobbleman and Harg, but nothing for Harpar. Now I was really worried. The receptionist slid back the window and I said, "Excuse me, when will Dr. Harpar be in?"

She looked at me, surprised. "I'm sorry, didn't we call you? Dr. Harpar won't be here this week."

"He's gone?"

"The doctor is in St. John at an important medical conference."

Yeah, right, I thought. Social workers and librarians had their conferences in Omaha. Doctors went to expensive Caribbean islands.

The receptionist seemed to sense my hostility. "We informed all his regular patients," she said. "Are you a patient of Dr. Harpar's?"

"Uh, no," I said.

"Then why are you asking?" she said, her eyes turning narrow and hard. "What are you doing in this office?"

"I'm . . . I'm in sales."

"The doctor does not see salespeople during office hours," she snapped, and shut the window.

I should have checked. I was careless. The killer was smart and careful. He would have checked Harpar's schedule and known he wasn't in town. He would wait until next week to kill him.

Unless he was after Boltz.

Boltz, the doctor who always said the wrong thing. Suppose he insulted the murderer? Didn't the Doc in the Box killer wipe out the entire radiation oncology department, a place known for its rudeness and insensitivity?

I grabbed my laptop and umbrella and left. The elevator was slow. I pressed the button twice, then decided not to wait. I ran down three flights of stairs and splashed through parking lot puddles until I found my car. The rain had stopped and the sun was coming out. It was eleven-fifteen. The killer would strike sometime in the next hour. I'd spent the morning in the wrong surgeon's office and now I had little chance of making Boltz's office before it was too late. Boltz was all the way downtown in the Doc in the Box building—where Brentmoor had been shot. The killer knew the building well. He could slip in and out easily. I had to get there, and get there in a hurry.

This was why I drove a Jaguar. I roared out of the doctors' lot, pedal to the metal, tires screeching. Ralph cornered beautifully. We were at the Highway 40 exit in five minutes. I plugged in my radar detector as I kept the accelerator down. It wouldn't catch every kind of radar, but this was one time a ticket was worth the risk. Ralph was fast and smooth. I was doing ninety, slowing only for an occasional lake-sized puddle, when I saw the jam at the massive I-270 interchange. Rows of brake lights were coming on as cars slowed to a crawl. Damn. The slowdown seemed to go on for miles, in all lanes. Police lights were strobing, sirens were singing. I slowed reluctantly.

As I got closer, I saw the cause: a three-car accident. One car had spun totally around and faced the other direction. Another was crumpled like a used Kleenex. The third was shoved off on the side of the road. A fire truck was parked next to it. An ambulance was pulling up beside it. Police had stopped all eastbound traffic so the other two stricken cars could be moved off the highway. It seemed to take forever for the tow trucks to get through the traffic and then move them. One lane opened at eleven thirty-three. I inched along past the accident scene. It was eleven forty-one when I was back on the open highway again, cruising at a sedate eighty. There was another slowdown at Brentwood and 40. I thought about getting off and taking Manchester Road, but the jam broke up suddenly and I had smooth sailing until I got off at Vandeventer.

Eleven forty-four.

Almost there. Almost there. A few more blocks and

I was almost there. Then, right before Lindell, almost in sight of Moorton Hospital, there was another huge jam, and more flashing police lights. I saw two big metal beasts from the seventies, hoods open like gaping mouths, radiators steaming. They'd collided head-on and were blocking the intersection. Greenish fluid leaked from them like lizard blood. How was I supposed to get by this mess? Traffic was backed up in all directions. It would take more time, and I didn't have it. It was eleven forty-seven.

I pulled a U-turn in the middle of the street, and half a dozen horns honked in protest. Then I hit the accelerator, cut off a cyclist, made useless mental apologies to him, and turned into the alley that ran parallel with the street. As I swung in, Ralph nearly clipped a Dumpster that was pulled too far out in the alley. He definitely hit an old tire and sent it rolling and bumping over the broken brick and blacktop surface. He squashed trash bags and scared a prowling cat. The cat jumped into a thicket of climber roses and a dog barked. I kept going, way too fast, splashing through puddles and avoiding an abandoned mattress and hoping no cars were coming from the other direction. How long was this alley?

Eleven-fifty.

Then, dead ahead, I saw it. Moorton Hospital. Thank god. I'd made it. It was seven minutes before noon. I might not be too late. Please, god, let me get there before the killer. I made a right turn out of the alley, and headed for the parking garage. Another half a block to go. If I could make a left into the parking garage, I would be there. I'd park in the first available spot, doctors' parking be damned, take the stairs, and be in the Doc in the Box building.

Just as I pulled onto the street, I heard the first siren. I checked the rearview mirror and saw a police car behind me, lights flashing. I pulled over to the curb to let him pass. It was eleven fifty-five.

A mother with a baby stroller heard the siren, too, and rushed out into the street, right in front of the speeding police car. The WALK light was on, and she was determined to cross, car or no car. The cop flashed his headlights, but she didn't slow down. She was using her baby's stroller like a cowcatcher on an old-fashioned locomotive, pushing her way across the street, right into the path of the police car. I couldn't look. The baby was going to be killed.

At the last minute, the cop car swerved. He almost sideswiped two cars to avoid her. He must have been on a serious mission, because he didn't stop to arrest the Mother of the Year. Another police car was right behind the first. Then another and another. I counted four police cars and two ambulances before I gave up. More were screaming down the street. All were going to Moorton Hospital.

It was twelve noon.

I was too late, I thought. Failure overwhelmed me. I should have told the police. I should have tried harder to make Dr. Boltz's assistant believe me. I should have gone to the right doctor's office. I'd wasted all morning in the wrong place. I should have driven faster, better, taken a different route. The Doc in the Box killer got here first.

Another doctor was dead.

13

It was an accident.

I followed the parade of police cars and ambulances to the hospital, and they roared into the emergency entrance, lights still flashing, sirens strangled off in mid-shriek. Doors slammed and opened, and the EMTs wheeled out a white-haired woman whose eyes were closed and two crying children. I didn't find out until later that the woman had run smack into a school bus.

But a quick glance told me these were not blood-spattered shooting victims. There were no gunshot surgeons. No injured men at all.

What was I thinking? Why would Boltz or Harpar arrive at Moorton by ambulance anyway? If Dr. Harpar had been shot, they would take him to the closest hospital, Katie's Palace on Ballas, St. John's Mercy. There was no reason to bring Harpar into the city. If Boltz were shot, they wouldn't need an ambulance. They would just wheel him down the hall to the Emergency Room.

I felt a rush of relief. Boltz was still alive. But it wasn't over yet. If Katie was correct, the Doc in the Box killer would strike today by twelve-fifteen.

It was twelve-oh-two. I whipped Ralph into the parking garage and pulled into the first empty Doctors Only spot. If I was saving their lives, it was the least they could do.

I took the second-floor walkway to the Wellhaven Medical Arts Building. Dr. Boltz's office was on the fourth floor. I didn't wait for the elevator. I ran up the two flights of stairs. The killer wasn't hanging out in the stairwell this time. No one else was using them.

I stood outside the door of Boltz's office for a moment, adjusting my slippery scarf turban and listening for screams, shots, or other sounds of chaos. Nothing. Inside, the place was packed but peaceful. I wasn't taking any chances. I checked with the receptionist to see if Dr. Boltz was in today. She said he was with patients, but running an hour behind, and the sign-in sheet was on the ledge.

I found a *Time* magazine from November and took a seat next to a large, lively woman wearing a bright red dress, dangling earrings, and a straw hat covered with red silk poppies. She hid her chemo baldness with flair. "Hi," she said. "Name's Rita. You look new. I'm one of the Nuts."

"The what?"

"The Nuts. We're all patients of Dr. Theodore 'Mr. Personality' Boltz. Get it? Nuts and Boltz?"

I got it, and laughed. She laughed along, earrings swinging like chandeliers in an earthquake. "We all see each other in the waiting rooms here at the hospital so much we formed our own club. You here for treatment?" she said, eyeing my turban.

"I'm waiting for someone," I said truthfully. I was grateful when the waiting room door swung open and

a tall, thin woman came in. The first two things I
noticed were her aluminum cane and her big smile.

"Hey, Denise!" the exuberant Rita yelled at her.
"You look happy."

"I am," Denise said, taking a seat nearby. "I get my
last chemo treatment this morning, after I see Boltz.
Then I won't be seeing much of you anymore, Rita.
My tests are looking good. I won't have to come back
except for checkups every three months. Won't even
need this thing much longer." She waved her cane.

"Congratulations," Rita said. "This is how we like
to lose club membership. Seen Rick yet this morning?"

"Here he comes now," she said, as the office door
opened again. "Hi, cutie, how are you doing?"

Rick was about twenty-five, a muscular handsome
tanned guy with longish dark hair, wearing a black
nylon lifting belt and blue coveralls. Was he the
killer? No. Cal was blond and lean. Harry was older
and going gray. Bill had curly dark brown hair, and
Rick's was straight. He also had large brown eyes and
long lashes that curled at the ends—and I'd swear he
never used an eyelash curler.

"My boss is being a bastard, but what else is new?"
he said. "I'm not barfing so much on this new chemo
program. So I can't complain."

A nurse called a woman, and the rest of us stared
at the waiting room TV. The local noon news was on,
and the anchor was reading the top stories. "She's a
real babe since she changed her hairstyle," Rick said.

"Shame on you," Rita said. "That's the problem
with women in the media. Everyone looks at their
hair and clothes, and nobody pays any attention to
what they're saying."

But I was hanging on the anchor's every word. "No new developments in the medical murders that killed six people, including four doctors," she was saying. "The FBI has been called in to investigate the serial killings . . ."

No new developments. That was just what I wanted to hear. No more doctors were dead. Yet.

I checked the waiting room once more for someone who looked like blond Cal or curly dark-haired Bill, or Harry the graying ex-cop. Someone average-looking, with average height. And an extraordinary desire to murder.

Besides Denise and Rick, who were both about five-nine, I saw a wheezy old man in a wheelchair. Sitting next to him was his daughter—at least I assumed it was his daughter. She looked like a younger version of the old man. Both were equally grumpy, but she didn't have the unlighted cigar butt stuck in her mouth.

Next to them was a pale, pretty young woman wearing a good blond wig. The grumpy woman and the pale blonde were both sitting, but they didn't seem very tall. Or very short. They were average.

The pale blonde sat across from an elderly, liver-spotted woman with a walker. Now, she was short—barely five feet tall, I'd guess. A young man, very thin with prematurely gray hair, sat next to the old woman, showing her some article in a magazine while she talked animatedly to him. He was straightening her fluffy pink sweater when the nurse called, "Mrs. Kaffee? Mrs. Henrietta Kaffee?"

Calling her name set off a burst of dithering for Mrs. Kaffee, the woman in the fluffy sweater. She couldn't find her pocketbook. She dropped her reading glasses. She wanted to take her magazine in with her, but didn't know if that was fair to the other patients who might want to read it. The young man helped her without complaint, found the purse, picked up her glasses, assured her that no one would mind if she took the magazine with her. When he gathered the last of her things, he said, "Tha-a-a-t's all, folks," and everyone in the waiting room laughed. That phrase reminded me of something. What was it?

The young man seemed to tower over the tiny woman. I'd bet he was . . . five-eight or nine. I looked at him closer. He had gray hair, but he was way too young to be Harry the retired cop or Cal the pawnbroker. He didn't have steely eyes, either, or eyelashes to die for, while I was checking out his eyes. I sat back and relaxed.

The young man helped Mrs. Kaffee make her way through the crowded waiting room, pushing the old man's wheelchair gently aside for her walker, while she talked nonstop. The man had the patience of Mother Teresa. I would have strangled the old woman after ten minutes, for the constant chatter alone. They were almost to the office door when I said to Rita, "That woman's son is really sweet. Look how he helps her."

"Son?" said Rita, looking puzzled. "Mrs. Kaffee doesn't have a son. She lives alone and comes here by cab. I don't know who that man is."

As the nurse opened the door to the inner offices, it created a breeze that set the man's clothes flapping on his thin form, and rippled the hair on his . . . wig. The guy was wearing a gray wig. It was obviously a wig. It had slipped slightly to one side. Where had I heard that phrase "his clothes were flapping in the breeze"? From Bill's neighbor, Agnes. Who told me Bill liked cartoons. Classic Warner Bros. cartoons. They ended with, "That's all, folks!"

This man with the gray wig didn't have long eyelashes, because he lost them to chemotherapy. Along with his curly dark hair.

It was Bill! He was here, and he was going to kill Dr. Boltz.

"Bill, stop! Stop!" I yelled.

Bill heard his name and took off running into the inner offices. I ran after him, knocking Mrs. Kaffee flat on her butt. Bill was heading down a corridor toward what I presumed was the surgeon's private office.

"Hey!" said the receptionist, but I couldn't tell if she was yelling at me or Bill.

"Wait! Stop! He's got a gun!" I said. "Call security!" I hoped they understood what I was saying.

Now Bill was sprinting, but not for the surgeon's office. He turned left down the hall and ran for the fire stairs. I followed. Where was security? Could the cameras see us on the stairs? Were the police waiting at the exits? I heard Bill clattering down the steps two flights ahead of me. He was running fast. The first-floor door opened with a modulated hiss. I was right behind him. He ran out on the first floor past an anonymous row of closed doors, then through the crowded hospital halls, knocking gurneys and wheelchairs aside, sending patients and visitors sprawling. A volunteer in a peach smock was knocked into the cart of flowers she'd been delivering, and water, glass, and flowers went flying. We had a near miss with a new mother and her baby, and a direct hit with a guy on crutches. He went down with a loud "oof!" and I nearly tripped on a crutch and landed on top of him.

Where was hospital security? I didn't want to chase an armed killer. I just wanted to keep Bill in sight. I'd be happy to let the guards tackle him.

Bill was fast for someone who was supposed to be half-dead. I managed not to lose him, even when he cut through the cafeteria, and sent trays of beef stew, fish sticks, and red Jell-O flying in his wake. The cafeteria was a mistake. The crowds slowed Bill down. I reached out and grabbed him by the sleeve when I slid on a sweet roll. Bill shook my hand free and was gone.

Where did he go? Through the door on the left? Out through the kitchen? Into the hall? Out the delivery entrance? There were a dozen ways he could go. Dazed people stared at the mess he left in his wake. Some were stepping over the food on the floor. Others were starting to go for help. I heard someone outside yell, "Hey, buddy, watch it."

Bill had ducked out a side door. I saw him running on the sidewalk. He looked back, saw me, and dashed into the street in front of the hospital, crossing against the light. A Jeep Cherokee slammed on its brakes and the driver hit the horn. I followed him, and heard an angry honk and a screech of brakes. The truck stopped so close to me, I could see my face reflected in the shiny grill, my hair hanging wildly out of that stupid turban.

"Jesus Christ, lady, watch it," said the driver, too frightened to be angry.

I didn't stop. I couldn't stop. Bill would get away. I couldn't tell if hospital security knew which direction we were going. I didn't know if anyone had called the police. All I could do was keep running. Bill had an uncanny way of darting into unexpected places. He made it across the street, and ran into the hospital parking garage.

Bill ran up the Down exit. I followed. The concrete ramp was freshly painted and slick with leaking motor oil. I slipped, and stopped to fling off my heels. I had better traction barefoot, but Bill was still way ahead of me. A doctor's big silver Mercedes roaring down the ramp blared at Bill to get out of the way. The doctor gave Bill the finger—must be a proctologist. On the next level, a battered station wagon pulled suddenly onto the ramp and nearly squished him. That driver was too surprised to react. Nothing stopped Bill, not honks, curses, or rude gestures. He ran and ran and I ran after him through the permanent twilight of the parking garage, up floor after floor. Our pursuit took on a dreamlike quality, one of those dreams where you run and run and nothing happens. I saw a constantly shifting collage of car fenders and hoods and brake lights, heard my own hard breathing and the drivers' furious honking. Then, suddenly, we were in blinding sunlight on the open upper deck. There were almost no cars up here. I chased Bill into the far corner. He must have thought there was a stairway there, but it was only a concrete storage area with a Keep Out sign on the door. He pulled on the door handle. It was locked. He looked at me. He pulled out a gun. I felt for the pepper spray in my pocket and pulled it out. Then I stood there, not moving.

"You won't shoot me," I said, with more confidence than I felt.

"You're right. I won't. I only kill people who deserve it," he said, but he still held the gun on me. His right hand shook, and he used his left hand to support it. He was breathing in long shuddery gasps. His wig was crooked and I saw that underneath he was totally bald. Bill caught his breath enough to continue, but his conversation was still punctuated with gasps. Once he started talking, he didn't want to stop.

"Francesca Vierling, isn't it?" he said.

"It is."

"I nearly killed you in the drugstore," he said. He coughed and tried to get more air. "But I couldn't find you and the police were coming. I ran off. Then I realized I only had so much time left. Chasing you would interfere with my mission. So I scared you a bit, to slow you down. But I let you live. Sporting of me, wasn't it?"

"How did you find out I was looking for you?" I said.

"I heard you talking to that nurse, Valerie, in the chemo waiting room. I took chemo, too. It couldn't cure me, but it keeps me alive for my mission."

"You were the bald man in the Cardinals cap," I said.

"That was me. Although some days I wore a curly brown wig, and I've been a blond, too. But I was bald that day. I was right there when Valerie gave you the answer."

"She did?" I was dumbfounded. "She was no help at all. She was just joking with me. She said for all she knew I was the killer, using Georgia as a cover to get in the doctors' . . ." I stopped. No wonder he was worried. Valerie gave me the solution to the puzzle. I just didn't recognize it.

"That's right," he said. "I shot Tachman as he was unlocking his door, but I needed to get inside the other doctors' offices, so I helped confused old people into Brentmoor's and Jolley's patient rooms. Once they were settled in the examining rooms, I let myself into the doctors' private offices. I hid in the closet in Brentmoor's office. I stood behind the door in Jolley's. I waited an hour or two, until they came back to their offices at noon. By that time, the old people I'd helped in were long gone.

"It was easy. I was used to waiting rooms, remember. I fit right in. I'd spent most of the last four years sitting in a chair next to a pile of old magazines, waiting for my name to be called. That's what I was doing when I heard you talking to Valerie. Waiting in a waiting room. I thought a smart gal like you would figure it out after what she said. I'd already run into you in the hall that day when I was going into radiation oncology. I was afraid you might recognize me. And then when Valerie told you how I did it, I was sure you'd put it all together and identify me. I began to worry. I still had some major names on my list back then. What if you stopped me before I finished? I decided I'd stop you first. I couldn't do anything that day. I was too sick after the chemo. But I thought about what I was going to do. I'd follow you out of your office, shoot you on the newspaper parking lot, and make it look like a holdup. It would be easy. Everyone knows the *Gazette* is in a bad neighborhood. I just read about those two twelve-year-olds who shot a guy at the gas station on the corner there.

"But the next night, I was in the Emergency Room. I had a rash from that round of chemo and I couldn't wait until morning to have it treated. I saw you sitting with that little blond woman again. I knew this was my golden opportunity. I got out of the Emergency Room before you did, but I waited. I followed you. I figured the doctor would send you to that all-night pharmacy. They almost always do."

"You came in there looking for me," I blurted. "You killed the store lights."

"I'm very handy," he shrugged. "I know how to do that stuff."

"You know how to knock around ninety-pound women, too."

"I'm sorry. That little store manager didn't deserve that. I couldn't even think of your name. Chemo does that to you. I was so tired that night I could hardly stand up. All I could think was that you were tall and that little manager kept saying there were no tall people there, which made me mad. But I'm glad I didn't find you that night. Killing you would have been a mistake. You've kept me going, you know that? I couldn't have killed all those doctors without you. It was like I had a partner to play against. Did you like the little present I left on your doorstep?"

"Used needles and bloody IV tubing. I could have been infected with AIDS," I said.

"Unlikely," he said. "The blood on the needles was not fresh. Even with fresh blood, the chances of contracting AIDS by a needle stick are point three percent."

"I don't understand how you found my doorstep. My home address isn't in the phone book."

"That was easy," he said, but I could tell he was proud. "Missouri drivers' licenses list home addresses. I called a friend who worked in a license bureau and he looked up your address for me. I told him I was giving you a present, and you wouldn't get it if I left it at the paper. That was all true." He laughed at his own cleverness, but the laughter turned into long, gasping coughs.

"I'm dying. Francesca. Soon. I have more bad days than good days now. Sometimes I don't feel like getting up at all. I'm so tired and I hurt so much, I just want to go to sleep. But knowing you might find me and stop me made me want to go on. I hit that little store manager and I regret it. That's all I regret. The others deserved everything that happened to them."

He was panting again. His skin was waxy white and pale. Sweat had popped out on his forehead. The gun shook in his hands.

"Why did they deserve it?" I said gently, hoping to keep him talking.

"Mind if I sit and catch my breath?" he said. He perched casually on the wide wall. His gun was still pointed at me, but I wasn't scared anymore. The stunning St. Louis skyline was at his back. It was a straight drop ten stories below him, but he had no fear. Why should he?

"I eliminated them in different order," he gasped, "but it will make more sense this way. Four years ago, my family doctor sent me for a sigmoidoscopy at this hospital. He said nothing looked wrong, but colon cancer runs in my family, and he wanted to be on the safe side. The doctor here made the procedure as painful as possible. He was bored and talked over me to a nurse. He hit on her while he worked on me, asking her for a lunch date. She said yes, and he turned off the sigmoidoscope light a little too early and didn't notice the tumor. I found this out later. I mean, that he missed the tumor. The rest I saw right then and resented it, let me tell you. He gave me a clean bill of health. 'You're fine,' he said. So I didn't worry anymore.

"My regular family doctor died soon after that, and I went to this new doctor my friends recommended, Dr. Dell Jolley. He was just like his name. He looked like the perfect family doctor. Older, gray-haired, with a face you could trust. I liked him. About three years ago, I went to him with a problem. He said it was hemorrhoids. But Dr. Jolley never performed a rectal exam on me. I learned too late that neglecting that exam was gross malpractice, like not using a lead apron shield when X-raying a pregnant woman.

"If Dr. Jolley had given me a proper exam, he'd have detected the tumor early enough that I might have survived. But jolly Dr. Jolley didn't like to get his hands dirty. So he treated me for hemorrhoids instead. After all, what were the chances of a man my age getting colon cancer? He gave me foam and salves and potions. Nothing much worked. I saw him at least once a month. For a whole year. I kept getting worse, and I couldn't understand it. Finally, I was so miserable I demanded to see a specialist. Dr. Jolley didn't like to make referrals. I found out later my HMO has an 'expected rate of referrals.' Doctors can refer all they want—the HMO party line is 'oh, we don't restrict our doctors'—but once doctors get over the magic number, guess where the money comes from? Their incentive bonus. Dr. Jolley didn't like to lose any of that money.

"I insisted on a referral. He handed me the HMO specialist list and said, 'Get yourself one and I'll write you a referral letter.' He didn't even tell me what kind of doctor I needed, and the HMO list didn't say. It just had the doctors' names and numbers. So I called twenty-five different doctors' offices and got laughed at by receptionists: 'We work on the other end. We're cardiologists, hee, hee.'

"At last, I called Dr. Boltz's office. I had to wait a month for an appointment. Then he told me I had a large tumor and only a forty-percent chance of making it. He said I needed to be operated on immediately, and I'd have to have chemo and radiation. I sat there in his office, too stunned to move. I did all the right things. I went to all the doctors, I took all the tests, and I was going to die anyway. It wasn't fair. Dr. Jolley had been treating me for something minor when I had cancer."

"I can see why you wanted to kill Dr. Jolley," I said. "Did Dr. Boltz do a bad job?"

"No, he was a good surgeon. I went after him for another reason. I'll get to that in a minute. I felt better after the surgery. Even with all the pain, I knew things were improving. I had hope. I went through chemo and radiation for eight months. The chemo nurses were lovely. Radiation oncology was run like a corner of hell. But at the end, when the chemo and radiation were over, my health was coming back. I thought I was going to get my life back. Then I went for one of my checkups six months later. They found another tumor, this time in my liver. But they put a chemo pump in the liver and I thought they whipped that one, too. Then a tumor turned up again, in the one place they couldn't do anything about—my colon. Dr. Boltz said there was nothing more left to take out. That was it. My number was up. I got this news on my thirtieth birthday. Happy birthday, huh?

"Okay, I was going to die. I thought I could take it like a man. The one thing that bothered me was my son, Billy Junior. His mother and I are divorced, but I'm crazy about that kid. We had shared custody until I got too sick to take care of him. I'll never see him graduate from high school. Never watch him go to the prom, or dance at his wedding, or hold my grandchild. All that was taken away from me by a lazy, greedy, incompetent doctor.

"But I thought I could live with that, too. I was going to sue old Dr. Jolley, and I knew I'd win, and I'd leave Billy enough money for a good life. He could go to college someday. His mother could stay home and care for him instead of working as a secretary and hiring sitters. I had it all planned out. There was no future for me, maybe, but at least my son had a future.

"Dr. Boltz ruined that. My lawyer talked to him about testifying. Boltz said that it really wasn't Dr. Jolley's fault. When my lawyer pressed him, he said, well, Dr. Jolley did wrong, but the extent of the damage couldn't be proved. To me, it seemed so clear-cut. But Boltz hemmed and hawed and excused and justified and explained it away. My own surgeon. He wouldn't testify against Dr. Jolley. He wouldn't break the code of silence. He knew that his colleague had screwed up. But Boltz said he had to work in this community. The other doctors, who were either friends of Jolley or Boltz, followed his lead. My lawyer said the suit wasn't worth pursuing if my own surgeon wouldn't testify for me. Maybe, if I wanted to spend two thousand dollars for an outside expert . . . but where does a bus mechanic with child support payments get that kind of money?

"Now I had nothing. No future. No money for my son. All I had left was revenge. I decided this wasn't going to happen to anyone else. I made sure no one else would go through what I did. I started killing the bastards. I began with the radiation oncology department because they were the worst."

"Been there," I interrupted. "They were mean."

I could hear people running up the garage stairs on the other side, and I wanted to move him on. Help was on the way, but I had to hear the rest.

"My oncologist, Brentmoor, was another one. He wouldn't testify for me, either. Said it was against hospital policy. But that's not why I killed him. He didn't have an ounce of compassion for his patients. I called his office early one morning, screaming in pain, and he never bothered calling me back. Not for eight hours. When I called again, after four o'clock, he'd left for the day. The doctor on call didn't get to me until five-thirty. This didn't happen once—it happened often. He was heartless."

"His other patients agreed with you," I said. I could hear the stairwell door open. Bill didn't seem to notice. He was still talking.

"Dr. Boltz was the last name on my list, but he really started it all. He ruined my hopes, you know. If he'd testified, none of this would have happened. I would have . . ."

I heard shouts and a commanding voice said, "Man with a gun. Drop it! Drop it now!" I saw two uniformed police officers running toward us and figured there must be more out of sight.

"Shoot me," Bill said to them. He never moved off the wall and he never dropped the gun. "It would be a kindness. Please kill me. Make it quick. It hurts too much to live."

I couldn't bear to watch this, or see him hurt anymore. "Put your guns down, officers," I said. "He won't shoot."

Bill looked at me, then looked at them.

"You're right," he said, "I won't," and he went over backward off the top of the garage.

Epilogue

I stared at the empty space on the wall where Bill had been sitting. There was nothing. No sign he'd been there. He'd simply tipped himself backward and gone over. The only sound I heard was the terrible wet thud when he landed. My Aunt Marie used to crack grocery store coconuts by dropping them out a window onto the sidewalk, two stories below. It was that sound.

I stood there, barefoot, my ridiculous scarf turban half off my head, unable to make a sound. Someone was speaking to me. "Francesca," I heard. "Francesca, it's me."

It was detective Mark Mayhew. "Talk to me, Francesca," he said, gently. "Tell me what happened."

"He—he—I—I." I made some kind of squeaky noise, like a rusty door opening, and then I started crying. I hoped I was crying for Bill, but I thought I was crying for myself. I wanted so badly to stop. I didn't want to cry in front of these people, in front of the police, in front of Mayhew. I never cried, not even when Lyle left me, but now I couldn't turn off the

tears. Mayhew reached in his pocket for a handker-
chief and came up empty. "A gentleman always car-
ries one," he said, "but I guess I'm no gentleman. I
forgot it."

"That's okay," I said, still sniffing a bit, my voice
wobbly. I rubbed my eyes and my hands came up
black with eyeliner. My scarf turban was now hanging limply around my neck like a bad fur stole. I
whipped it off, dried my eyes and blew my nose.

"That's disgusting," he said, but he sounded
amused.

"You want disgusting, you should have seen it on
me," I said, and set the scarf on the parking garage
wall. A spring breeze grabbed the scarf. It billowed
out like a sail, then wafted over the side. It was gone,
too, but I didn't look. I didn't want to look down ten
stories. I knew I'd see the people swarming frantically
around Bill's body, like ants on a piece of meat.

Mayhew took me to the elevator and out the front
entrance of the garage, so I wouldn't have to see Bill's
body. I heard the sirens and saw some of the police
cars, but that's all. We crossed the street into Moorton. Someone gave us an empty office and a couple of
cold sodas. I sat down on a chair, and the questioning
started. I told my story, many times. The only part I
left out was Katie's role. But no matter how often I
repeated it, I couldn't quite make it real. When I finished, and Mayhew had his signed statement, all I
wanted to do was sleep for a thousand years. But I
couldn't. I had to write Bill's story. I was in no shape
to drive, so Mayhew dropped me off at the *Gazette*. I
showed up in the newsroom, barefoot and half-drunk
with shock, but I wrote one hell of a story. I don't give
myself much credit for it. I didn't have to do anything

but write down what Bill said. No fancy flourishes, no witty remarks, just straightforward reporting. The strange thing is that I can't remember most of what he said now—I have to reread my own story. But I still remember how he went backward off the wall. I still remember the long silence as he fell. And most of all, I remember that empty wall, with nothing there.

Everyone told me Bill's death was for the best, it was over quick, he didn't suffer. They were wrong. He did suffer. He'd suffered for three long years. I was sorry he didn't get to say good-bye to his son. I was sorry Billy Junior would see his father branded as a murderer. That's what Bill was. But I made sure everyone knew what made him that way. I told the story of what happened to the man who did everything right and died anyway.

Did I approve of what Bill did? No. But I understood it. Oh, yes I did.

So did most of my readers. There was a real outburst of sympathy for Bill. Many of them had had cancer, or they loved someone who had, and all too often the sick person had been treated like Bill. Some had been treated worse.

A few readers chewed me out for not having more sympathy for the victims. They were right. I usually do. And I tried this time, I really tried. But I didn't like them. I didn't like the sadistic receptionist, who used her little bit of power to torment sick people. I didn't like the unfeeling radiation oncologist and the tech who worked with him, cracking jokes over the surgically maimed bodies of hurting people. I didn't like Dr. Tachman, who used the easiest and roughest means to examine patients, because it was convenient for him. If Tachman had spent a little more time with his patients, if Tachman hadn't been so eager for a quickie with a secretary, Bill might be alive today. So might Tachman, for that matter.

But Tachman's faults were at least human.

It was Dr. Brentmoor who made me the angriest. Brentmoor, who didn't bother to call back patients writhing in pain. Brentmoor, who was too arrogant to answer the questions of a frightened patient. The worst part was that Brentmoor wasn't unusual. Georgia's oncologist did the same thing. A cancer doctor without compassion was a shell of a human, in my book. When Bill shot Brentmoor, I thought he had killed a dead man.

Dr. Jolley was the one I almost felt sorry for. Almost. He was growing old and careless and he neglected a basic exam. But at least his patients loved him, and he seemed to sympathize with them. Except where that HMO incentive bonus came in. Dr. Jolley held the line on those costly visits to specialists, and made sure they didn't cut into his nice little bonus. His greed killed Bill, just as surely as if Jolley had put a gun to his head. But a gun would have been quicker and kinder.

Of course, as the doctors' defenders liked to point out, the victims weren't there to speak for themselves, and that was true. But I knew Bill was telling the truth. Katie had seen his medical records, and they confirmed his sorry story. I'd talked to other patients of the dead doctors and heard their stories. And I'd been there with Georgia. I knew Bill wasn't exaggerating.

I did call the one survivor, Dr. Boltz, and ask him for a comment about what Bill said for my story. Boltz said he didn't want to talk. That's what nearly got him killed, but it made a nice counterpoint in my story. His own silence condemned him. I wondered if Boltz felt any guilt about not testifying for Bill. His peers, like Katie, were in awe of his medical mastery. But he was one of the good doctors who kept silent and allowed the bad ones to flourish.

Georgia drove me home that night, when I finished the story. She also lent me enough cash for a cab the next morning. I took the cab to Moorton to pick up my purse and car. I found my purse at Dr. Boltz's office, and no money or credit cards were missing, a minor miracle. Boltz's assistant, Kristine, saw it on the waiting room floor after Bill's dramatic run, and put it away in the safe for me. I asked after Mrs. Kaffee, the woman who got knocked flat on her fanny when I bolted after Bill. Kristine assured me she was fine. In fact, she was basking in her new celebrity status. Mrs. Kaffee was interviewed on TV that night. She told the reporter that she knew Bill was a killer. She could tell by his eyes.

Kristine thanked me for saving the doctor. Boltz never bothered.

My car was gone when I got to the garage. At first I thought Ralph was stolen, but he had been ticketed and towed for parking in a Doctors Only zone. The hospital said it was sorry, but the parking garage was a private concession, and they couldn't do anything about the ticket or the towing costs. The *Gazette* wouldn't pay for them, either. They came to one hundred fifty dollars, total. I paid them and put them on my expense account at the rate of three dollars a week, for almost a year. I put them under parking.

• • •

I took Katie out for a thank-you lunch, and this time it wasn't at McDonald's. She was back in her healthy mode again, and munched a salad at O'Connell's Pub. She seemed pleased with how her efforts turned out. "You know," she said, "Boltz was the only doctor out of that bunch worth saving."

"His gratitude has been touching," I said, sarcastically.

Katie shrugged. "I don't care about that," she said. "I just want him around in case I ever need a surgeon."

She had the right attitude—surgeons existed for her, and not the other way around.

I wanted to get Katie something for all she did, some acknowledgment of her help. After all, she risked the most to save Dr. Boltz's ungrateful neck. But what do you get a country girl who liked dogs and guns and pickup trucks? A box of bullets? A new set of mudflaps? Finally, I heard her talking about a medical society banquet she was going to attend. It was a formal affair, and she was getting some kind of honor. I saw just the gift for her in a Tiffany's catalogue and ordered it. She called me the day she got it.

"It's perfect," she said. "Fits right in my little beaded bag. Sterling silver, too. It's the evening accessory every woman should have."

No woman should be without a formal pocket knife.

I saw Jack, the former Leo D. Nardo, in the Clayton Schnucks' supermarket, wearing a wedding ring and about six hundred dollars worth of Ralph Lauren. He was pushing a shopping cart and looked very happy. He and his bride went through a tough spell with her children after they came back from their honeymoon. Rutherford and Althea—those are the kids—didn't like the prenuptial agreement that gave Leo a million dollars. The rest of Nancy's fourteen-million-dollar fortune was theirs, but it wasn't enough for them.

Rutherford, a real prune, declared that his mother must be crazy to marry a common stripper. His sister Althea was shocked that her stepfather was half a century younger than her mother. I wondered how someone as lively as Nancy produced such a pair of prigs.

Rutherford and Althea hired a bunch of lawyers. Their mother, Nancy, hired a bunch more. At the sanity hearing, Althea and Rutherford's shrinks testified that their mother was batty as a barn owl. Nancy's shrinks said she was sane.

After all the experts yammered away, the judge asked Nancy why she'd married Jack. "For sex, your honor," she said. The judge, a woman with a young face and gray hair, declared Nancy sane. So did every woman in the courtroom. Nancy promptly changed her will. The bulk of the estate was going to her beloved husband, Jack. Each child would get "only a million," which they regarded as a poverty-level income. I could have probably eked out a decent life on a million bucks, but then I was a South Sider and used to making do.

Heather, the nurse Dr. Brentmoor was supposed to marry, gave birth to a nine-pound, six-ounce boy. DNA tests confirmed that Brentmoor was the father. Heather promptly sued the Brentmoor estate on behalf of her son. Brentmoor's wife, Stephanie, hired herself a real shark. The suit was dropped when Brentmoor's parents agreed to support the child in exchange for generous visiting rights.

Stephanie had a fling with her attorney, who was recently divorced. She kept her house in Ladue, but moved into his condo in Clayton. She said he promised to marry her, and gave her an engagement ring. He said the ring was a farewell gift. All that is known for certain is the lawyer took up with a thirty-year-old nurse he'd deposed in the Brentmoor case, and Stephanie was out on her ear. The resulting palimony suit gave Stephanie plenty of ink in Babe's column, but I don't think she wanted it. Stephanie spent most of the money she got from Brentmoor suing her lawyer lover. The last I heard, she was selling real estate in West County. She was good at it, too.

Bill comes back to me in my dreams sometimes. I hear him say his final words and I see him fall backward and I hear the long silence before he landed. And scariest of all, I see that empty wall. That's the part of the dream where I wake up with a pounding heart. When I see nothing.

The insurance company wanted to get out of paying death benefits to Billy Junior, claiming his father's death was a suicide. I guess it was by their definition, but I considered it medical murder. I wrote a story about how the insurance company was leaving an orphan destitute. Readers felt so sorry for Bill's son, they sent me money for him. I talked with his mother in Tampa. She used it to set up a college fund for him at a local bank. Billy had a future after all. His father's death accomplished that much.

My dreams about Bill began to fade after that.

Maybe because Bill could finally rest, now that his boy was provided for. Maybe because I didn't have to spend any more time at Moorton Hospital.

Georgia had finished her course of chemo and radiation after eight months. At her last chemo session, the nurses came into the room cheering and waving sparklers and blowing bubbles. She looked embarrassed and pleased at the attention. They presented Georgia with a nicely lettered Certificate of Achievement.

"What the hell am I supposed to do with this?" asked Georgia on the way home.

"Keep it," I said. "You earned it."

"I didn't do anything but stay alive."

"That's enough," I said.

She's gained back most of the weight she lost and all of her foul-mouthed high spirits. She looks good. She's been cancer-free for a year. Four more to go, before the cure is official. She's sure she'll make her five-year anniversary. I am, too.

Georgia needed reconstructive surgery after the surgery healed and the radiation was over. She decided to have breast implants while she was at it—the saline kind. "Hell, why not," she said. "The insurance company's paying for it. Never too late to have tits."

Speaking of tits, Charlie, my reptile of a managing editor, quit giving me sleazy stripper assignments after I cracked the Doc in the Box case. My series on the subject created quite a stir. I gave a lot of speeches about the killings to the Kiwanis and other groups, which the paper considered good PR. The audience, unless it was a bunch of doctors, was sympathetic to Bill.

The doctors, or the doctors' relatives, would get all hot under the collar when I mentioned Dr. Jolley's misdiagnosis. They'd say it was easy for any doctor to forget the basics, and I'd say, "For a whole year?" Or they'd try to explain away a cold fish like Brentmoor. "Isn't it better that we have the doctors' knowledge to save lives? Do we need their feelings, too?" they'd say. We did, I said. Many of the chemo nurses managed to have both brains and feelings. The nurses were far from perfect, but a lot more of them were recognizably human. I could hear the men in the audience snort at the radical notion that nurses might handle anything better than a doctor and see the women nod their heads in agreement.

And if doctors couldn't deal with their patients' pain, I'd add, maybe they should be in research. Slides and test tubes have no feelings. This was when some guy, usually older, would say that the oncologists saw so many bad things, they needed to "protect themselves." But it wasn't protection, was it? The doctors were dead, weren't they?

They were as dead as my love life. I spend a lot of time thinking about Lyle, and what we had and what we lost. I tried to pick up my life after we broke up. I went out with other men. My friends fixed me up with "nice guys" who were so nice, I had to struggle to stay awake when we went out. They weren't men I could ever love. So I stopped going out. It was better that way. There are women who can be content with minor romances, but I'm not one of them. I'd rather have nothing.

I had my work, and that was enough consolation.

Especially since my Doc in the Box series was a finalist for the McNamara prize for distinguished feature reporting.

"Congratulations," Georgia said, when I got the phone call from the prize committee. "This is the big time."

"It's an honor just to be chosen," I said with uncustomary humility.

"Bullshit," she said. "It's a bigger honor to win. And you'll get twenty thousand dollars if you do."

The awards dinner was at the Sheraton New York in Manhattan. The *Gazette* offered to pay my fare and room—if I won. Georgia and I figured they had a good chance of popping for my trip. The other nominees were a *Los Angeles Times* series about police brutality, a *Des Moines Register* series on fraudulent home repairs, and a conservation magazine series about a Canada goose. The two exposés were solid stories, but not groundbreaking. The goose story wasn't in the same league.

At the awards dinner in New York, Georgia and I and the *Gazette* brass all sat at the same table: Charlie said his wife, Nails, was home with the baby. My editor, Wendy the Whiner, ignored me and talked with Smiley Steve, the assistant managing editor for scummy stuff. Georgia tried to make conversation with me, but I was too nervous to talk coherently. I cut my sixty-five-dollar chicken into little pieces and pushed my food around on my plate. I wore a smashing Ungaro dress, and Georgia said I looked every inch a winner.

But I didn't win. I lost to a heartwarming series about a state conservation agent named Gus who hand-raised a baby goose. The gosling imprinted Gus as his parent and followed him everywhere. Everyone said it was a charming story. The judges agreed.

Charlie looked relieved when I didn't win. I was trouble enough as it was—I'd be insufferable if I had won a big prize. After I lost, the brass left the table quickly, as if my failure embarrassed them.

Georgia and I went to the nearly empty hotel bar and for once in my life I set out to get plastered. "Here's to Gus and his fucking goose," I said, hoisting my glass of white wine. "I hope he winds up on a platter at Christmas."

"Awww, he was kind of cute," Georgia said.

"What?" I couldn't take this final betrayal.

"I was pulling your leg. Besides, the guy who won is living with a goose, for chrissake. You want goose shit all over the house? You know how slippery that is?"

I said nothing.

"That was a joke, Francesca. Can't you laugh about anything anymore? You need to lighten up. Lyle was the only one who could make you laugh. The task of cheering you up has become too much for me."

Lyle. My other major failure. I couldn't believe she would mention him tonight. I felt low enough already.

"When are you going to call that man?" she nagged. "You're not seeing anyone else, and neither is he. You're crazy about him and you know it."

I could feel my face turn to stone. "I. Am. Not. Calling. Him."

"I know," she said. "That's why I brought him here."

I turned around and there he was, standing at the entrance to the hotel bar. I hadn't seen Lyle in a year.

I did not know what to say. I did not know what to feel. Until he came forward and took me into his arms and kissed me.

"Oh, baby," he said. "I missed you so much."

"I missed you, too," I said. "Don't leave me ever again." The words that had been so hard to say slipped out so easily now.

"Never," he said, between kisses. "Never, ever."

I wrapped my arms around him, pressed my body against his, and felt just how much he missed me. How did I ever think I could live without him? All my anger and the awful year in the chemo ward melted away with his kisses. I felt the silky hair on the back of his neck, put my arms around his broad back, felt his strong arms around my waist and now going down to my . . .

We were interrupted by a tap on my shoulder. "You two better go to your room," Georgia said. "You're creating a spectacle, even in New York."

For once, I listened to my editor.

About the Author

Like her series character, Elaine Viets is a six-foot-tall newspaper columnist. Her thrice-weekly column is syndicated by United Feature Syndicate in New York. She was named Florida Author of the Year for her third mystery, *The Pink Flamingo Murders*. Elaine is president of the Florida chapter of the Mystery Writers of America, and was a judge for the MWA's coveted Edgar Award for Best Novel 2000.

The St. Louis native now lives in Hollywood, Florida, with her husband, Don Crinklaw. Before that, she lived on Capitol Hill in Washington D.C., where her dishwasher was repaired by the same man who fixed Al Gore's washing machine.

Please e-mail Elaine at eviets@aol.com